# T

# DROUGHT

## Steven Scaffardi

Pen Press

© Steven Scaffardi 2011

First published in Great Britain by Pen Press

All paper used in the printing of this book has been made from wood grown in managed, sustainable forests.

ISBN13: 978-1-78003-192-7

Printed and bound in the UK
Pen Press is an imprint of
Indepenpress Publishing Limited
25 Eastern Place
Brighton
BN2 1GJ

A catalogue record of this book is available from the British Library

Cover design by Jacqueline Abromeit

For Jade –
The brightest light in my life

# Acknowledgements

Massive thanks to Lynn Ashman and everyone at Pen Press, especially Claire Spinks for your editing skills and pointing out my obvious errors, Jacqueline Abromeit for your patience and fantastic work on the cover, and Linda Lloyd for your invaluable reader's report.

Very, very special thanks to my personal book review club: Martin, Preyan, Dylan, Muna, Ortis, Kwame, Angellica, Matt, Little Bill, Angela, Jim, Potko, Schofe, Zeke, and Dee Dee. I really appreciate you all taking the time to read that first draft back in September 2009 and for all your advice, support, inspiration and feedback along the way. Thanks also to David and Lynne Harrison for your kind and encouraging words, Tim Rider for casting your eye over the book, and Luke Dolan for your help creating that promo video!

Thank you to Matt Whipp at printweek.com for letting me blog about this journey, and Daniel Poulter at Advanced Web Creations for the excellent website you created for me.

A special mention for Jade, who put up with me typing away for hours on end, and kept me fed and watered! Thank you for your patience and your love.

And last but by no means least – mum and dad – thank you for all your love and support, and for always believing in me.

# About the author

Steven Scaffardi was born in Tooting, south London in January 1978. A former journalist, *The Drought* is his first novel, and has already received praise from television personalities and journalists alike. He currently works in advertising, but since January 2011, he has been a regular on the London open mic stand-up comedy circuit. His brand of comedy combines witty observation with self-deprecating humour; incorporating tales of relationships, dealing with life in his 30s, and the situations he encounters as a man.

For more information on Steven Scaffardi visit:
www.stevenscaffardi.com

# Contents

Chapter 1: The End 1
Chapter 2: 47 Messages 8
Chapter 3: The Break-up 19
Chapter 4: Back to Work 32
Chapter 5: Black Sabbath 46
Chapter 6: Out of Practice 56
Chapter 7: First Date 67
Chapter 8: Valentine's Day Massacre 81
Chapter 9: Visiting the Folks 96
Chapter 10: Office Dares 110
Chapter 11: Up in Smoke 120
Chapter 12: Beer Talk 132
Chapter 13: Amazing Grace 144
Chapter 14: Little White Lie 157
Chapter 15: Jack's 10 Commandments 168
Chapter 16: Road Trip – Friday Night 177
Chapter 17: Road Trip – Saturday Night 188
Chapter 18: Extreme Makeover 209
Chapter 19: The Dating Game 223
Chapter 20: Shop Horror 234
Chapter 21: Paul's Birthday 245
Chapter 22: Kelly's Hero 257
Chapter 23: Jack Hammered 266
Chapter 24: The Betrayal 278
Chapter 25: A New Beginning 292

## Chapter 1: The End

*Sunday, September 13, 2009 - 12.47pm*
*Drought Clock: 255 days, 23 hours, 50 minutes*

I guzzled down the remainder of the vodka and coke left in my glass, wiping away the liquid that escaped my lips and trickled down my face, staining the neck of my white T-shirt.

"Same again, darling" The barmaid was polite enough to at least pretend to ignore that I now had an equal amount of alcohol on my top as I did in my throat.

"Yes please, and a bib if you have one," I responded, attempting a witty comeback to cover up my embarrassment.

She shot me a cheeky grin and let out a little giggle, as she tended to prepare my drink. Then eye contact, and another smile. Hold on, what did we have here? A mutual attraction perhaps? Well, sort of.

Okay, so maybe she was a little overweight and wore her hair up in that strange side ponytail that some girls of a certain stereotype go by. You know, the one where they scrape their hair back so tightly it looks painful because of the constant agony they must be in from the stretching of skin from the hairline to their forehead. This was all held in place by the obligatory neon-coloured scrunchie, of course.

She wasn't the usual type of girl I would normally go for. In fact, she looked like the type of girl my dad would say had been around the block a few times. In this case, the prisoner cell block by the look of those tattoos on her forearms.

I guess I normally went for the more natural and pure look in a girl, as opposed to the aggressive and potentially violent look this barmaid had managed to perfect. I think

1

she even had a bit of a limp too, like one leg was shorter than the other or something.

But who was I kidding? On current form I was certainly no Casanova and was in no position to be picky. I was experiencing the worst drought of my life. It had been over eight months since I had last managed to get my leg over. I didn't know if I should laugh or cry half the time. Eight months without sex. People had committed crimes and been given lesser sentences. It was the worst slump I'd experienced since losing my virginity seven years ago. With each passing day I had gone without sex, the further my self-esteem seemed to spiral downwards. But today's events had tipped me over the edge.

I caught a glimpse of myself in the mirror behind the bar. There I was – Daniel Hilles. I stared at my reflection but I was unrecognisable to my own eyes. I had become a desperate man, and the strain was beginning to take its toll. `I might not be the best looking bloke in the world, but I'd like to think I could pass for a 7-out-of-10 on a good day. But now I was starting to look a shell of my former self. My stylish messy dark brown hair now looked, well, just plain messy. Three days of not shaving had not given me the desired effect of designer stubble. Instead my face looked more like a used Brillo pad. My eyes were bloodshot and glazed over, but that could have been the alcohol.

An hour ago I'd hit rock bottom. Just when I thought things couldn't have got any worse, they had. And this time it went much deeper than trying to get a girl into bed. I'd walked into the White Horse on Balham High Street with one intention – to get as pissed as quickly as possible.

The White Horse was your typical old man's pub. Dark and gloomy, and full of drunks who wanted to get as much cheap alcohol down their throats as quickly as humanly possible. The wallpaper was red and white stripes. The white stripes were no longer white; instead they were nicotine yellow, while the red was a strange velvet material. It was the type of wallpaper your parents may have had on the living room wall back in the 1980s. The rest of the bar furniture was dark oak, and the lack of music meant the only noise that could be heard was the inane alcoholic chit-chat. The perfect venue to drown my sorrows.

I thought this would be a safe place; a place where I could forget about what had just happened. It was also the last place on earth in which I thought I would find myself in a position to have to try and impress a girl in a lame attempt to get her to shag me. But now faced with an opportunity in the shape of Vicky Pollard's twin sister, I thought to myself why not? Beggars can't be choosers as they say.

Besides, she had some redeeming qualities. The little bit of extra weight she was carrying had certainly enhanced her buxom appearance, and she wasn't exactly shy when it came to trying to hide those two fabulous assets busting out of her pub-issued white shirt. Granted she was probably wearing one too many sovereign rings on her fingers for my liking – seven to be exact plus two amazingly large Pat Butcher-esque gold hoop earrings. But at that moment I had a good feeling about this.

That feeling could have been the bulge that was starting to develop in my pants as I found myself staring for a tad too long at her fantastically large breasts jiggling with every movement. But she didn't seem to mind me looking, and with the right amount of coaxing I could be on to a winner. The four double vodka and cokes I had downed in the last 45 minutes were also helping guide my judgement on this one.

She placed the drink down on the coaster, leaning towards me and giving me even more of an eyeful with a devilish look across her hard features. The dirty little minx – she wanted me to look. I handed her the money and held

3

onto her hand for just a second or two long enough to be playful.

Brad Pitt eat your heart out. I don't think I could have played it any cooler. I knew it, she knew it – even the old man slumped at the end of the bar drinking the cheapest bitter on tap knew it – she wanted me bad. "Keep the change, sweetheart," I told her with a wink and flashed her that old winning smile which had been missing for far too long.

Yep, I was certainly back on form. She wiggled her way over to the till, before turning and heading back over towards me. I was ready for the next stage of where this was heading. I'd crack a few jokes, we'd flirt a bit, and she'd probably playfully hit me at some point in that way girls do when they fancy you. God knows why I had been worried about getting back into the game for all this time. I just had to be myself and stop listening to other people. This one was most definitely in the bag.

"You're 40p short," she said, that cheeky grin now fading away. Bollocks. A minor setback, but don't panic I said to myself. I made a quick joke about telling her to keep the change and offered to buy her a drink instead. I pulled out my small change pouch and started to dig around at the copper and silver coins.

"Is that a purse?" she sarcastically asked, her grin now replaced by a mocking curl of the lips.

"No," I shot back. "It's a pouch actually," I continued, as I tried my best to savour whatever masculinity I had left holding the stupid leather purse that displayed a picture of a tiger in fake gem stones and plastic diamonds.

Why the hell had I listened to Rob when he advised me to buy the damn thing? *"It's the height of fashion; all the footballers have got one of these bad boys,"* he told me. I had that same look on my face the barmaid now displayed when Rob had said this to me. *"It's bloody gay"* had been

4

my exact response. I should have gone with my first instinct.

"Well it looks like a purse – a man purse," she laughed. "And is that a picture of a cat?"

"It's a tiger *actually*," I said as manly as possible, not wanting to concede the fact that I was indeed holding a purse.

"It is a cat!" she said, pretty pleased with herself. "That makes it a pussy purse!" And she started to cackle uncontrollably. "Hey John, have you seen one of these before?" I was delighted with the fact she had decided to share this awkward moment with her colleague. "This guy has a pussy purse."

John's booming laugh alerted other patrons in the bar, and he wasted no time informing the two workmen he was serving, who were now looking over, pointing and laughing.

"It's not a purse, alright?" I managed to sputter out as I shoved the coins into the palm of her hand, hoping to put an end to this conversation immediately.

She studied the change. "This is only 37 pence. You owe me another three pence. Anything else in that purse of yours?" she enquired, looking at me like I was the biggest tosser she had ever had the misfortune of laying her eyes on. From the look of the clientele in this establishment, she had seen a fair few in her time and I wasn't exactly thrilled to be at the top of that pile.

I don't know why I was surprised this was happening to me. One way or another, all female contact I had experienced in the last few months had resulted in some form of humiliation. Why should this be any different?

Panicking, I rummaged around in my pockets, praying I had the lousy three pence somewhere so I could at least salvage some dignity. Impatiently she rolled her eyes at me, knowing full well I didn't have the money. "Could I owe you the three pence?" I pathetically asked.

"Whatever," she sighed. I scooped up the drink and drank. I wanted to get out of this bar as quickly as I could. But with the final swig, a piece of ice about the size of the one that brought the Titanic down, slid into my mouth and lodged itself in my throat. I coughed hard, and in doing so managed to not only dislodge the iceberg, but also spray the barmaid with a mouthful of vodka and coke.

"Oh shit, I'm so sorry," I blurted out, before in my infinite wisdom deciding it would be appropriate to help dry her vodka and coke soaked chest with my man purse. If the scraping of fake gems and plastic diamonds against flesh wasn't enough, I somehow managed to wedge the purse in between her cleavage. The tiger's face now looked as though it was peering out over two eggs.

I didn't see the punch coming, but I did feel the full force of her heavily sovereign-ringed fist make crunching contact with the side of my face. And it wasn't the playful variety of hit I had anticipated earlier either. I stumbled back, tripping over a bar stool, and came crashing down flat on my back.

As I lay there looking up at the smoke-stained ceiling, the last eight months flashed before my eyes. How had it come to this? I used to be a pretty cool guy. Perhaps not the coolest, but I got by. Now look at me – lying flat on my back in a stinking old man's pub, beaten up by a girl. And to cap it all off I still had a semi hard-on from where I had been staring at her tits.

I was snapped out of my trance by another blow to the head, this time the barmaid was considerate enough to use the fist with just the three sovereign rings. She followed up with a kick to the groin, causing me to yelp like an injured puppy.

"Get up!" she shrieked in her glorious south London twang, grabbing a handful of my hair to help me to my feet. What a way for my life to end; all because I was three pence in debt to Queen Chavette of Balham. I wondered what my mother would think when they found my body with an injured semi in my pants.

With the finesse of a Kung-Fu master, she twisted my arm halfway up my back and frog marched me towards the door. A toothless old hag laughed at me as I was dragged past her to add further humiliation to this already sorry scene. Using my head as a battering ram to open the door, the barmaid flung me out on to the busy high street pavement. Passers-by gawped and gasped as I crashed into the steel railings alongside the road.

"Don't come back unless you want another beating! You're barred!" The barmaid cried out. "And take your man-purse with you!" She launched the purse at my head as the final insult.

Momentarily I checked for any broken bones. I was still alive – she had spared me. But at that moment I might as well have been dead. I was at the lowest point I had been in the last eight months. I wasn't too sure how I should feel as I sat myself up on the pavement. Anger? Sorrow? Bitterness? Maybe all of them. Maybe none.

All I knew for certain was that I was throwing in the towel. I'd had enough of the knock-backs and the disappointment. I was sick and tired of the bad advice and the ridicule I had suffered. I had managed to get myself into more near-death experiences than Evel Knievel. And the obsession with internet porn I was starting to develop couldn't be healthy either.

But despite everything that had happened in the last eight months, one thing stood out as the hardest pill to swallow. It was something I honestly had not seen coming. After all the rejection, the despair, the disappointment, it was the betrayal that had hurt the most.

Perhaps I had better start at the beginning.

## Chapter 2: 47 Messages

*Thursday, January 1, 2009 - 8.47am*
*Countdown to start of drought: Two hours, 34 minutes*

"Wakey, wakey, rise and shine!" Rob slapped me a few more times to try and arouse me from my drunken slumber. Immediately the sensation of my pneumatic drill headache signalled this was the worst hangover I had suffered since the time I stuffed myself with 27 pieces of vodka jelly.

"What time is it?" I was barely able to get the words out as my tongue was stuck to the roof of my mouth. It was so dry it felt as though I had eaten an entire pack of crackers while stranded in the middle of the Sahara Desert.

"It's nearly nine," Rob said nudging me with his foot. "It's Greasy Spoon time, just what the doctor ordered. A nice bit of fried bread on this fine New Year's morning will do the trick."

The thought of food made my stomach churn, and I pulled the pillow over my head in a feeble attempt to get Rob to leave me alone. A sharp pain lodged itself permanently down the centre of my skull. Even breathing made me feel sick. What a way to start the New Year.

"I'm going now, baby, thanks for a great night." I managed to pull the pillow down from my face and force my right eye to squint open to see who the unfamiliar female voice belonged to. I worked my gaze up from the long tanned legs, to the tight leopard print miniskirt hugging the firmest peach-shaped arse I'd ever seen. And the view just got better. Packed into a tight low-cut black top were two fantastically round breasts, and a perfect mane of blonde hair.

Rob leaned in and kissed the sexy blonde stranger. "Give me a call next week and we'll hang out," he told her as he put his number into her phone. They kissed again and then she left.

"Who was that?" I drooled, suddenly my mouth not so dry anymore.

"That was Kirsty, no Karen," he replied still with a puzzled look on his face as he tried to remember what her name was. "No, it is Kirsty. She was the girl I picked up in the pub before we came back here last night."

God I hated guys like Rob Devlin. I hated how his sandy blonde boy-band hairstyle always looked inch perfect. I hated his dedication to put hours in at the gym to sculpt and tone his athletic physique. I hated that he had a style all of his own and always looked like one of those male models from an Abercrombie and Fitch advert. And I *really* hated the way he was able to effortlessly pull girls that most blokes only dared stare at from a distance; just long enough to memorise them for the wank bank later on.

He had also been my best friend since we were six-years-old, and I loved the guy to bits. He was super laid-back; so much so that he was in danger of falling over sometimes. He had a real charm about him, especially with the ladies, and you rarely heard anyone say a bad word about him. In fact, the first and last time we fell-out was as nine-year-olds when Rob kissed Debbie Chopman in the playground during a game of kiss chase. I loved Debbie, and had obsessed over her for at least two weeks without doing a thing about it. Rob knew I liked her, and would even hold her down during kiss chase, urging me to come over and plant one on her lips. But even then I was useless with the opposite sex, and could normally be found hiding behind a tree. Eventually I guess Rob got bored and decided to kiss her himself; just to prove how easy it was. I was devastated and refused to speak to him for a full three days, until he invited me to his house to play on his new games console. I guess even Debbie Chopman couldn't compete with a Sega Mega Drive.

"Come on Danny boy, get dressed. We're leaving in five minutes," Rob continued. "And do me a favour – cover yourself up."

I cried out in shock horror as I stared down at my morning glory in, well, all its glory. "Where the hell are my boxer shorts?" I gasped as I cupped myself to hide the shame.

"I think you took them off during the drinking game. You were pretty wasted. Last time I saw them, Ollie was wearing them on his head," Rob said gazing out of the French door windows of his living room, his face scanning the garden for the missing underwear. "Maybe they're on the roof of the shed?"

Oh of course, why didn't I think of that? Missing pants always turn up on top of garden sheds. "Why the hell would they be on the garden shed?" I pulled the pillow down to cover my modesty before I continued to whine. "And why did you let me just lie here with my Rock of Gibraltar hanging out with Karen in the room?"

"Her name's Kirsty," Rob corrected me. "And I don't think she noticed." He grinned as he took a sip from the cup of tea in his hand. "Besides, don't you have *bigger* things to worry about?" he said nodding at my phone. "Like Stacey for example?"

Shit, Stacey! I shot straight up ignoring the headache and the noises coming from the pit of my stomach, swirling around with the contents of copious amounts of Jägermeister bombs and tequila shots. I reached for my mobile sitting on the side of the table and hit the on button. The phone took what seemed like an age to come to life, and right on queue the screen flashed up: *You have a voicemail*. I clicked the call button.

*Welcome to Orange answer phone. You have 47 new messages. First new message received today at 12.47am.*

"I can't believe you have done this to me," Stacey wailed into the phone. "You're such a bastard. You left me on my own on New Year's Eve. I fucking hate you. Tonight you heart-raped me!"

Heart-rape? Who says things like that I hear you say?

Ah, allow me to introduce you to my girlfriend. Stacey could not be content with accusing me of breaking her heart. Oh no, I had to be labelled a rapist of the heart. A rapist, for crying out loud! She had probably already contacted *Crimewatch* and described what I look like to a police artist. I clicked the end call button and decided I would need to mentally prepare before I listened to the remaining 46 abusive messages that surely awaited me.

"What a night!" Ollie enthused as he walked into the living room and slumped into the couch, that big dopey grin on his face. He rubbed his hand through his short curly light brown hair, and pulled a cigarette out from behind his ear.

Jack followed him in and sunk down beside Ollie on the couch. They both jostled for position. "Please someone tell me they remember the beast Ollie pulled last night," Jack started up. "I swear to God it was Sloth from *The Goonies* with long hair!"

Ollie grabbed Jack in a headlock, the unlit cigarette hanging from his mouth. "You're just jealous," Ollie replied. "Go on, smell my finger!"

Jack struggled as hard as he could to avoid Ollie's index finger lingering precariously close to his face, summoning all the strength he had in his five-foot-four frame to push himself to the far end of the couch and out of the reach. "You big, sick freak," Jack said trying to catch his breath and rubbing his short, cropped brown hair back into place. Ollie grinned and lit his cigarette, blowing out smoke rings.

11

Rob and I met Jack and Ollie on the first day at high school and the four of us had been inseparable ever since.

Ollie Pemberton wasn't the sharpest tool in the box, but at six-foot-three and 14 stone of muscle he didn't need to be. Even at school the teachers had been nervous to point out Ollie's obvious stupidity at times because of his sheer physical presence. He had known his partner in crime, Jack, since primary school. The difference in size between the two was comical in itself, with Jack being nearly a foot shorter, and we often made references to the 90's film *Twins* that starred Arnold Schwarzenegger and Danny DeVito.

Jack Chatham was definitely the joker in our pack. We nicknamed him Jackie Cheatham because of the amount of times he had strayed from his long-suffering girlfriend Anna. It wasn't that we condoned Jack cheating on his girlfriend – we had all attempted to intervene on countless occasions. But in a man's world it is commonly agreed that if your friend is still capable of looking you in the eye to tell you he knows exactly what he is doing, then that absolves you from all responsibility. Fact.

Although I'd probably never say it to Jack, I did feel bad for Anna. It wasn't just the playing around behind her back, it was the fact that even Anna couldn't escape his wicked sense of humour and schoolboy banter. Two weeks ago Jack asked Anna what she wanted for Christmas, and she replied: "If you loved me then you would know what I want." Jack bought her *The History of the World Cup* – a set of 18 encyclopaedia's and bonus DVD's. One for each tournament.

Oh, and it cost him £250.

But he was just one of those guys other guys liked to be around. He always had that mischievous twinkle in his blue eyes. He could come out with the most outlandish of things, but he never failed to raise a smile.

12

"So what's the plan?" Ollie asked, scratching his balls and pulling at his underwear. "These boxers are really uncomfortable. Rob, can I borrow a pair of yours before we go out?"

"Hey!" I yelled. "Where did you get those from?" I looked on in disbelief, finally realising why I had found the blue and green pattern so familiar. "They're mine!"

"Why are you not wearing your own pants?" Rob chipped in.

"I found these in the kitchen," Ollie offered as an explanation. "My pants are on the roof of the garden shed. Do you want them back?" Ollie started to slip them off.

"No! I don't bloody want them back! I'm not going to wear them now."

"Why not?" Ollie asked as serious as the day is long, a puzzled frown on his round face.

"This is priceless. I've got to get a picture of this," Jack chuckled as he got his camera phone out. "So you two are sharing pants now? You twisted bastards. Do you want us to leave the room?"

"Let's all leave the room," Rob quickly interrupted. "Come on, outside in five minutes. Let's go eat."

Rob wandered into the kitchen to put his mug in the washing up bowl, while Jack and Ollie disappeared upstairs to get dressed. I slipped on my jeans, trying to remember if I'd ever gone commando before now, and careful not to catch my bits in the zip.

We met outside and climbed into Rob's Peugeot 306. The weather was far too cold to have the roof down on his blue convertible, and we urged him to switch the heater on before he had even put the key into the ignition.

As we pulled out of the drive, I took my phone out of my pocket and took a deep breath before making the plunge to listen to the remaining 46 messages. Most of them followed a similar pattern. Stacey would wail uncontrollably, scream

13

down the phone, or say in a calm matter-of-fact tone that we were over. A lot of the messages were incoherent and sandwiched in the middle was one from my mum wishing me a Happy New Year, and reminding me that I had to come round for lunch soon.

With a bit of encouragement from my friends, I played them my top three favourite messages.

**1.42am – the angry message:** "If you don't switch your phone on I will smash your stupid fucking PlayStation into little pieces. Who do you think you are? You can't treat me like this. You're not a real man. You're pathetic."

**2.23am – the hysterical message:** "I can't believe you have just left me on my own (inaudible). This is the worst night of my life. I'm all alone (inaudible) nothing but that shit DVD set you bought me for Christmas. And you... And you... And you... (pause and then more sobbing and sniffing) You just left, and I'm all alone. (more sobbing)"

And my personal favourite:

**3.46am – the calm message:** "Daniel Hilles. (pause) You are a wanker."

Like any good group of friends, my boys rallied around me. And found great delight in the almost inevitable break-up of my relationship.

"That last message was classic," Jack said choking back the tears. "I can't believe it has taken her three years to realise how much you love to hand jive. We've known for years you're a real grade A stroker!"

"Okay, let's go over this again," Rob said as we approached our destination. "What happened last night? What did you do to her?"

14

"That's the thing," I started. "I didn't really do anything."

Rob pulled the car up and we got out. The streets of South Wimbledon were dead; the glow from the Greasy Spoon the only sign of life in a row of closed estate agents, kebab houses, and newsagents.

"You must have done something, or was that just her way of talking dirty?" Jack said as we moved in pairs towards the inviting warmth of the Greasy Spoon.

"Piss off," was about the best response I could muster, my head still pounding.

Eileen greeted us with her usual warm smile as we entered the cafe. "Hello boys, sit down and I'll bring you over some tea."

The Greasy Spoon had become our regular morning-after pick-me-up ever since we discovered the place last year after a particularly heavy night that involved two bottles of tequila, a crate of Stella, and a half-Mexican, half-Korean guy surprisingly called Owen, who had taken us to an underground rave in Shoreditch.

Come rain or shine, Eileen and her husband Bob opened up every morning at 6am. It was an old-fashioned cafe, but immaculately clean – a rare thing for a cafe in south London these days. But it was the food that kept us coming back. You simply couldn't beat it.

We took our usual table in the corner by the window and Eileen brought our tea over and took our orders, which didn't take long seeing as we always had the same thing – Full English with the works.

A partygoer from the night before was slumped at a table across from us wearing a blue and yellow paper crown. His friends, or whoever he had the misfortune to have seen in the new year with, had kindly stuck a piece of paper to his chest which read: *If found please deliver to 21 Evelyn Road.*

"Right, spill your guts, Danny boy," Rob demanded.

Finally succumbing to the fact they were never going to let up, I took a sip from my hot mug of tea and attempted to make sense of the events that had resulted in my girlfriend accusing me of being a rapist, albeit one of the heart.

"Everything was fine until we left the pub after midnight," I began. "I decided to go to the cash point so I could buy some booze to take to the party."

"I remember that," Rob said. "I think I joked about turning you away from my house if you turned up empty-handed."

"Well, Stacey took that as you not wanting her at the party."

"What? That's ridiculous," Rob said half in disbelief, half defensively.

"I know it's crazy," I reassured him. "I told her that, but she wouldn't listen. She got it into her head again that you guys don't like her and she wasn't welcome at the party."

"Bloody women," Jack said raising his eyebrows. "You should have given her a slap," he said joking.

"She really went into one," I continued, shaking my head as I thought about it. "She stormed off, saying it was my fault. I tried to reason with her, telling her she was being silly but she wouldn't listen. There was no way I could let her walk home by herself, she was too drunk. So I just followed her to make sure she got back okay. When we got back to her flat she was screaming at me, F'ing and blinding, and calling me a C U Next Tuesday."

"You arranged to see her next week then?" Ollie questioned.

The stupidity of his question took me aback. "No, I didn't arrange to see her next week," I shot back. "She was calling me a... never mind."

"So what happened?" Rob said trying to get me back on track.

"For a while I tried to calm her down, but that just made her angrier and she started lashing out. It was at that point my patience ran out and I totally lost it. I told her that she was right – nobody liked her when she behaved like this and nobody wanted her at the party in this type of mood. I was so angry. I stormed off but she kept calling me and abusing me down the phone so I switched it off and came to the party."

I sat back letting my own words sink in. It was a horrible situation, and I didn't really know what else to do. I only hoped my friends would have the answers.

"Well, at least she knows the truth now, that none of us like her." Ollie's comment was met with stunned silence. I saw Jack kick him under the table and screw his face up at him. I looked at them all, scanning their faces and reactions to Ollie's bombshell.

"It's not that we don't like her," Rob was the first to try and explain, "It's just that she can be a bit... intense sometimes."

"Like when you were in Paris last year and she got jealous because you were staring at that woman in the Louvre," Ollie said.

"That was the painting of the Mona Lisa," I corrected Ollie.

"Exactly," Rob said making his point.

"Or the time she cock-blocked me when I was trying to chat up that older bird she was with at that party last year," Jack said.

"What party?" I was puzzled.

"The one at the big house in Kent."

"That *older bird* was her mum, and we were at a funeral."

"Well, her mum was bang up for it," Jack responded, taking a mouthful of his tea.

17

We all burst into laughter and the tension that had been briefly hanging in the air was broken immediately. Stacey hadn't exactly endeared herself to my friends in recent months, and her behaviour last night was becoming too much of a common thing. But things hadn't always been like this, and that is what made this situation all the more difficult to fathom.

"So what happens now?" Rob asked me as Eileen came over and placed plates of bacon, egg, sausage, beans, toast, and fried bread, in front of us.

"I guess I'll have to go round there and face the music."

## Chapter 3: The Break-up

*Thursday, January 1, 2009 - 10.43am*
*Countdown to start of drought: 38 minutes*

I'd been with Stacey for just over three years. We'd met at university and the first two years of our relationship had been pretty smooth sailing. Don't get me wrong, we'd had our moments during that time like any couple, who doesn't? But there was a time when I honestly believed she could be *the one*.

I can still remember the first moment I laid eyes on her during Freshers' Week. Drinks had been arranged for everyone on our marketing course so we could get to know each other. Stacey wandered into the bar late, having got caught in one of those famous British summer showers. She was soaked to the bone, but was still the most attractive girl there in my eyes.

"Hi everyone," she said as she sat down in the seat opposite me. "Sorry I'm late, I was washing my hair." We all broke out in laughter, and I knew I liked her instantly.

"Can I get you a drink?" Dean Marshall asked her. It was a simple question, but one I ultimately regretted not asking myself. Dean had played his cards early, so I decided to turn my attentions to Ellie Thornton. After all, this was university and there were plenty more fish in the sea, as my mum used to tell me.

Still, I grew fond of Stacey in our first year of university and we became close friends. We were both from south London, and had a common bond in that we both agreed *Danger Mouse* was undoubtedly the most underrated superhero of all time.

By this time she was already seeing Dean, but that didn't stop my heartbeat quickening every time she smiled. She had an edge to her and didn't suffer fools gladly. I liked that about her; that she was able to stand up for herself, but at the same time she could be soft and vulnerable, none more so than the time Dean dumped her at the end of our first year at university, and I was left to pick up the pieces of her broken heart.

It didn't happen instantly but over time I think we both realised our feelings toward each other went deeper than just friendship, and within weeks into our second year we shared our first kiss.

From that moment our uni lives became entwined. We had the same friends, we went to the same parties, and we were on the same course so we studied together. Despite spending so much time together, it never felt claustrophobic.

But the moment we left university something changed. We had lived in the same bubble for so long, and Stacey found it more difficult to adjust than I did.

At the start it was subtle things, like giving me the silent treatment if I had been on a night out with my friends without her. "Why do you exclude me from nights out with your friends," she would moan. "Why can't I be involved in that part of your life?"

I tried to involve her when we first moved back to London, but she would spend the whole night moaning that there were no other girls to talk to, and she hated the two Jack's in my life. "Why do you drink Jack Daniels? It turns you into an idiot," she would say of my newfound taste for the Tennessee Whisky. "And I don't trust your friend Jack. Doesn't he have a girlfriend? He tried chatting up my friend Sophie last week."

And there was my problem – Sophie. We had never seen eye-to-eye. In the three years we had been at university, I had only ever met her best friend Sophie once, and it was clear from the start that she didn't like me. To be fair, that was partly down to Stacey. Sophie was slightly older than

Stacey and I, and during the course of our first meeting she had asked me to guess her age. Getting a woman's age wrong is never a good thing at the best of times, so I decided I was going to play it safe and say she was the same age as me. But at the last second Stacey lip-synced the number 30 to me, so I went with it.

"You think I'm 30?" Sophie growled at me as Stacey giggled. "Do you have shit in your eyes? I am 24, you cocky little twat."

From that moment on I think it is fair to say Sophie hated my guts, and it was only when we returned to London I started to notice the influence she held over Stacey, especially after they decided to flat-share together. Maybe it was because she was older, but Stacey literally hung on every word she said, and that combined with Sophie's obvious disdain toward me, definitely had an effect on our relationship.

I noticed Stacey drank more around Sophie, and in her drunken state, Stacey started to pick fights with me over the most pointless of things. I tried to avoid confrontation as much as possible, telling Stacey that we would sort things out in the morning. But with Sophie in her ear egging her on, she'd go on and on, to the point where I would get pissed in an attempt to drown out her constant whining. Eventually I'd succumb to the goading and we'd have the most explosive rows. She'd end up in tears and I'd have to apologise. For weeks she would emotionally blackmail me by reminding me of the night I made her cry. And I'd apologise again.

Back at university, Stacey was quite happy to sit and read while I watched a game of football on the television, but with Sophie throwing in her two pennies worth that all changed.

21

"Sophie doesn't understand the point of watching football matches when you don't even support either of the teams playing," Stacey now whined at me.

"You love football more than you love me," Stacey screamed at me during one particular heated debate on the subject.

"Correct," I stupidly responded. "Now go and collect your prize in Scotland and leave me in peace."

Stacey was furious. She grabbed the remote control from my grasp, and informed me: "This is my flat so we'll watch what I want to watch." I tried to grab the control back from her but she wouldn't release it from her grip. Eventually I grabbed my coat and declared I was leaving, only for Stacey to launch the remote control at my head, causing it to break on impact.

The football argument surely has to be one of the most common and annoying debates girlfriends insist on having with their boyfriends. Let me try and clear this one up right now, and I speak for men up and down the country when I say this – we like football. End of. There is no mystery. No need to send Scooby and gang in to solve this one. Girls like mind-numbing rubbish like the *E! Entertainment* channel, while men watch things that matter, like sport.

Although in saying that, I didn't tend to put up too much of an argument when Stacey used to insist on watching *Girls of the Playboy Mansion*. You don't have to be a rocket scientist to work out why.

In recent months Stacey's personality under Sophie's watchful eye had transformed her completely. The girl I had fallen in love with at university was slowly becoming a stranger to me, and that was the most difficult thing to take.

*

It had been about 20 minutes since I'd left the boys at the Greasy Spoon to make my way to Stacey's flat. I turned on to her road and my mind started to race. Was this really the end? Three years was a long time to be with someone, and I wanted to make sure in my mind this was the right thing to do. I wanted to reassure myself that I had done everything to make this work.

I tried to think about the good times, but then my mind would be clouded with recent events. Her behaviour last night was just another in a long line of recent performances that had drawn me to the conclusion our relationship was a bit like watching England at the World Cup: it starts with a lot of promise but inevitably it ends in tears and disappointment.

I hit the buzzer and waited. The door opened and her flatmate Sophie stood in the doorway in her white dressing gown and green socks, a scowl on her face. Her big wild hair looked even more untamed than normal, and her eyes told me in no uncertain terms that she was not going to make this easy for me.

"She doesn't want to see you," Sophie greeted me in her own charming way, arms folded across her chest. She had always insisted on sticking her nose into our relationship. At least she was being consistent I thought to myself.

"A pleasure as always Sophie, you are looking radiant this morning," I sarcastically responded. "Can you tell Stacey I'm here please?"

"You have got some nerve turning up here after what you put that poor girl through last night."

"And you look like you haven't bleached that moustache in quite some time," I couldn't help myself. I leaned over her and started to shout. "Stacey! We need to talk."

"If you think I am going to let you in here..."

"It's okay," Stacey's voice interrupted and cut Sophie off mid-sentence. Stacey appeared from behind her

23

flatmate, opening the door wider. There they both stood –
my nemesis and my significant other, whatever the hell that
meant. "I'll take it from here," Stacey said. Sophie cut me
one final look, and I met her gaze full on. She then squeezed
Stacey's hand as a way of telling her to be strong. Sophie
moved away from the door but couldn't help herself as she
mouthed the words, "I'm watching you", pointing at her
eyes with her two fingers and then pointing them back
towards me, before returning back to the darkness from
whence she came.

It was at this point I was able to really look at Stacey for
the first time. She had her brown hair clipped back away
from her face. She was wearing the *Little Miss Naughty* T-
shirt I'd bought her. Her eyes were red and puffy, and she
looked like she had been crying all night. My heart sank.
Despite everything, I still had feelings for her and didn't
want to see her like this, especially when I knew that I was
the cause of the hurt.

"You'd better come in," she said avoiding eye contact.
She led me upstairs to her bedroom. She sat down on the
bed as I closed the door. I turned back to her. The TV was
on in the background, but the sound had been muted. The
clothes she had been wearing from the previous night were
strewn across the floor.

"Are you okay?" I hesitated to sit down on the bed next
to her.

"What do you think?" She sniffed, wiping her nose with
a tissue. "You left me alone on New Year's Eve."

I was willing to let that one go, deciding it would be best
not to drag up the who was right and who was wrong
argument.

"And you obviously never gave me a second thought by
the smell of you," Stacey said wrinkling up her nose at me.
"You smell like a brewery. I hate it when you get drunk and
turn into *that* person."

I bit my tongue to stop myself responding with what I really wanted to say. I didn't want this to descend into a slanging match at such an early stage. I sat down beside her on the bed and took her hands in mine.

"I'm sorry for what happened last night. The last thing I wanted was for us to end up having a row." I stroked her hands.

"It's a bit too late for that now," she pulled her hands away from me and stared me straight in the eye for the first time as her tone reverted to one of bitterness. "You made the choice to go and hang out with your friends without me."

She really knew how to push my buttons. She had this annoying habit of being able to lull me into a false sense of security and just when she had me where she wanted, she would unload. I felt the rage slowly start to build up inside me, but again I took a deep breath.

"That's not really fair," I tried to reason with her. "I tried talking you into coming to the party. You were the one who told me to go. You said some pretty harsh things. What did you want me to do?"

"Not leave me on New Year's Eve," she snapped back. "It doesn't matter now anyway. What's happened has happened. You had a good time – at least one of us did."

"But you were screaming at me to leave you alone," I could feel my voice starting to rise. "What else was I supposed to do?"

"Don't shout at me. This isn't my fault," she paused. "You did this," she said jabbing her finger into my chest, her eyes narrowing at me accusingly.

At that moment I could have exploded. I think the only thing that stopped me was that I was still nursing the hangover from hell, and didn't physically have the energy to rise to the bait. However, Stacey obviously had no problem forcing the issue.

25

"You don't give me the same level of attention like you used to," she continued with her verbal attack. "But you have no problem spending time with your mates."

"That is ridiculous," I protested. Stacey had unrealistic expectations that our relationship should continue in the same vein as it had done during the first 12 months; an expectation Sophie had no doubt drilled into her to create this wedge. But I managed to restrain myself again; somehow I knew pointing that out would not help the situation.

"Is it?" Stacey fired back at me. "I suppose you think it's *ridiculous* that Sophie and I smashed up your PlayStation last night as well then?"

"Come on Stace, we can sort this..." I paused, suddenly taking in what she had just said. "You smashed up my PlayStation?" And it was at that moment I noticed the broken pieces of my beloved games console sitting in Stacey's bin.

"This is worse than that time you ruined my birthday," Stacey suddenly blurted out, moving my attention away from the bin and back to her.

"What?" I couldn't believe what I was hearing. This was the same story she had been throwing in my face for nine months. The power of restraint was obviously not a strong point for Stacey.

The story of the night in question wasn't my finest hour. I had drunk myself into oblivion to block out the boring inane chit-chat I was being forced to endure at the hands of her dry work colleagues. I have very little memory of the night. All I remember is waking up the next morning to discover a wall of pillows separating Stacey and I.

Dazed and confused, and after much begging and pleading, I finally managed to coax Stacey into telling me why she was giving me the cold shoulder.

She explained how we had arrived back at her flat and proceeded to have what she described as "incredible sex." She told, in great detail, how she moved on top of me and proceeded to deliver her best impersonation of Sharon Stone in *Basic Instinct*. And just as she was about to explode in pure unadulterated pleasure, it happened.

I was snoring – so loudly that I snorted like a pig.

Stacey tapped my face a couple of times to rouse me, but it didn't work so she hit me instead. Apparently I responded with 11 words that would haunt me for the rest of our relationship: "Get off me. You're too heavy and I'm trying to sleep." I topped it all off by pushing her off me and rolling over. And farting.

I knew I was in trouble, and for weeks I did everything I could to make this up to Stacey. I bought her flowers, took her out for dinner, and even took her away for the weekend, but nothing was ever good enough.

Nine months on and she was still using this against me. I was starting to think she had made the whole thing up just so she could bring it up whenever we had a disagreement or row. I even tried using man logic but that didn't help things; it just made it worse. I would tell her that anything that happened over six months ago is inadmissible in an argument. And when I was feeling particularly brave I would inform her that all comments and actions become null and void after seven days.

"That was nine months ago," I pointed out the obvious as I had done on numerous occasions.

"You ruined my birthday, and now you have ruined New Year."

Suddenly any guilt I had felt slowly started to evaporate. The Stacey I had met at university was no longer the same person. She was never going to change, and in a strange way I felt relieved.

"We can't carry on like this," I said after taking a deep breath.

She opened her mouth but the words wouldn't come out. After all this time even Stacey was exhausted from the constant fighting. She looked at me and I could see tears starting to well in her eyes. "I know," she said letting her guard down.

Something hit me in my chest. It was an ache I had never experienced before. I could feel a lump in my throat. This was really it. We hugged each other, and held on tight. We both knew this was goodbye. I pulled my head back and wiped the tears from her cheeks. She stroked my face and a small smile appeared through her tears. I looked into her eyes and saw the Stacey I had fallen in love with three years ago. We kissed.

Things moved on to the next stage pretty quickly. So quickly that we were in danger of losing some teeth as our lips clashed together. She reached straight for my belt buckle and started to unzip my fly. She pulled my jeans down to my knees and arched back on to her bed. She didn't seem to notice my complete lack of underwear and I decided it wasn't the best time to explain why I had gone commando. I pulled her thong down and she let out a moan. Her moans became louder and louder as she demanded I thrust harder. I would have loved to have obliged, but I was really feeling the effects from the previous night's drinking and began to lose steam quickly. I made one final thrust and lay on top of her, breathing heavier than I really should have been after just one minute and 57 seconds. I lifted myself up and slumped beside Stacey on the bed.

I slowly began to catch my breath. Staring up at the ceiling I started to think how that was the last time we'd ever make love to each other. Not that I would have called that making love. In fact, does any man actually call it making love? Please can we never mention that I referred to sex as making love? It was a goodbye shag. The type of thing couples need to do one last time before they finally go their separate ways. Almost like a *well done* for giving the relationship a go. You get to leave things on a positive note. Not that I would normally consider one minute and 57 seconds a positive, but I think we both appreciated what had just happened. After three years it was time for us to walk off into the sunset in different directions. A two-minute memory in our back pockets.

"I'm glad we sorted this out," Stacey said cuddling up to me. "I forgive you."

What did she say? I started to panic. She thought this was *make-up* sex, not *goodbye* sex. I cursed myself for being so stupid. Goodbye sex would have been tender and soft, something we could both take away and remember. And longer than 117 seconds. We just had classic animal, aggressive make-up sex. This was awkward.

"But I thought that was goodbye sex..." I said it out loud without even thinking.

"What?" Her tone was more anger than shock.

"I thought... I mean..." I stuttered and stumbled.

"Get out!" She screamed so loudly I was sure the Russians on the space station could hear her. I tried to explain again, but suddenly the door to her bedroom burst open and there stood the wild-haired Sophie, holding a baseball bat. "I fucking warned you!" she screamed at me.

Sophie launched at me, swinging the bat with a crazed look in her eye. I dived across the room as she smashed the bat into the pillow where my head had been lying just seconds before. I still had my jeans around my ankles so I could only hop and shuffle towards the door like a penguin.

"Get him!" Stacey shouted. What the hell happened to forgiveness?

Sophie was up off the bed in a flash and swung for me a second time, this time crashing the bat into the door frame

29

as I ducked and headed toward the stairs. Sophie was right behind me and as I took the first step on to the stairs I lost my balance and tumbled head first, landing in a heap at the front door.

Sophie stood at the top of the stairs looking down on me like raging bull. She started down the stairs toward me. Frantically I dragged myself up and grabbed for the door latch, pulling it open just as Sophie threw herself on top of my back.

We rolled out onto the pavement, my jeans still swinging around my ankles. The bat went flying off to one side as we hit the floor. I tried to make a run for it, but she grabbed the top of my jeans. Scrambling to my feet I turned to push her away but she grabbed hold of my testicles and squeezed tightly.

My face went purple and then a shade of green. I tried to scream but couldn't get the sound out. I kicked her in the shin and she fell back clutching her leg. I crumpled to my knees in a heap, the colour slowly returning to my face. I sluggishly pulled my jeans back up and looked up to see Stacey now on the doorstep.

"Sophie! He is getting away," she cried out to her pit bull.

I pulled myself up and leant against a car, still doubled over in pain. Sophie was now back on her feet and had retrieved the bat. She swung it above her head like a cavewoman swinging her hunting club, and moved quickly towards me. I ducked at the last spilt second, and heard the glass from the passenger seat window shatter, setting off the car alarm.

"You crazy bitch!" I screamed, still trying to catch my breath, but had to quickly roll to safety as she attempted another bat attack which crashed into the tarmac.

This time I took off as fast as I could. Sophie made chase for about 50 yards before giving up and standing in the middle of the road; the bat raised above her head. "If you ever come near her again I'll kill you!"

I didn't look back. I kept running until I was certain I was clear and free. And that pretty much brought the curtain crashing down on the most meaningful relationship I'd had in my life up until that point.

It would also prove to be the last day I would have sex for a *very* long time.

## Chapter 4: Back to Work

*Monday, January 5, 2009 - 9.17am*
*Drought Clock: 3 days, 21 hours, 55 minutes*

Monday morning. Back to work and in the office. The festive holiday was well and truly over, in more ways than one.

It had been four days since I'd broken up with Stacey and stared death in the face. I had dared not tell the boys what really happened. They would crucify me with their taunts if they knew how the baseball bat-wielding Sophie had nearly decapitated me. I wasn't quite ready for their onslaught of ribbing and banter just yet.

But I had been desperate to talk to someone, and I knew I could trust Kelly to be the voice of reason and offer some words of consolation.

"That is the funniest thing I've ever heard," Kelly somehow managed to get the words out through fits of hysterical laughing, holding her stomach. So much for being the voice of reason.

"It's not funny," I smiled. "I could have been seriously injured. Or worse. Dead!"

Kelly held one hand over her mouth to try and stem the flow of laughter while she waved the other hand at me apologetically. Her long brown curly hair bounced up and down as she tried to control her giggling. "I'm so sorry, babe," she managed to finally calm herself down.

I had worked with Kelly Campbell for a little over four months now after she came on board as a sales executive at Maxwell Media through a graduate scheme. We sold online advertising to a range of different industries across the three business-to-business websites. I had been with the company a little shy of a year, but I'd been bored shitless before Kelly arrived. She was bright, bubbly, and had this infectious laugh. She was an easy person to get along with. Before meeting Kelly I had never bought into the theory that a man and a woman could *really* just be friends. I'd had female friends before, but inevitably one person would always fancy the other person. Normally I was the one who did the fancying.

But with Kelly it was different. Don't get me wrong, she was attractive, but I think the fact we were both in relationships meant that neither one of us felt the need to try and impress the other person. There was no pretence. No bravado. Kelly had been with her boyfriend Paul for nearly a year now, and I had met him a few times when he had come to meet her after work. He was a good guy and they seemed really happy together.

"So, how have you been doing?" she asked genuinely.

"I don't know really, it all feels a bit empty," I said. "I still think it was the right thing to do, but it still feels a bit strange."

"That's normal," Kelly reassured me. "You were with each other for a long time. You get into a routine. It takes time to adjust to the change, especially when things happen so quickly."

Kelly was right. For the last three years my daily routine had always revolved around Stacey in one way or another. I was now in an unfamiliar situation not seeing or talking to her every day. With no contact, I couldn't shake the feeling that something was missing, almost like not being able to remember where you last saw your keys. But no amount of head scratching and searching under the sofa would remedy this issue.

"I thought about contacting her but I'm not sure that would be the best thing to do," I said.

"Too soon?"

"Gut instinct," I said. "Plus this text I received from her last night."

33

I got my phone to read the text out to Kelly. "You will never find anyone as good as me. I can't believe I wasted three years of my life with you. PS – your small cock never satisfied me."

Kelly burst into laughter again. "I'm sorry, babe," she managed to say.

"Got time for personal calls, have we, Hilles?" Richard Mussel slapped both hands on both my shoulders from behind. "Good strong shoulders," he said massaging me. "I would have thought you'd have loads to catch up on after being out of the office for two weeks."

"Yes, Richard, I was just..." I tried to offer before I got cut off.

"How many times do I have to tell you?" Richard said. "I prefer Dick."

It was bad enough having to call my boss Mr Mussel, even though he insisted it was pronounced *Moo-Cell*. Who was he kidding? His preference to the name Dick left me with a comical dilemma when you put the two names together. "Okay, Dick," I said trying to keep a straight face.

"I need those sales plans on my desk before midday," Dick said in his irritating middle-class monotone twang before dashing off to ruin someone else's morning.

"Happy New Year to you too," I said under my breath. Kelly poked her tongue out and flipped Dick the finger behind his back as he stomped off towards the editorial department.

"Okay, Campbell," I said in my best Dick impersonation. "Pick those phones up, update those boards. I want to see you driving this business forward. And will you please refer to me as Dick Mussel."

I insanely typed at the keyboard and picked the phone up and down during this little charade. Kelly laughed, but suddenly her expression changed, but I was too caught up in my improvisation to notice. Then I felt those hands clamp down on my shoulders for a second time.

"Midday, Hilles. If I don't have that sales plan on my desk we will need to have a little chat," Dick informed me. "And update those boards."

"Why didn't you warn me," I threw a piece of paper at Kelly as Dick marched back to his office like a bear with a sore head.

"I tried," Kelly protested, throwing the piece of screwed up paper back in my direction with a wink.

I smiled and got up to update the boards, grabbing a piece of tissue and wiping away December's figures. I reached down for a red board marker and that is when I saw her. I froze on the spot. At that precise moment, nothing else mattered. She was a picture of pure unadulterated beauty. An untarnished image of an angel that would melt the coldest of hearts. Her black hair swayed like she had stepped out of the perfect shampoo advertisement, while her dark smouldering eyes burned a glowing passion inside her.

"Dan, close your mouth," Kelly whispered. "You're practically drooling."

I knew Kelly was speaking because her mouth was moving and words were coming out, but I was completely transfixed with the vision before me. She wore a white silk shirt, unbuttoned to the third button, hugging her slim athletic body. It was tucked into a tight-fitting black skirt that forced her to take each stride like a catwalk model.

And then it happened. It might have only been a split second, but at that precise moment it felt like an eternity. It was a moment I would later relive over and over in my head. It was a story I could boast about to the boys down the local. Hell, I might even tell my grandchildren about this one day. Because at that moment, as this vision of sex on legs walked past, I swear to God she looked straight at me. And it wasn't a run-of-the-mill type of look either. It was an

35

eye-fuck – a 100 per cent genuine bona fide unspoken look of lust.

"Who *was* that?" I gushed.

"That is Dick's new PA," Kelly said. "Her name is Shaila Saxena."

Shaila Saxena. Even her name was hot. She looked like an Indian Goddess. The type of girl you fall in love with the moment you lay eyes on her.

"Did you see that?" I asked Kelly. I needed confirmation that someone else had just seen the future Miss World give me the *look*.

"I saw you standing there with a strange crooked grin on your face and your tongue hanging out of your mouth like a demented dog," Kelly replied raising her eyebrows.

"No way. She looked at me. She gave me the *look*."

"What?" Kelly said in a slightly high-pitched voice. "She barely glanced at you."

"Hey, it was a look, okay?"

"Daydreaming again are we, Hilles?" I turned and saw Pete Crowford the IT geek. He was wearing a white short-sleeved shirt with four different coloured biros in his top pocket. His five strands of hair were stuck to the top of his head in a Bobby Charlton style comb-over.

"What do you want, Crowford?" I asked.

"That is one sweet piece of candy," Pete said pushing his thin-framed spectacles back up the bridge of his nose. "But word of warning," Pete continued, straightening my collar. "I saw her first."

Kelly let out a laugh and Pete shot her a look. "Don't worry, Kelly," Pete said, tilting his head so he could look over his glasses at her. "There is plenty of love to go around in the IT department for you too."

"Oh, please," Kelly said almost insulted, flicking her hair back.

"Get the hell out of here, Crowford," I said pushing Pete away and kicking him up the backside in the process. He threatened me with a back-hand before slowly slinking off back towards the IT department gently rubbing his butt.

I turned my attentions back towards Shaila who had now taken her seat at her desk outside Dick's office. "I'm telling you, Kelly, she *looked* at me."

"Well whatever it was, it's probably not going to get Dick off our back." Kelly paused in thought and then turned back to me. "You know, it doesn't matter how often I say that sentence it still sounds wrong, you know?"

I finally snapped back to reality and looked at Kelly who was grinning. "You have got a filthy mind, Campbell," I smiled as Kelly pulled a face as if to say *what me?* "Come on, we'd better get on the phones then."

Like so many graduates fresh out of university I had no idea what to do with my life and had fallen into the career path of a Media Sales Executive. Searching for that perfect job in the *Media Guardian* I'd stumbled across Media Sales. The job descriptions sold themselves fantastically well. Looking back I shouldn't have been surprised seeing as they were written by sales people:

*Develop new business dealing directly with those responsible for advertising and marketing budgets. We are looking for someone who wants fast career progression with high levels of drive, enthusiasm, initiative, and commitment. You need a strong personality and a determination to succeed, and will be working across both digital and print media.*

Technically that description is true. However, in the case of my job it failed to mention one or two important aspects:

37

*Far from being glamorous as the job title suggests, your soul will no longer be your own. You will be working for a slave driver, who will constantly berate and belittle you. You will be speaking to arseholes on the phone all day who will treat you like a piece of scum on the bottom of their shoe. You will slowly start to loathe your boss and your job, and become one of those zombies who live to work.*

The first day back at work after a holiday always drags, but today was particularly bad. I managed to complete the sales plan by 11am and had emailed it to Dick. I spent the next hour on the phone. The most annoying part of my day was trying to speak to the person who held the purse strings. The key was to get past the gatekeeper, in most cases some low-ranking jobsworth who follows their instructions and procedure to the letter. Often just to piss you off and to make them feel important.

A typical conversation goes like this:

**Me:** Good morning. I was hoping you may be so kind to help me out. Who do I need to speak to with regards to any decisions on advertising?

**Jobsworth:** I'm afraid I can't give out that information.

**Me:** Is it possible to be put through to the marketing department then?

**Jobsworth:** You can email me the information and if the marketing department is interested they will be in contact.

**Me:** And who am I speaking to?

**Jobsworth:** My name is Jayne, I work on reception.

Knowing full well that Jayne the Jobsworth would never pass my email on, I take a new approach. Type in the company name and "marketing manager" into Google and chances are you will find a contact. We then have to go through the process again.

38

**Me:** Good morning, could I speak to Mr Matthews please?

**Jobsworth:** Who's calling please?

**Me:** My name is Daniel Hilles and I am calling from Maxwell Media.

**Jobsworth:** Mr Matthews is not interested.

**Me:** You don't even know why I am calling.

**Jobsworth:** What is the nature of your call?

**Me:** Advertising.

**Jobsworth:** Please hold.

At this point I would like to take the opportunity to point something out to all the jobsworths up and down the country: just because you put your hand over the receiver, it doesn't mean I can't hear you asking Mr Matthews if he will speak to me.

**Jobsworth:** I've just checked and Mr Matthews is not in the office today.

**Me:** But I just heard you speaking to him.

**Jobsworth:** If you would like to email me the information I will forward it to him and he can then decide whether or not he would like to take you up on your offer.

It doesn't matter how long you work in the job, that conversation will always leave you seething with the same level of frustration. If I had my way, that conversation would go a little more like this:

**Me:** Good morning, could I speak to Mr Matthews please?

**Jobsworth:** Mr Matthews is not available. Please email the information to me and...

**Me:** Listen to me bitch. If you screw with me, I will come down to your office, bend you over and screw you right back.

**Jobsworth:** I beg your pardon?

**Me:** Beg? You'll be begging alright, you minimum-wage old hag. Now put me through and don't make me come down there and shove that headset straight up your....

"Hilles!" Dick interrupted my daydream by bellowing across the floor. "My office. Now!"

Kelly raised her eyebrows and stretched her mouth to the side. "Good luck," she said as I took a deep breath and made my way across the office. Whenever I was summoned by Dick I swear I could hear the death march whistling through the wind outside the window. I readied myself for the inevitable. It didn't matter how good my sales plan was, he would find something wrong with it. I often wondered if he had any work to do himself with the amount of time he kept me locked in his dungeon.

"Sit down," Dick instructed as I entered his office. I closed the door, took my seat, and braced myself.

Dick leaned across his desk, peering over his glasses, his eyes levelled straight at me. "This is not what I asked for." He waved the sales plan in his hand before throwing it into the dustbin at the side of his desk. "Are we jousting with feather dusters here, Hilles?"

I had absolutely no idea what he meant.

"I have been looking at last year's figures and is it correct we missed budget by £4,000 in quarter four?"

"Yes," I nodded. "The credit crunch really caught up with us in the build-up to Christmas."

Dick shook his head and held his finger up to his lips. "There is *no* recession," he announced. It was one of those ridiculous statements he often made. While the rest of the world suffered from the economic downturn, Maxwell

40

Media was oblivious to any financial constraints in the world of Dick.

"The problem is you are not hungry enough. You do not drive this business forward out there on the floor," he sat back in his chair, his hands locked behind his head in one of his typical power poses. It was a line I had heard all too often. It was all part of the so-called motivational repertoire he had in his locker.

"In all seriousness, that is a sackable offence," Dick announced pointing towards my screwed up sales plan now taking pride of place in the dustbin. "Missing budget by such a small amount I mean."

"Don't worry, I plan on missing budget by a much larger amount in the next quarter." I couldn't help myself. He sat forward, both hands on the desk, glaring at me. I attempted to hold my ground and hated myself for diverting my eyes.

"I want you to go back and do this report again, this time with a plan on how we are going to make up the money you lost!" Dick snapped at me.

"Yes, Richard," I said, and got up and left his office.

"I prefer Dick!"

I stepped outside and Shaila was staring straight at me. She must have heard the whole sorry thing. I tried to shrug it off and hand gestured how Dick had droned on by bringing my fingers and thumb together. But Shaila simply turned her attention back to her computer screen and went about her day. That was not a good sign.

My face must have given it away when I came back to my desk.

"That bad huh?" Kelly asked.

*

Lunch break could not come soon enough. I needed to get out of the office and cool down. I headed towards Liverpool

Street. I had quit smoking about eight months ago, but at that moment I was tempted to buy a packet just so I could have a quick puff to de-stress myself.

"Hi, excuse me," the gorgeous brunette startled me. "Have you got five minutes?"

Five minutes? I'd give this girl five hours. "Yeah, of course. How can I help you?"

"I'm working for a charity helping children in Africa. Did you know that 19,000 children die in Africa each day?"

Bollocks. I'd walked into a minefield of charity street workers – charity muggers or *chuggers*. Groups of animated young people, carrying clipboards and trying to separate you from your money, all in the name of a good cause. Don't get me wrong, I am not a heartless bastard. I give money to charity. Three pounds comes out of my wage packet each month in a *Just Giving* scheme set-up by work. I felt terrible that there were children living in Third World countries who were starving.

It's just that I only had an hour for lunch.

I kicked myself for being duped by her looks and fantastic legs, exposed by black leggings under a frilly mini skirt. The blue bib with the name of the charity scrawled across it in big bold white writing should have given it away, but sometimes you miss the small details.

"For just £15 a month you could sponsor a child, offering them a better life," the pretty brunette continued. I nodded, desperately trying to pretend I was interested in what she was saying, but in reality I was only interested in what was under the blue bib. Sordid little thoughts raced around my brain, ricocheting from one side to the other like a bumper car. Then it struck me. For the first time in three years I was single, and here I was standing opposite a really hot girl. I started to think what would Rob do in this position? Of course he'd be so super cool it would make me sick. But I had seen him in action, loads of times. Surely I could muster a small fraction of that Rob magic.

"Excuse me, what's your name?" I cut her off as she was explaining how my money could help send a child to school.

"Carla," she said, somewhat perplexed.

"Look, Carla, I would love to do more for the children of Africa, but perhaps I could spend the money on taking you out instead?" Even Rob would've been proud how I had just handled that. Pretty damn smooth if I do say so myself.

"What?" she raised her eyebrows, hands on her hips, and head slightly cocked to one side. Immediately I realised how my question could be viewed in slightly bad taste.

I panicked. "No, what I meant was if I sponsor a child then you have to have a drink with me." Casanova could not have put it better himself.

"So, now you are blackmailing me into going for a drink with you?"

"No, what I meant was..."

She held her clipboard up to my mouth. "I wouldn't go out with an insensitive prick like you if you were the last man on earth."

That seemed pretty final, but just when I thought things couldn't get any worse, Carla decided to announce my faux pas to her colleagues. "Hey, this guy will only help the starving children of Africa if I allow him to get into my pants."

Technically that isn't what I had suggested, although if the children of Africa could see this girl I think they would understand. Still, facing a sea of angry clipboard holders and fellow city workers, I decided to cut my losses and make a dignified exit.

I ran.

I got back to the office as quickly as I could. What the hell just happened? I tried not to dwell on it. After all, I had

43

only been single for four days. I just needed to dust the cobwebs down and get some match practice in and I'd be as right as rain.

Clearing my head, I got back on the phone. The second half of the day seemed to pass more quickly than the first, and by the time 5.30pm rolled round I realised I had not even started on the second draft of my sales plan.

"I'm off now, Dan," Kelly said. "Are you coming?"

"Nah, I've got to finish this report," I told her.

"You sure there isn't anything I can do to help?"

"Thanks, but I'll be okay."

"Okay, have a good evening. Don't stay too late."

I sat back and stared at the screen. One by one people started to leave the office. I cracked my knuckles and decided to get stuck in. But before I could get into my flow I was interrupted by the voice of an angel.

"You're Don Hilles, aren't you?" Shaila said looking at a piece of paper, and then glancing back at me.

"That's... er... that's right," I sputtered out. Hey, Don was close enough for me. This girl could call me whatever she wanted.

"I need to tell you something," Shaila continued. This was it. She was probably going to tell me that she too had shared our moment earlier today, but had been too shy to say anything before. Maybe this day wasn't going to end up as a total disaster after all.

"I will need that report emailed to me first thing in the morning so I can put it together for Mr Mussel with the other sales plans for his board meeting."

"Oh," I replied, the disappointment clear in my tone. I tried to sound more upbeat so I didn't come across like some sort of loser. "Yeah, sure. I'll have this bad boy done in a jiffy." I wasn't too sure if I should be more embarrassed by the fact I had referred to a sales plan as a *bad boy* or that I had used the word *jiffy*. Either way, Shaila simply nodded, pulled the strap of her handbag over her shoulder, turned on her heels and headed toward the exit.

"Tough luck, Hilles," Crowford said slapping me across the back of my head as he followed in hot pursuit of Shaila out of the office. I stared back at my computer screen.

Completing the sales plan seemed to take an eternity. Even the cleaner and the buzzing of his vacuum were long gone by the time I finally finished at 7.47pm. I emailed the report to Shaila, sat back in my seat and stretched. I couldn't help but smile to myself as I thought about how 2009 had started. So far I had exposed myself to a stranger, broken up with my girlfriend of three years, escaped death by baseball bat, been threatened with the sack, accepted Don as my new name, and ran away from a girl. Twice.

Not exactly the perfect start to the new year. At least I was safe in the knowledge that things couldn't get any worse. Right?

## Chapter 5: Black Sabbath

*Sunday, January 25, 2009 - 9.02am*
*Drought Clock: 23 days, 21 hours, 40 minutes*

The break-up of a long-term relationship is never easy. It was certainly one of the hardest things I'd ever done. You miss so many things. Intimacy, companionship, friendship. You miss having someone to share your day with; your dreams and hopes.

Me? I missed the bloody sex. No one warns you before a break-up how much you take for granted having regular sex on tap when you have a girlfriend. You start looking back and cursing yourself for how blasé you were when you had the opportunity to pretty much shag whenever you wanted.

All those missed opportunities. With Stacey I had once gone a whole month without having sex with her and thought nothing of it. A whole fucking month! What was I thinking? Three years equated to 1,095 days. I calculated that if during that period we had had sex an average of twice a week, we would have only had sex 312 times. That means I missed out on 783 day's worth of shagging!

Now, three weeks into being all on my lonesome I was already having withdrawals, and that had only been 23 days. How the hell had I managed to dismiss 783 days so easily?

The mornings were the toughest. Every day I would wake up and there he was, tall and proud. I felt guilty for not giving him any attention. After all, it wasn't all his fault. We had been in this together. But for the past three weeks I had resisted any contact with the one-eyed snake; almost as if I was punishing myself for all those wasted opportunities when I was with Stacey.

But this Sunday morning was different. I'd woken up with a boner so hard it was verging on being painful. I'd decided that little Dan had been punished enough, and he had a long overdue date with Palmala Handerson.

The art of mental masturbation is a skill that does not get the press it deserves. With no visual or audio aid to assist, a true pro-stroker will take a dip into the resource pool that is the wank bank; in this particular case the hot red-head who sat opposite me on the bus on Thursday evening.

I got myself comfortable on the bed, kicked off the covers, and prepared mass murder on millions of tiny defenceless sperm. Anyone who tells you that spit-shining the water pump is a dirty act should consider this: if Hitler had been into masturbation instead of murder, all the millions of deaths caused by his acts would have not upset the world.

I started off slow, but soon lost interest in making the act last. After all, this was not a spectator sport. Just as I felt myself coming to a climax, an unexpected noise put me off my rhythm. I glanced across the room and felt the colour drain from my face just as quickly as the blood started draining from little Dan.

"Rosalie!" I was horrified to see the cleaner tip-toeing around the bedroom, a feather duster in one hand. "I clean round you, no worry," she said in her thick South American accent, and continued to dust the shelves. I desperately tried pulling for the covers but it was too late and I ejaculated across the bed; an eruption of three weeks' worth of frustration.

"Naughty boy," Rosalie giggled. "I clean, I clean."

"No!" I shrieked in horror. "Please leave it Rosalie. I'll take care of it."

She reached for the bed cover and before I knew it I was involved in a tug-of-war for the sperm-soaked sheets. "I clean, I clean," she kept saying over and over again in broken English, a big smile on her olive-skinned face.

47

Rosalie eventually lost her grip, but the momentum of me yanking on the duvet sent me flying backwards; my legs flailing skywards and the cover landing on top of me, covering me in my very own love juice.

"Señor Hilles, so sorry, so sorry!" Rosalie clasped her hand over her mouth. "I clean?"

"No Rosalie," I managed to answer quite calmly. "I'll finish off here. You can start in the kitchen if you like?"

"Si señor. Gracias." Rosalie disappeared quickly out of the room, still dusting as she left.

I'm not too sure how long I sat there for. Maybe hours. Maybe days. Or maybe just five minutes. I had completely forgotten that I had hired Rosalie just before Christmas to come in once a month to clean the flat. Something told me I wouldn't forget again in the future.

I quickly showered and got dressed. Rosalie was just finishing off in the living room when I finally got up the courage to come out and face her. She was in her mid-40s and I had managed to work out that she was from Venezuela.

"Hi Rosalie," I sheepishly greeted her.

"Ah, señor Hilles. Naughty boy, naughty boy," she wiggled her finger at me.

"Yes, naughty boy," I said rubbing my hand through my hair and trying to avoid eye contact. I could feel myself going bright red again. "I'm really sorry about that. It won't happen again, I promise."

"It happens again?" She paused to think, one finger against the corner of her mouth. "No problem, no problem. I clean round you," she had obviously completely misunderstood what I was saying.

"No, it *won't* happen again. That…" I trailed off pointing towards my bedroom, "…won't happen again," I mirrored her accent, like that would make a difference in her understanding English, and slowed the pace of my words. "That... won't... happen... in... there... again." I then pointed towards the bedroom. And then in my infinite wisdom towards my groin.

She seemed to pause in thought before shrugging her shoulders. "You want me in bedroom? Ok." And she started to shuffle in the direction of the bedroom.

"No, no!" I said leaping in front of her to block her passage towards my room. "I'm saying it *won't* happen again. Ever." I waved my hands in front of me. "Okay, comprende?"

"Si, comprende," she nodded.

I pulled my wallet from my back pocket and handed her the money for cleaning the house, praying that she knew this was her wages and not some sort of indecent proposal or something sleazy.

"Gracias. Bye bye." She took the money and made her way out.

"Adiós," I said, falling backwards onto the sofa, pulling a cushion across my face.

*

I barely moved from the sofa all day, only getting up for toilet breaks and food. To say I was bored was an understatement. I'd been stuck in the flat all week. It was a week before the January pay day. Everyone was skint; a common occurrence at this time of the year. The early pay day in December coupled with the money spent at Christmas pretty much meant January was a write-off.

I'd been renting the small one-bedroom flat in Balham for about ten months. It cost me slightly more than I would have liked, but it was better than living back with my folks. Don't get me wrong – I love my parents. I just don't love living with them. Something happens after you have lived away at university for three years. You return home from

49

uni with your worldly belongings packed in boxes, including your independence. That box remains unpacked when you move back in with your folks, and stays that way until you make the plunge to move out.

My mobile phone suddenly vibrated into life, and it was a welcome distraction to the dross that was on television.

"Hello," I answered.

"Hello, love." It was my mum.

I sat bolt upright, preparing myself for the Spanish Inquisition. I hadn't spoken to my mum since I'd broken up with Stacey. I wasn't exactly avoiding her; I just knew she'd be disappointed. I was an only child, which meant my mum had all her hopes pinned on me making her a grandmother at some point. When I was five-years old I married my next-door neighbour Nicola, which was fine; a lot of kids pretend to marry. But not all kids have their mum proudly preside over the ceremony.

We got through the usual chit-chat: work was okay, dad had been doing the garden, the dog had to go and see the vet. And then, like a POW officer integrating a captured soldier, she got to the point.

"So have you got any news to tell me? You don't sound very cheerful. Is everything okay with you and Stacey?"

God, this woman was good. I should have known that I would not be able to avoid the subject forever. My mother had a sixth sense when it came to these sorts of things.

"Yeah, about Stacey," I started, trying to think of the best way to deliver the news. "We kind of broke up."

"What do you mean you *kind* of broke up?"

"Things had been pretty strained for a while and we just decided that it would be for the best if we went our separate ways." I intentionally left out the actual specifics of the break-up.

"But why?" she asked, her tone demanding more information than I really wanted to give. "I thought things were going well between you."

I knew she wasn't going to let up, so I told her about the arguments, and how Stacey had become unreasonable. I opened up to my mother and explained how we just wanted different things in life. I knew she would understand.

"Is there someone else?" she asked me sternly.

"No, nothing like that. It's just one of those things." For a moment I thought about lying and telling her that Stacey had cheated on me. It would have immediately got her on my side, and the questions would have taken a much-needed new direction. In the end I decided to see it through like a man. Albeit a man who for three weeks had been afraid to tell his mother the truth.

"You never tell me anything anymore. I have to force it out of you. I bet if I hadn't called you tonight, you would not have told me anytime soon."

"Of course I would have called you. I was going to call you in a day or two," I lied. There was more chance of me calling in a year or two.

"Are you okay?" Her tone softened.

"Yeah, I'll be okay. As I said, it's just one of those things."

"Okay. You will have to come over soon. We haven't seen you since Christmas."

"Sounds good. I'll call and we'll sort something out."

"Good. And if you need to talk..." she purposely trailed off.

"I'll give you call."

We said our goodbyes and I hung up, letting out a huge sigh of relief that I had finally got that out of the way. The call had sapped the energy out of me and I simply lost what little motivation I had left to get up from the sofa. The hours drifted away as I watched re-runs of old 80's sitcoms and

51

music videos, before the dozens upon dozens of channels all morphed into one. Before I knew it, the day had turned into night.

Sunday night is my least favourite part of the weekend. It means you are edging closer and closer to Monday morning as every minute passes. I sprawled across the sofa flicking through channels aimlessly. A discarded pizza box sat on top of the coffee table.

I managed to prise myself up and looked at the clock. It was 10.28pm. I had wasted the day away. I was sick and tired of sitting indoors. I picked my phone back up and typed in a text: *Anyone up for beers next Saturday?*

A couple of minutes passed before the first reply came back: *Ollie + beer = yes.* Rob was only 10 minutes behind with his response: *Sounds good buddy, it has been too long.*

The end credits to the film I had been watching on Channel 4 appeared on screen when my phone beeped for a third time. I scooped it up and almost dropped it when I saw the name: Stacey.

*Hi how r u? x*

I stared at it for a while, my mind trying to process the complete randomness of the text. We had not spoken since New Year's Day when Babe Ruth had tried knocking my head out of the ball park.

I placed the phone back on to the table without replying. I would be lying if I said I hadn't contemplated contacting Stacey over the last three weeks. Despite everything that had happened, I still wanted to make sure she was okay. Kelly had been spot on when she had said how hard it could be adjusting from a routine you had become so accustomed to. It felt strange going from daily contact with Stacey for three years to having no contact whatsoever. Maybe Stacey was feeling the same way and that is why she had sent the text.

The phone beeped again. I picked it up expecting it to be Jack's reply but it was Stacey again.

*R U mad with me? x*

I sat forwards, my elbows leaning against my knees, and brushed my hand through my hair. Her question baffled me. What the hell did she expect me to say? That I was pleased for the exercise after having to run for my life to avoid certain death at the hands of her pit bull flat-mate? Still, curiosity got the better of me and after a couple of minutes I decided to reply.

*Hi, I'm good. How r u? I'm not mad, just a bit confused.*

Within seconds the phone beeped: *Why are you confused? You're the one who used me for sex and then dumped me.*

Immediately I regretted replying to her. I'd fallen into her trap too easily. I knew the exact pattern of conversation that would follow if I replied. I had lost count of the number of conversations that had started like this during the last few months of our relationship. I sat back in my seat, pissed off that she was trying to drag me back into another pointless argument. When we had been together I had tried desperately to avoid situations like this, but she always managed to drag me into her web just like a female black widow spider preparing to eat her male equivalent after they have mated.

But then I smiled. We weren't together anymore. I didn't have to put up with this. I was free. No longer did I have to engage her in this bullshit. So I ignored her. This may sound immature, but I don't mind admitting that I got an enormous amount of satisfaction knowing that my silence would be driving Stacey crazy. My instinct was proven correct when she sent me a fourth text: *Too scared to face the truth? You're not a real man.*

If ever I needed proof that I had made the right decision, there it was. Stacey was not the same person I had once

53

known and fell in love with, and I knew that moving on was the best thing for me. Stacey on the other hand had different ideas, and not content with sending me abusive texts, my phone started to vibrate with her name flashing up on the screen. I contemplated sending her straight to my voicemail but I had already learnt my lesson with the 47 messages at New Year. I wanted to nip this in the bud now.

"What do you want, Stacey?" I abruptly answered.

"Don't speak to me like that," she was drunk. "Who do you think you are?"

I could hear Sophie egging her on in the background. I could just imagine her big mop of frizzy hair waving around like Medusa's snake locks.

"What do you want, Stacey?" I asked again.

"I just want to let you know that I'm so over you. I've found someone else and he is more of a man than you ever were."

"So you're dating Sophie, then?" I managed to stifle my laugh.

"You think you're so funny, don't you? You'd better hope you don't see me out because next time you won't be able to run."

"Hold on Stacey, I have got someone here who wants to talk to you. Say hello to my mate tone." And I clicked off.

I sat there for a while wondering how things had gone so wrong. Why had Stacey allowed herself to be manipulated by that witch Sophie? The girl I knew at university seemed like a distant memory, but I couldn't dwell on it any longer, and I certainly wouldn't blame myself for what had happened.

My phone beeped and the fifth text from Stacey came through. It was short, direct, and to the point: *wanker.*

I switched the television off and decided to call it a night. I got into bed and started to think about what Stacey had said. It really played on my mind. Not the part about me being a wanker obviously, but the fact she had met someone. I hated to admit it but it had got to me. Had she really met someone so soon or was she just trying to be spiteful and get a reaction out of me? It was probably the latter knowing her.

My phone beeped again. This was now getting beyond a joke. What sort of monster had she turned into? How long was this going to go on for?

*The 10th annual cock sucking and deep throating contest is this Friday. Don't bother coming mate, we've got girls to come this year. Thanks anyway champ! Yeah, I'm all over it buddy! See you Saturday. Come on!!*

I smiled. Jack was on board for drinks next week.

# Chapter 6: Out of Practice

*Saturday, January 31, 2009 - 7.35pm*
*Drought Clock: 30 days, 8 hours, 13 minutes*

Sitting in my flat in Balham, I stared at the computer screen, clicking my way through the pictures in the photo gallery. I had toyed with the idea of removing Stacey as my friend on Facebook. It was pretty clear that we were never going to be friends in the real world again, so why bother being cyber friends?

It presented a constant reminder of what she was up to. That is probably the worst thing about social networks on the net. Your private life is no longer private anymore. Even Jimmy Mercer – who I only vaguely remembered as the fat kid from primary school who used to sit at the back of the classroom sniffing Sherbet Dib Dabs – had constant access to my every move.

And now, looking at Stacey with her tongue down the throat of some Neanderthal with two huge gold hoop earrings, I was starting to think I had made a mistake by not cutting all ties with her.

"Come on, mate, don't do this to yourself," Rob said swigging at his bottle of beer.

"I can't believe she has moved on so quickly," I continued flicking through the pictures. It had now been four weeks since we had split up. The photo gallery I was looking at was titled *Friday night @ Oscars* and had been uploaded this morning.

I stopped on one picture of Mr gold earrings – tagged Dave Rowett – sandwiched in the middle of Stacey and Sophie. He had his hands on Stacey's chest while Sophie maniacally laughed behind him.

"She knew I'd see these pictures," I said pointing at Sophie, who had posted the gallery online.

"Forget about it, and turn the computer off," Rob handed me a beer. "Come on, drink."

He clinked his bottle against mine. I took one final look at the screen, gulped down a mouthful of beer and shut the computer down.

"Atta boy," Rob slapped me on the back. "Tonight I am making it my personal responsibility to get you hooked up. And she'll be a damn sight prettier than that goon Stacey was assaulting. I can't believe you used to kiss that mouth."

I laughed hard, nearly spitting out the contents of beer swishing around in my mouth. I needed a good laugh. I had not been out since New Year's. A combination of working late and waiting for pay day to roll round had kept me stuck indoors.

"Come on, take your beer with you," Rob said putting on his brown designer leather jacket. "I told the others we'd meet them at eight."

There was a cold bite in the air as we made our way down to Balham Station, and Rob had a mischievous look about him. "This is where it begins, Danny boy."

"What are you talking about," I asked him.

"Single life," he said it as though that was meant to clear everything up. Obviously the look on my face told him I still had no idea where he was going with this.

"Danny, for three years you have done a very honourable thing. You gave your penis to just one woman," Rob patted me on the back. "Honourable, but fucking stupid at the same time."

"Eh?" was about all I could muster as we entered the tube station.

"You were what 19, 20, when you hooked up with Stacey? Do you know how sad it is that I slept with more girls at *your* university than you did?"

Rob had a point. Every time he came to visit me he pretty much cleaned up.

"You wasted a lot of opportunities," he told me. "Luckily for the girls you went to university with I was willing to take one for the team. But I never allowed myself to get tied down to any of them, and believe me when I say that a few of those girls were into that sort of thing."

As we stepped onto the escalator, Rob turned to face me. "Single life, Danny," he said like it was the greatest thing in the world. "Take our current setting, for example," he said waving his arm around the tube station. "How many times have you been on the Tube on the way to work and seen a really hot girl and thought to yourself 'if I was single, I would talk to her?'"

"A few I guess," I answered. And by a few I meant none. Yes I'd seen plenty of good-looking girls on the Tube, but I would never have the balls to approach any of them – single or not. I just wasn't one of those guys who were capable of pulling off something like that. We made our way down the platform and Rob continued to educate me on the delights of my newfound single life.

"Tube stations are a great place to meet women," Rob enlightened me. "You just need to be confident," he said scanning the platform. "What about her?" he said pointing towards a girl wearing a long cream coloured coat.

"She's cute, I guess."

"Go and talk to her then."

"What?" I responded like he had asked me to place my hand in a blender.

"Go and talk to her. Just say hello."

"And then what?"

"Something will come to you," and he pushed me in her direction. I turned back to him but he waved me on. "If you're lucky, she'll bite."

A strange uneasy feeling began to come over me. My palms began to sweat. She caught sight of me coming towards her out the corner of her eye. I stopped and turned back to Rob but he kept urging me on. Before I knew it I was standing next to her. I needed to say something quickly before this got even more awkward.

"Excuse me," I nervously said.

"Yes?" she faced me, a subtle pink lip-gloss made her lips look luscious.

"Erm, I was just standing over there with my friend," I actually pointed towards Rob. "And I just wanted to say hello."

"Hello," she smiled. Yes, she smiled! She could have pepper sprayed me, but instead she smiled. A good sign. Things were going well. I decided to follow this up with...

... the longest pause known to man. I drew a complete blank. I puffed out my cheeks as if somehow that would help the situation and rubbed my hands excessively down the side of my jeans. We were experiencing an awkward silence and this wasn't even a first date. Eventually she broke the unbearable silence by asking "Was there anything else?"

"No. I mean, yes." Say something more meaningful than this for fuck's sake I thought to myself. "You're getting a tube, then?"

There are days when I look back at this moment and wish I had asked her if she came here often. Anything else than asking her if she was getting a bloody tube while she waited on the platform at a tube station, directly opposite a map of the Northern Line.

"Er, yeah," she replied, now with a slightly nervous tone to her voice as the southbound tube thundered into the platform. "This is my tube," she said almost relieved to be putting an end to my misery. "Nice speaking to you." And with that she hopped on, not even giving me a second look, sitting down with her back to the window.

"So, how did it go?" Rob asked as I shuffled back over to him. "Did you get her number?"

"No, and if you have any more pearls of wisdom tonight please keep them to yourself," I pleaded, more than asked.

The northbound tube pulled into the platform and we got on to make the short two-stop journey to Clapham Common. As we took our seats it was pretty clear Rob was not going to let this go so easily. "Don't worry about what just happened. You're just out of practice; it's ring rust that's all. After being stuck with the same girl for three-years you have simply forgotten how to chat-up girls. It'll all come flooding back, trust me," Rob told me confidently before smiling at a strawberry blonde opposite us, and then engaging her in conversation like it was the easiest thing in the world.

Maybe Rob was right. Before Stacey I'd had a decent track record with the ladies. Clearly not a track record like Rob; he just needed to look in the direction of a female and she seemed to drop her knickers for him. I just needed to get back into the saddle – it's like riding a bike as they say.

God, I really missed riding.

Ollie and Jack were already waiting outside when we got to Clapham Common. Jack was on his mobile phone. "I told you I was out Saturday night, darling," he said down the phone in his over exaggerated cockney accent. "It's going to be a messy one – I've brought the big guns out tonight." Jack spotted us and winked in our direction.

"Who is he on the phone to," I asked Ollie.

"Anna," Ollie responded.

"No idea what time I'll be back, sweetheart." Jack looked back over to us and used his hand to simulate a mouth chatting by bringing his fingers and thumb together repeatedly. "Okay, don't wait up."

He clicked the phone off. "Hello boys, ready for some carnage tonight?" Jack shook our hands and embraced us.

We headed into Murphy's Bar opposite the station, and Rob got the first round in. He left two pound coins in the silver tip tray left behind by the barmaid. She smiled and thanked him as she took the tray away.

"Why the hell did you do that?" Jack questioned.

"Because when the bar gets busier later on, I won't have any problems getting served," Rob offered as an explanation. "That two pounds just bought me quick and efficient service for the rest of the night," he winked at the barmaid who smiled back. "And probably a blowsie from her at the end of the night."

"It just bought you one less beer is what it bought you," Jack replied, rolling his eyes.

We took our place at a table towards the back of the bar. It was our usual spot; just far away enough from the speakers for us to still hear each other over the loud dance music.

"So what happened to Kirsty from New Year?" I asked Rob.

"She was nice enough Danny, but nice isn't always what you want, if you know what I mean?" Rob said.

"She wouldn't let you slap her on the face with your cock huh?" was Jack's delightful input to the conversation, and improvised the movement just to drive his point home.

"I love dirty women," Ollie said.

"What the hell are you talking about? You only do the missionary position," Jack said before mimicking Ollie's voice: "If missionary was good enough for my old man, and his father before him, then it's good enough for me."

Rob and I laughed as Ollie tried to argue back. "Shut up, I do other positions," he said.

"Like what?" Jack taunted him.

Ollie took a long pause and a sip of his pint, presumably to try and recall his extensive knowledge of the karma sutra before replying.

"Up the arse."

"Nice," I commented, raising my eyebrows.

61

"Yeah, I get her in the position to do her doggy style, and then I just slip it in," Ollie said explaining the art to his technique.

"Doesn't the girl notice?" Rob asked him.

"Yeah, but I pretend I haven't realised and tell her I'll be finished in a minute anyway."

"Touché," Jack raised his beer to Ollie.

"And who said romance was dead?" Rob said shaking his head. "Maybe I'll have to try that one myself sometime." We all laughed.

Suddenly all of our eyes locked on a stunning blonde who entered the bar with a group of friends. She was wearing knee-high fuck-me-boots and a snake-print dress. They took up a position directly opposite us at the bar.

"That bird is absolute," Jack said, his eyes bulging out of his head, and the accustomed one finger index salute he made when paying a girl the compliment of calling her *absolute*.

"Go and talk to her Dan," Rob said.

"Are you nuts? I'm not talking to her." What the hell was he trying to do to me? He had already witnessed the car crash at Balham tube station.

"Yeah, go and talk to her Dan," Jack egged me on.

"Why don't you go and talk to her?" I fired back.

"I would, but I'm just waiting for the right moment," Jack said rubbing his hands together.

"Ladies, ladies. I'll go and talk to her," and Rob got up and made his way over. We all watched the master in silence.

"Excuse me, I don't mean to interrupt," Rob started, confidence oozing from his body language. "I know this might sound really schoolboy, but... I'm so embarrassed, I can't believe I'm doing this."

"Don't be embarrassed, what is it?" she responded, already seemingly hanging on his every word.

He lowered his head, and rubbed his brow, but constantly sporting that big white smile. "Do you see my friend over there?" He pointed in my direction.

She looked straight at me. "What the hell is he doing?" I asked the others. Ollie and Jack shrugged their shoulders as they kept their eyes firmly locked on the blonde who was now playing with her hair.

"He wants to know..." he paused for just the right effect. "He wants to know..."

Please don't do this to me I thought, we're not back in the playground playing *my mate fancies you*.

"He wants to know... if you fancy me?"

What?! I want to know if she fancies *him*?!

"Why doesn't he ask me himself?" she teased, keeping her eyes permanently locked on Rob. I doubt she even knew what I looked like. Or cared.

"He's shy," Rob responded.

"Sure," she smiled. "You're not *too* bad," and she playfully rubbed her hand across his face.

And just like that Rob proved his point. He spent the next 10 minutes flirting outrageously with her while Jack kept cursing him for not bringing her over with her friends. "What is he doing?" Jack asked us. "I've got the right horn for that dark haired bird. She keeps giving me the eye."

"I think she just has a nervous twitch," I taunted him.

"I don't care which one I have. I'm up for anything," Ollie confessed. "Do you want the fat one Dan?"

"Funnily enough Ollie, I don't," I said.

"That is fine with me; I'll take her. Fat birds tend to put a bit more effort in as they don't know where the next shag is coming from."

"This is ridiculous," Jack declared. "I'm not waiting any longer. Oi, Rob!" Jack perched his small frame up on to the seat. "Bring the birds over here – we've got plenty of room."

63

Faced with such a charming invitation, how could they resist? Rob led the girls over and made the introductions. The blonde who Rob had been talking to was Katie. Jack immediately made a beeline for dark-haired Jessica, while non-fussy Ollie started up a conversation with fat Kathy.

Friend number four slid into the remaining seat next to me, but I certainly wasn't disappointed with what I had been left with. She was petite, with full lips and auburn coloured hair in bob cut. She had pretty little freckles on her nose.

"Hi, I'm Grace," she extended her hand, "I guess you're stuck with me."

"I guess so," I stuttered as I shook her hand. "I mean, I'm pleased I'm stuck with you. Not that I feel that I'm stuck with you. I probably would have chosen you."

Get a grip I told myself.

"You really know how to make a girl feel special," she smiled and took a sip of her bright coloured cocktail.

Say something I thought. Everyone else had engaged in some sort of conversation. Jack was overly animated and talking with his hands, while Ollie had no shame in basically talking to Kathy's chest. I started to feel the same type of anxiety I had felt on the tube platform earlier. What was wrong with me?

"What is that you are drinking?" I eventually blurted out.

"Sex on the Beach. Wanna try?" She offered me the straw.

I took a sip. "Mmm, not as sandy as last time."

"Sorry?"

"Not as sandy as last time I had sex on the beach," I cringed the moment the last syllable of the sentence dribbled out of my mouth.

"Oh, right." She sort of let out a weak laugh, and then abruptly turned away and started looking around the bar; a sure-fire sign I had managed to put her off me in record

64

time. This was not going well. Rob must have sensed my desperation. He gave me the thumbs up as a way of asking if I was okay, but I just shook my head. I was really annoyed how easily I'd given up. Stacey was right, I wasn't a real man – I was pathetic; doomed to walk the rest of the earth a singleton.

"Hey Dan, what's the name of the place where we went snowboarding last year?" Rob suddenly asked out of the blue.

I was taken slightly aback but managed to answer, "Lake Tahoe."

"Oh my god, you snowboard?" Grace was genuinely interested. "That is *so* cool."

Rob simply smiled and winked at me before he slipped back into his conversation with Katie with great ease. It was simple things like this that showed that thin line between a friend and a best friend.

"Yeah, well at least I try," I turned back to Grace who was now leaning towards me, her chin resting on her hand. "I fall down a lot," I said as she giggled.

And just like that I was back on track. It felt like a weight had been lifted off my shoulders. We talked for ages and I started to feel comfortable again. It turned out to be a great night, the first one I'd really had this year.

Rob was as smooth as ever, and had Katie eating out of the palm of his hand without even breaking sweat. Jack was his usual loud self, making sure he was centre of attention and he continuously had us laughing at his jokes. Ollie had drunk himself into a stupor, and nestled his head across Kathy's ample breasts, who didn't seem to mind too much to be fair.

At the sound of the last orders bell we walked the girls to the nearest mini cab station. We paired off again as we waited for their taxi to arrive. Katie had Rob's leather jacket draped over her shoulders and he wrapped his arms around

65

her to shield her from the cold. Jack and Jessica locked lips, while Kathy pinned Ollie up against the wall and was practically eating the poor boy in what was clearly the most disgraceful public display of affection of the evening. Maybe fat girls were more grateful I thought to myself.

"It's so cold," Grace said, shivering.

"Where are my manners?" I took my jacket off and placed it over her shoulders. I hesitated to put my arm around her. Instead I almost ended up leaning my arm against her, before she made the move to snuggle herself against me.

"I had fun tonight," she said looking into my eyes.

"Me too," I hesitated again. Just ask her out – stop being such a pussy. "Perhaps we could go for a drink sometime," I finally summoned the courage to ask.

"Yeah, I'd like that."

The taxi pulled up and the girls got inside. As we waved them off Rob turned to me. "So, are you going to see Grace again?"

"Yeah, we said we'd meet up for a drink."

"You got her number then?"

Damn it.

# Chapter 7: First Date

*Saturday, February 7, 2009 - 7.40pm*
*Drought Clock: 36 days, 7 hours, 18 minutes*

Rob came to the rescue again. Embarrassingly I got him to text Katie asking for Grace's number. It probably cost me some serious points in the cool stakes, but I hoped the banter we had exchanged over texts throughout that week had repaired the damage. Plus we'd arranged to meet up the following Saturday so I'd have another crack at redeeming myself. Perhaps we would even laugh about the whole phone incident in bed after sex. Or at least that is the scenario I was wishing for.

But as the week wore on, the nerves had started to get the better of me. The build-up to the date had put me on edge. I started to get the same feeling as the night I lost my virginity.

I was 17 when I finally popped my cork. It was the summer of 2002 and me and the boys had travelled to Magaluf for our first ever lads' holiday. We picked the destination mainly because Ollie's older brother Brian had been there two years previously and often referred to it as *Shagaluf*. That was enough to sell it to Rob, Jack, Ollie, and me.

Six nights into a two-week break I met Rebecca. She was 18, tanned, with long golden brown hair. She could have just been 18 and female and that would have been enough.

She wasn't perfect by any stretch of the imagination. For example, she had an annoying habit of widening her eyes whenever she finished a sentence, making her look a bit like a frog. But two hours' worth of alcohol later, including six shots of something blue that tasted like aniseed, she took me by the hand and ordered me to take her back to my apartment.

This is when I made schoolboy error number one. I boasted to my friends that I was about to get *some*. I was going to "get my nuts in deep" is how I remember romantically describing it. I grabbed the wide-eyed Rebecca by her hand and marched her out of the bar like a man possessed.

Almost instantly the warm night air roused me from my drunken state and the enormity of this situation started to fester on my teenage brain. I was going to have sex. This was really going to happen. But wait – what if I was no good? What if I got too excited and squirted before I had even got my pants off? Or what if I got her pregnant? Shit, where were those condoms?

I quickly flipped my phone out and texted the boys to find out where the six packets of condoms were that we had brought along on this trip (only one had been used so far – by Rob obviously). Within seconds I got a reply from Jack informing me of which drawer I could find the *Randy van Warmers* in, as he liked to refer to them as. Little did I know that I had just made schoolboy error number two.

We arrived at the door to the apartment. Rebecca passionately kissed and nuzzled my neck as I fumbled to get the key in the door. She whispered how much she wanted me, which only served to make me feel more anxious. Finally I got the key in the door and we were in. She shoved me down on to the bed and leapt on top of me, whispering further delightful treats such as *stick it in me.* I reached across to the drawer where Jack said the condoms were stashed.

What was I going to do once I had a condom anyway? Did I put it on straight away or did I wait until she instructed me to do so? And what if she wanted to go downstairs for some foreplay – did I put it on before or after? I was so confused.

But the condoms were nowhere to be found. I panicked. What if I couldn't find them? Would she still let me stick it in?

I didn't have much time to think about it though as suddenly the door swung open. It was then my schoolboy errors came home to roost as standing in the doorway were the laughing teenage figures of Rob, Jack, and Ollie.

"Go on my son!" Jack shrieked. "You'll need these," and he threw the condoms at us. I was horrified as the packet bounced off Rebecca's head. She screamed at me to get them out, and I jumped up without thinking. The laughs grew louder as I stood naked in front of my so-called friends, with a penis as tall and proud as ever, and ushered them out. I could still hear their laughter outside as I turned around and scooped up one of the condoms. I ripped the packet open and struggled to roll the latex balloon down my penis. Luckily Rebecca was on hand to tell me I was doing it the wrong way.

As soon as I was strapped I jumped back into bed. Screw foreplay – I didn't know how much time I had left. Ignoring the giggles outside the front door I proceeded to lose my virginity. *Awkwardly*. But things were about to take an unexpected turn.

During the course of that day I had visited the local shop and returned with bread, ham, and cheese. My fantastic idea was that we would save beer money in our final week by making sandwiches for lunch. In my head, this was a fantastic idea and I would return home a hero. In reality, it is a well-known scientific fact that boys are immature at the best of times. Seventeen-year old boys on their first holiday are probably at the most immature level the male species can reach. Instead of praising my well-thought out plan of making sandwiches, they ridiculed me mercilessly and started to throw slices of ham, bread, and cheese around our apartment to show their appreciation.

I don't think I will ever forget the moment 30 seconds into losing my virginity that I noticed the piece of ham stuck to side of Rebecca's face. "What the hell is this?" she screamed upon realising she had a smelly, cold, piece of processed meat attached to her cheek. Her horror caused her muscles to tense, which caught me by surprise, and is still the reason I maintain to this very day why I only lasted 36 seconds during my first ever sexual experience. And if you don't believe me you can always watch the whole sorry incident on Jack's camera phone as luckily he was at the apartment window filming every last pathetic detail.

*

This was the first date I'd been on in over three years. After being with one person for so long, it was almost like I had no recollection of the rules of dating.

Luckily though, the boys had been on hand during the course of the week and were kind enough to offer their expertise on first dates, and how to impress a girl.

Where to take her:

**Rob:** Too many guys take girls to the cinema on a first date, but that is no good. You want to go somewhere where you can talk and get to know each other. You can't go too wrong with a romantic dinner. But don't take her to Burger King for crying out loud.

**Ollie:** There is that new Kung-Fu film on at the cinema. I bet she'd like that. Or even better, take her to a horror because she'll be all over you. You might even cop a feel in the back row.

**Jack:** Wherever you go, make sure you arrange to meet somewhere out in the open so you can get a good look at her beforehand. I'm sure Grace is a good-looking girl, but we all had our beer goggles on that night. She could be a right old bow-wow. In which case, ditch her there and then. Give me a call and we'll go for a beer instead.

Start of the date:

**Rob:** Make sure you arrive early and compliment her. Tell her how fantastic she looks before you say anything else. Girls love compliments, but don't go too overboard because they will start to lose their effect, and you'll come across as a desperado.

**Ollie:** Get a few shots in; it will help you relax. But don't have too many, you don't want to get drunk too early. Seven or eight shots should do the trick. Maybe drink a pint of milk before you go out just to line your stomach. Or maybe a dairy-based alcoholic beverage like Eggnog. That will kill two birds with one stone!

**Jack:** Don't play your cards too early – keep a few aces up your sleeve. You don't want to slip a Manchester United shirt on and call yourself Roy Keane. Girls hate it when guys are too keen. The last thing you want to do is be hanging on her every word and come across too *Roy*.

During the date:

**Rob:** Listen to her and ask questions. Keep your focus, attention, and conversation solely on her. Be interested in what she has to say and get to know her. Make her feel like she is the only person in the room that really matters. But don't stare at her tits though; unless she encourages that sort of thing. If she does – winner!

**Ollie:** I would advise against farting in front of her. The only time you can really do that is after you have slept with her a few times and then you can trap her head under the covers. She is officially your girlfriend when you get to the stage of forcing her head into the Dutch oven.

**Jack:** Make sure you crack a few jokes throughout the date. Birds love a guy with a good sense of humour. Say things like, "Want to come back to mine for pizza and sex? Why not? Don't you like pizza?" She'll be all over you mate, trust me.

The end of the date:

**Rob:** Some girls don't kiss on the first date; some will be disappointed if you don't at least try to kiss her goodnight. There is no easy answer for this one. You'll have to try and gauge the situation from her body language and go on your gut instinct. Not once have I ever failed to get a goodnight kiss, but this is you we're talking about.

**Ollie:** I insist on two things when I go back to a girl's flat: a cooked breakfast in the morning, and a lift home.

**Jack:** If she bites it, smack her.

Loaded with such brilliant advice, how could things possibly go wrong? I'd arranged to meet Grace in a bar in Leicester Square at 8pm. I was planning on getting there about five minutes early, but my enthusiasm to make sure I was on time meant I ended up getting to the bar 20 minutes too early.

I decided to go in and scope the place out. I spotted an intimate table in the corner and slipped my jacket across the back of the chair, like a lion marking my territory. I decided to get a drink in, something a lion probably wouldn't do.

"Vodka and coke, please," I said to the barmaid. I watched as she poured in a double measure of vodka and then sprayed the coke on top; the ice clinking against the glass as she sat it down in front of me.

"That's seven pounds and 20 pence please," the barmaid said. Bloody West End prices. I started to think that I hadn't thought this through very well. Inevitably I was going to end up paying for this date, with that being the gentlemanly thing to do. This was going to cost me an arm and a leg.

I handed her a £10 note and she placed the change on one of those little silver trays in front of me. I remembered Rob leaving the barmaid a tip last week, and his plan had worked – he never had to wait longer than a couple of minutes to get served whenever he went to the bar. So I scooped up the silver coins and left the barmaid two gold ones.

"Thank you very much," she said smiling as she collected the money. "I'll be able to get myself a drink when my shift ends at eight." Bollocks I thought to myself. My two pounds had earned me just 15 minutes worth of immediate service. Not exactly money well spent.

I had time to kill. Looking around the bar, I started to get that paranoid feeling that people were looking at me like I was some kind of loner. Of course, no one was paying me any attention, but that didn't prevent the burning desire I had inside to prove I wasn't alone, and was in fact waiting for someone.

I constantly checked my watch, and squinted as I stared into crowds of people, trying to make it as obvious as possible I was looking for someone.

My mobile came in extremely useful in this situation too. What did people do when they were waiting for someone before mobile phones came along? I pretended to text. I even started to write conversations with myself. Before realising it I had typed out sentences like *Where is she? I hope she turns up soon.* I glanced around to make sure no one had seen this and quickly deleted the messages.

I thought about calling someone, but who would I call? If I called my mates they would take the piss saying I had been stood-up. If I called my mum she would want to pry; and calling your mum on a first date isn't something I could imagine a 21st century James Dean doing. Instead I pretended to make a call.

I finished my first drink and went to the bar and ordered another; getting my money's worth for the one and only time that night as the same barmaid served me another double vodka and coke in record time. I sat back down and looked at my watch: two minutes past eight.

As the minutes passed I resisted the urge to text Grace. She had probably got caught on the Tube or something, knowing how bad public transport could be. Still, by the time 8.15pm ticked by I was onto my third vodka and coke and starting to worry.

"Hey, need some company?" The barmaid I had bought a drink earlier plonked herself down in the seat opposite me reserved for Grace.

"I was just waiting for someone," I stuttered.

"You've been waiting for quite a long time. Has she stood you up?"

"No, I just got here early," I told her, now nervously looking towards the door. I was pretty sure that sitting here with another woman was not going to be viewed too favourably on a first date.

"I see guys get stood up in here all the time. They sit around waiting for ages like right losers. But you bought me a drink so I thought I'd take pity on you."

The nerve of this girl. She couldn't have been more than 19 and here she was making assumptions that I was this sad loser who had been stood-up and needed her company. Had she not seen my little act earlier which made it perfectly clear I was waiting for someone?

"I am not a *loser*, she is just running late," I told her.

"How do you know? Has she called or text you?" she said, sipping on the drink I had probably bought her.

"Well, no..."

"She hasn't even contacted you? You have definitely been stood-up." She giggled.

"I have not been stood up. And even if I have, I don't care because..."

"Hi Dan, I'm so sorry I'm late," out of nowhere Grace was now standing at the side of the table. "Who's this?"

Before I even had a chance to reply the barmaid got in there. "He thought you had stood him up."

"No, I didn't think *she* had stood me up," I frowned at the barmaid before turning to Grace with a nervous smile on my face. "I didn't think you had stood me up."

"Anyway, I'll get off now you're here. Thanks for the drink," the barmaid said before leaving me the most cumbersome start to a first date I think I could have imagined.

"I'm sorry about that, she just came over and..." I started to explain.

"No need to apologise, it's me who's late." Grace said as she hung her coat and scarf over the back of the chair.

Wow, she looked amazing. More gorgeous than I remembered. She was wearing a black sleeveless silk jersey top, shiny dark grey leggings, and black heels.

"You look nice," she said as she sat down.

75

Damn it, she had beaten me to it. All I had left in response was a pathetic "Thanks, so do you." I groaned inside at how lame that sounded. "Can I get you a drink?"

"Yes please. Bacardi, lime, and slimline tonic."

As I carried the drinks back to our table I realised that I was already now on my fourth double vodka. I would need to pace myself if I was going to get through this date.

I sat back down and surprisingly eased into conversation with her. The drink seemed to have a calming influence on me. She told me all about her job in market research, but her dream job would be to run her own bar in the Caribbean. She loved RnB music and romantic comedies. She had an older sister, and a pet cat called Smokey.

She laughed at me. Not literally at me, but at my jokes. I had to pinch myself that I was sitting here with such a stunner. I noticed other guys around the bar looking at her and I grew in confidence at the fact that she was *my* date. I started to grow in other places too when she slid her finger around the top of her glass and then sucked the liquid off.

I was so engrossed with her that I hadn't realised how busy the bar had got while we talked. The people around us had formed a mini dance floor next to the table where we sat, and it was growing in numbers.

"Let's dance," she said, her eyes widening with a big smile on her face.

This was not good. When the big man upstairs had been handing out rhythm, he neglected to bless me with the dancing gene. I was so bad I looked like Frankenstein on acid when I hit the dance floor. My movements resembled that of a Daddy Long Legs. I had no coordination or thought to my movements, and would simply remain in one spot with too much arm movement. It wasn't a pretty sight.

The DJ had started to play a full-set of the latest RnB and hip-hop tracks. I have a rule I lived by – no white man

76

should dance to RnB, unless you are Michael Jackson of course.

It is not natural for your normal run-of-the mill white guy, especially when you gyrated like a pensioner after a hip operation like I did. And if you were on the verge of being drunk then it was a total no-no. A drunken white guy dancing to RnB is never going to have a happy ending.

"Maybe later, I'm not really in the mood right now," I lied. I would never be in the mood. Ever.

"Okay," she said sitting back and curling her lips downward, playacting how disappointed she was.

"Maybe after a few more drinks," I stupidly said.

With that she leapt to her feet. "Right," she said. "In that case we had better get you another drink!"

Five minutes later she returned with *another* double vodka and coke, and two shots of Sambuca. "Down it," she demanded with a sexy little smile on her face. We both slammed the drinks back. She then slid the vodka and coke towards me. "This one as well. We need to loosen you up."

By now I had drunk seven double vodka and cokes and a shot of Sambuca, and I was starting to feel light-headed. She took my hand and led me on to the dance floor. She moved like serpent, her body moving in time to the beat. She pressed herself up against me. "Relax," she whispered into my ear. But all I could think of was *please don't get a boner.*

I was sure that all eyes were on her. Inadvertently that also meant that all eyes would be on me and my total lack of rhythm. I attempted to limit my movement, sticking with the simple sidestep routine. But the more paranoid I felt, the stiffer my movements became. To complement the shuffled sidestep I started to bounce my shoulders up and down. I must have looked like a puppet on a string.

Eventually she put me out of my misery, leaning towards me and kissing me on the cheek. "Thanks for the dance," she said and she took my hand and led me back to the table.

"I'm just going to the bathroom," she said excusing herself.

I've blown it I thought to myself. I was worried she might not even come back. I hated myself for not being able to just let go. Grace was right; I did need to loosen up. I finished my vodka and coke, and made my way to the bar and bought two more shots of Sambuca and another round of drinks for us.

"Snap," Grace said as she got back to the table, holding two more Sambuca shots in her hand. We downed the shots and I took a gulp of my vodka and coke. I wiped my mouth, and took Grace by the hand. "Come on," I said with a determined look in my eyes. "Let's dance."

I led her onto the crowded dance floor and decided to let it all go. I started to feel the music and moved in time to the beat. After years of making such a big deal about not dancing, I was now making love to the music and it felt great. If God is a DJ then I was his disciple. A surge went through my body. For the first time in my life, I threw my inhibitions to one side and danced like man had never danced before. There was an edge to my performance and all eyes were definitely on me.

Unfortunately for all the wrong reasons.

In reality, I was completely pissed. I looked like an octopus that had only two tentacles left and was trying to compensate for the missing six. One leg remained completely stiff, while the other leg had a mind of its own and performed some sort of strange convulsion. At one point I busted out my version of the running man, then into the worm, completed with a roly-poly into the disco finger. My face was a picture of pure concentration as I bit down on my bottom lip and nodded my head to the bass line. A

78

frown appeared across my brow to show my fellow dancers that I meant business.

Not content with that, I followed up with a shimmy directed to different sides of the dance floor. I finished off with the lasso, ripping my shirt off and swinging it around my head, like a cowboy trying to snare cattle.

The memory is nothing but a blur to me, but sometimes at night I wake up in a cold sweat from the nightmare of the complete horror performance I must have put on. Someone once sang a song called *Murder on the Dancefloor.* That night, that song became my anthem.

I didn't notice Grace slip away through the crowd that had now gathered around me and were egging me on to attempt the Macarena. I couldn't exactly blame Grace. I can only imagine her embarrassment at having to dance with John Revolting. To top it all off, I decided to be a crowd pleaser and performed my version of Macarena. And if you can believe it, I somehow made my version even worse than the original.

Finally I ran out of steam and staggered back to our table. Grace was nowhere to be seen. People were patting me on the back and congratulating me on a job well done, as they held back tears of laughter. I pulled my shirt back on, minus three buttons, and headed over to the bar. It was packed solid and I swayed in my vodka and Sambuca fuelled-state before pushing my way to the front. I obnoxiously waved a 10 pound note towards the bar staff. It took me an age to get served, and when I finally ordered my drink I decided to leave the new barmaid a tip so I would not have to wait quite so long next time. But a tall guy with long hair and a dark tan picked up my tray. I grabbed his hand. "That's not for you," I slurred. "That is for her."

Don't worry, I'll make sure she gets it," he replied and tried to pull away, but I kept hold of his arm.

"No, I want her to have it." I forcefully said, my finger swaying in the barmaid's direction.

"Let go of my arm," the barman said sternly and tried to pull away again. I made a grab for the silver tray and he tried pushing me back. "He is trying to steal your tip," I shouted to the barmaid, somehow believing she would see that I was fighting for her honour and come to my aid.

Instead she called the security staff over. Two burly doorman grabbed me; one holding me by the arms while the other lifted my legs up. They scooped me off the floor and carried me through the bar. I tried to resist, but even if I had been sober I was no match for these two behemoths. We reached the fire exit and they launched me at the doors, forcing them to crash open before I was dumped outside in the rain.

I skilfully managed to land in a puddle in such a way that 80 per cent of my clothing was soaked through. From the distance a bright white light approached. For a moment I thought it was God. But instead it turned out to be a taxi. It skidded to a halt beside me, splashing the remaining content of the puddle into my face. The window wound down. "Dan?" I heard a familiar voice say. I looked up and Grace was looking down at me. "Is that you?" she said.

"Grace, I'm glad I've bumped into you," I said, dragging myself up from the gutter. "Do you fancy meeting up next week?"

"Drive on," I heard her say as the taxi pulled away and disappeared into the distance.

## Chapter 8: Valentine's Day Massacre

*Saturday, February 14, 2009 - 8.01pm*
*Drought Clock: 43 days, 16 hours, 36 minutes*

A week had passed since the now infamous first date with Grace. I had sent her a text the following morning to apologise and, unsurprisingly, I had not heard back from her. I couldn't even keep the incident under wraps as Katie had told Rob the whole story. She even told him things I couldn't remember. At one point I had apparently spotted someone taking the piss out of my dancing and had engaged in a heated exchange with them, only to realise it was my reflection in the mirror.

So in the aftermath of what had been the worst period of my love life to date, the last thing I needed was Valentine's Day. I really didn't want to go out. The thought of spending an evening being reminded that everyone else was getting some did not really appeal to me in the slightest. But I'd promised Ollie I would meet him for beers. Rob had a date with Katie, while Jack was taking Anna out for a meal. Ollie had as many options as I did for Valentine's Day and had nagged me to meet him for a drink as he reasoned that alcohol was better than any woman.

I was meeting Ollie in a pub in Wimbledon called the Three Crowns. Unlike the dozens of trendy wine bars and gastro pubs that had cropped up in the town over the last 10 years, this was more of your traditional English pub. It was in desperate need of a paint job, with black and white photos on the wall capturing images of life in Wimbledon a century ago. It sold proper ale on tap rather than stocking the shelves with fancy coloured bottles of alcopops. I was confident this was just the place where we would not be exposed to countless romantic couples out celebrating their love for each other. Ollie was already at the bar when I

81

walked in, nursing a pint, and pretending to text someone so people wouldn't think he was on his own.

"What time do you call this?" Ollie asked as we exchanged handshakes. I winced as he crushed my hand as he always did, not realising his own strength.

"Sorry, mate," I yanked my hand away. "Got here as quick as I could." He already had a pint waiting for me. "So how's work?" I asked taking that first satisfying gulp of the evening.

"Not bad, you know how it is," Ollie said, pretty much summing up his life as a postman. I nodded at him and raised my glass back to my mouth. I glanced around the pub as the silence between us grew in the air. We both knew what the other was thinking but neither one of us wanted to say it. Here we were, two single guys out on Valentine's Day. Together. It didn't get any sadder than that. We were on a man date. It was a sorry state of affairs. I was about to ask Ollie whether he delivered his own mail, but luckily he had a much more interesting topic of conversation.

"I've been shagging this housewife lately," he said with a big grin. "She's a right Milf."

This was more like it. "How did that start?" I enquired, quite excited.

"You know how it goes, mate. I start by slipping the post through the letterbox, and then I move on to slipping her one."

And it didn't really need any more of an explanation than that. As men, we didn't need to examine everything with a fine-tooth comb. No need for the little details. Ollie was shagging an older woman. That was all we needed. I raised my glass to him on a job well done.

Obviously, that is a complete lie. He told me some disgusting stories about what he had been doing to this poor, lonely housewife. A gentleman never tells, but we were far from being gentlemen.

Ollie's revelation opened up the door to our first topic of conversation for the evening – women. Cars and football would come later. We turned our lack of female companionship on the most romantic day of the year by engaging ourselves in a bit of women bashing. It wasn't *our* fault we didn't have dates tonight. We didn't even want a date. Moaning about women made us feel much better about our own inadequacies of not being able to actually find one.

"Why do girls insist on chatting continuously when you're watching the footy, but as soon as the adverts come on they shut up?" I said.

"Yeah, that is what the adverts are there for. That is their chance to speak, otherwise, please be quiet," Ollie said.

"And why do they always expect you to know what's wrong with them? If you ask them and they say nothing, then don't expect us to press any further on the matter."

Ollie chuckled, "The thing is we know they're lying when they say nothing but we just can't be arsed with the hassle."

We both took the time to gulp down another mouthful of lager before Ollie kept the debate going. "You remember that girl Sue I was seeing last year? The one that was always sick?"

I remembered Sue quite well. We all did. She was the one girl Ollie had managed to pull who seemed quite normal compared to his usual conquests. And she seemed completely oblivious to Ollie's complete lack of a brain. But she just disappeared one day and no one knew why. Even Ollie didn't know. We all took the piss of course, saying she had finally cleaned the shit from her eyes and seen sense. But this was news to me that she had been ill and I suddenly felt very guilty for taking the mickey all those times. "I didn't know she had been sick, mate. Was it serious?" I asked with a concerned tone.

83

"I'm not sure really," Ollie said, both hands pressed against the bar. "She would get these headaches. They always seemed to flare up at night when we would get into bed. In the last couple of months we were together they got really bad. She would be in so much pain that I couldn't even touch her."

"You mean she got headaches when you wanted sex?" I asked, suddenly seeing where this was going even if Ollie didn't have a clue.

"It got worse than that," Ollie continued. "It got so bad that she couldn't even talk to me on the phone because it would make the headaches more intense. Then one day I called her number and it was no longer in use. I never heard from her again after that."

Ollie went back to nursing his pint with a look on his face like he was still trying to search for the answers. I felt I should probably put him out of his misery and break it to him gently that Sue hadn't been sick. There were no headaches, she just took the easy way out; a bit like a man would.

"Mate," I started, putting my hand on his shoulder. "I think Sue was probably lying about the headaches?"

Ollie looked at me and frowned. He needed answers. "So you think..." I watched his expression change as it finally dawned on him what had really happened. "You don't think she died, do you? Would that make me a widow?"

For a split second I thought Ollie was joking, but his face was deadly serious. Then I remembered it was Ollie I was talking to. Here is the guy who believed Jack when he told him that Winston Churchill was the bloke who sold insurance on TV adverts. At that point I gave up and decided that perhaps the truth wasn't the best option. "I'm sure she is fine, mate," I reassured him. "You're not a widow," At least that seemed to cheer him up.

"So I heard you got a bit drunk when you took that Grace out last week," Ollie said with a smile.

"That's one way of putting it." I said avoiding eye contact. I really wanted to change the subject. I'd already had Rob and Jack give me plenty of stick over this. The last thing I needed was the widow throwing his two pennies worth in. Time to unleash old faithful I thought to myself. "Hey, I think that bird over there is looking at you."

"Where?" Ollie turned round scanning the pub. It didn't matter how many times I played this practical joke on him, he always fell for it. Hook, line, and sinker.

"She just turned away when you looked," I swigged down some of my lager. "Quick, she's looking again."

Ollie spun around as fast as he could, but of course no one was looking. "You missed her again, sorry mate," I told him.

"I don't believe you," Ollie said still looking around the bar out of the corner of his eye just in case there was a chance I was telling the truth. "You're just winding me up," and he punched my arm, immediately making it go dead. "I'm going to take an eyelash. Get the drinks in." He downed the rest of his pint before heading off to the toilet.

I was only halfway through my pint and knew I was in for a long night if I was going to keep up with him. I ordered us another two pints, and attempted to sink as much of my first pint as I could before Ollie returned.

"Well, look who it is," someone said bitingly behind me.

I knew that voice. I knew it all too well. I closed my eyes tightly hoping it wasn't who I thought it was, but no such luck. I turned around to be greeted by Stacey.

And her new boyfriend Dave.

"Hi Stacey," I said trying to be grown-up about the situation. I nodded and half-smiled towards Dave, extending my hand to him. Stacey slapped my hand away immediately.

"I don't think so," she growled, her face all screwed up. "I've already told Dave all about you so don't go thinking you're going to be mates."

Dave just stared at me, a crooked smile on his face. "I don't have a problem with you, Stacey, and I really don't want any trouble," I told them both.

"Trouble? If you want trouble, mate, I can give you trouble." Dave added his intellectual input to the conversation. The guy was a real piece of work. His big gold earrings looked thick enough for a gymnast to swing off of. He had a small ginger goatee and a tattoo across his shaven head. He was short, but stocky, with a small scar across his cheek. No doubt a proud battle scar.

"I said I *don't* want any trouble," I repeated just to reiterate my position. I'd never been a great fighter. I'd struggle to fight my way out of a wet paper bag. But I really didn't want to back down, especially as I knew how much satisfaction it would give Stacey. Then again, I didn't want to take a beating either. I liked my face. It wasn't the best looking face as it was, and I was pretty sure Dave was not interested in enhancing my appearance.

"Well, maybe you don't have a choice," Dave said positioning himself in front of me so we were nose-to-nose. First Sophie, now Dave. I wondered how many more people Stacey had lined up to inflict injury on me. I wouldn't have been surprised if she had started a Facebook group called *Death to Dan Hilles*.

I tried my utmost to stand my ground. Dave snarled at me, the left side of his lip curling upwards like a rabid dog flashing his fangs. I attempted an equally menacing look to try and cover up the fear that was slowly building up inside me, but I probably looked more like a stroke victim. I was praying for the best but expecting the worse.

"Is there a problem here?" I had never been so pleased to hear Ollie's voice in all my life.

"This is between me and him," Dave said not taking his eyes off me. I stood my ground, growing in confidence now I had Ollie next to me.

"If you have a problem with him, then you have a problem with me," Ollie told him, manhandling me out of the way to square up to Dave. Ollie towered over him. My masculinity took a slight knock, but under the circumstances I was willing to live with that. I merely poked my head over Ollie's shoulder to eyeball Dave. I'm not too sure it made much difference, but Dave backed away slowly with Stacey pulling at his arm. Part of me likes to believe that my iron stare from behind Ollie's broad frame had Dave running scared.

"Come on, Dave, he's not worth it," Stacey whined.

"I'll catch up with you when your boyfriend isn't around, Danielle," Dave said, sarcastically blowing a kiss at me before exiting the pub.

Ollie glared at the door a second longer before returning to the bar and nonchalantly sipping at his pint. "Well, you shit yourself, didn't ya?" he said grinning.

"Nah, not really..." I stuttered. "I had it under control." We both laughed. "Thanks mate," I said to Ollie. "I could have dealt with that, but..."

"No problem. I know you could have, I just wanted to make sure it didn't ruin your night."

"Come on, boyfriend, let's drink up and get out of here before dangerous Dave comes back."

\*

The next part of our plan was simple – ruin Valentine's Day for as many couples as possible. We started by constantly calling and texting Rob and Jack, but soon got bored of that when they switched their phones off and we had left them three voice messages each. Next, we decided to annoy

87

people we didn't know. We stood opposite an Italian restaurant and took the piss out of some poor guy as he spoon fed his girlfriend ice cream. The look on the guys face as he clocked us pointing and laughing from the other side of the glass was a picture.

We stopped at every bar or pub we passed and got a drink in. We would stagger past tables where couples were sitting together enjoying intimate moments and insist we sing them a love song. Drunken renditions of *I Wanna Know What Love Is* by Foreigner went down a treat. Well, we thought it was funny. We must have been in seven or eight bars before we made our way to South Wimbledon tube station with a kebab in hand to finally call it a night. But the call of more alcohol whistled in the air.

"Shall we have one for the road?" Ollie asked, pointing at the Kings Arms opposite the station.

"Why not," I replied and we staggered across the road.

Inside there was a live band playing 60's and 70's rock songs to an older crowd than we had been used to tonight. We sat at the bar and ordered our tenth beer of the night and sang old rock anthems until our throats were hoarse. All in all, it was turning out to be one of the best Valentine Day's I'd ever had. And it was just about to get better.

"Look at her," I gasped nearly falling off my barstool. I spotted a pretty little strawberry blonde who was sitting on her own. She looked over at me and I smiled at her. She shyly turned away, but then returned my smile. Ollie didn't really take much notice of me, and instead was singing away with a grey-haired hippy he had befriended who was wearing a black skull and crossbones vest top and showing off faded tattoos on his arms.

I kept my gaze fixed on the girl. I took another mouthful of lager, wiped my lips with my shirt sleeve, and plucked up the courage to go over. "Can I sit down?" I asked her. She smiled and nodded as I introduced myself.

Her name was Chloe. She said she was 18 and at college. She looked so pure and so out of place in an establishment like this. I struggled to hide how pissed I was, but she didn't seem to mind, so I didn't let it bother me. After a few minutes of chatting I asked if I could buy her a drink and she agreed.

"I'm well in over there," I said to Ollie as I returned to the bar to buy Chloe a Malibu and pineapple juice. "You don't mind if I crack on with her, do you?"

"Not at all," Ollie slurred. "I've got Frank to keep me company," and with that Ollie and Frank broke back into song.

I gave Ollie a wink and headed back to Chloe, only this time she was not alone. "Hello," I said to the woman with peroxide blonde hair and a fake orange tan. She must have been in her 40s at least. She was attractive despite her hard features, but dressed cheaply in a short denim skirt and a top that left little to the imagination.

"Who are you?" she barked at me rather aggressively.

I saw Chloe nudge the woman and give her a look. "I'm Dan," I said handing Chloe her drink, and offered the woman my hand. "And you are?"

"I'm Chloe's mum," she said snatching the drink out of Chloe's hand and smelling the content. This was not good. I'd heard about these mothers who went out on the pull with their daughters. "What are you doing giving my daughter alcohol? She is only 15."

I was immediately taken aback. I looked at Chloe, who looked at her mum. "Mum!" she said in horror.

"I'm so sorry, I thought she was 18," I pleaded my case.

"You sick little pervert," Chloe's mum said swigging back the Malibu and pineapple juice I had bought for her underage daughter.

"I swear I didn't know," I said again trying to calm the situation down. "Sorry, Chloe, but you're too young for me." Chloe looked crushed. I made my excuses and headed back to the bar where Ollie was still singing with his new friend.

"Drink up," I said. "We need to get out of here."

"But I thought you were gonna bone that girl over there," Ollie said, shouting over the music.

"Shhhh," I said holding my hand up to his mouth and looking around the bar in case anyone had heard. "You're gonna get my head kicked in."

I felt a hand on my shoulder and turned around to see the mum. "You like chatting up little girls, do you?" she asked me, still drinking the Malibu I had bought.

"No, it was a mistake. She told me she was 18," I tried to explain again.

"That is what they all say," she said, stumbling slightly as she slammed the glass down on to the bar.

A few people around us were now looking over. "I promise I didn't know she was 15," I said.

"You were trying it on with a 15-year-old?" Ollie suddenly decided to quiz me.

"No, you idiot," I shouted back at him, before turning back to the mum. "It was just a misunderstanding."

"You should try going after a real woman instead of chasing schoolgirls around," she said shoving an accusing finger in my face.

She was getting louder and I was starting to panic that I was going to get lynched and put on the sex offenders' register. "Look, I'm really sorry but it wasn't my fault. She shouldn't be in here if she is 15. It was a mistake."

But she wouldn't let it go. She just got louder and kept prodding her finger into my chest. Even the band was now staring in our direction, while Ollie and his hippy friend watched on like it was some sort of sporting event.

"What exactly is your problem?" I snapped after one too many pokes to the chest.

"I can't help it if I like shagging young boys," she abruptly blurted out, before grabbing the back of my head and forcefully pulling me towards her, shoving her tongue down my throat and grabbing at my crotch.

I stood there like a rabbit caught in the headlights, too afraid to move. "Go on, my son!" I heard Ollie bellow out behind me. I let her finish, and as she pulled away she told me in no uncertain terms, "You're coming home with me."

This was not the response I expected. One minute you're being labelled a kiddie fiddler, the next minute you are copping off with someone old enough to be your mother. I probably wasn't in the best state of mind, but I heard myself agree to go back with her. Partly because I was too scared to turn her down, and largely because I hadn't got my leg over for six weeks now. Taking me by the hand, she dragged me out the pub. An old guy with a receding hairline and a bushy moustache stared daggers at me and made a cut-throat sign with his thumb. I could only imagine that he was in there with the peroxide mum before I arrived on the scene. I glanced back at Ollie who was still sitting at the bar giving me the thumbs up.

"What is your name?" I asked as we walked back, realising I couldn't call her *mum* all night, especially during the wild throes of passion. That would just be weird.

"Toni," she replied. "Come on Chloe, keep up!" she shot at her daughter who shuffled behind us, quietly sobbing that her mum had stolen the guy she had been chatting up just minutes ago. I had a feeling this was not the first time this had happened. I wasn't exactly proud of myself, but I was a desperate man and desperate men do desperate things. Plus I was really pissed.

After a 10-minute walk, we arrived at a house with a red door and paint peeling from the wooden frame. Chloe ran upstairs and slammed her bedroom door shut behind her. I thought about making a run for it myself, the fresh air had sobered me up slightly and I was now starting to fret over whether this had been a good idea.

"Shouldn't you see if she is okay?" I sheepishly asked.

"She'll live," Toni said with a fag hanging out of her mouth, and grabbed me by the arm and pulled me into the living room. She pushed me down on to the sofa and stubbed her cigarette out in an ashtray already overloaded with fag butts.

"Please," I said pathetically holding my hand up to her, "be gentle."

A wicked grin appeared across her face and within seconds she was on top of me, kissing me in quite a violent way. She finally let me up for air and squeezed my cheeks with her right hand. "Let's have a drink," she announced as she playfully slapped me across the face.

I was relieved to catch my breath. She poured me a straight whisky and lit up another cigarette. She sat next to me, blowing smoke in my face, and caressing my thigh. "You're so tense," she said in her gravelly voice, no doubt from years of too many cigarettes. "I know something that will make you feel better." She rose to her feet and took the drink from my hand, gulping down the remainder of the whisky in my glass.

She unbuttoned my jeans and unzipped my fly, shoving her hand into my pants. She was not exactly gentle and toggled it back and forth like it was a joystick. "You like that, don't ya?" she said with a wild look in her eyes, cigarette still clenched between her teeth.

Like it? I was genuinely worried she was going to pull it off. Did she think I was somehow impervious to pain? I prayed she would eventually get bored and let go, but she just kept going. She started to do it quicker and rougher. I held my breath trying to stifle the pain and my impending screams. But with one tug too many she flicked her wrist, and I let out a howl before smacking her hand away. "What the hell are you doing?" I winced. "Don't treat little Dan like that."

"What is your problem? Most men would kill for a hand job like that," she declared.

"Kill or be killed?" I snapped back rubbing my crotch.

"Mum, is everything okay?" A deep voice shouted from upstairs.

"Who was that?" I said anxiously. It certainly didn't sound like Chloe.

"That's my son," Toni said, oblivious to the long trail of ash from her cigarette finally dropping off and landing on the carpet, creating a miniature puff cloud.

"Your what?" Footsteps were now coming down the stairs fast. I managed to put my mangled penis back into my pants and zipped myself up. "How old is he?"

"Is everything okay, mum?"

I knew that voice. But surely it couldn't be, could it? I slowly turned my head, every part of my being wishing I was wrong. But I wasn't. I sensed the rage in the air the moment he stepped into the light of the living room doorway, and the sheer horror of the situation took over me.

"You!" Dave menacingly hissed and started stalking towards me.

"I can explain," I desperately said trying to buy myself time, while rising to my feet and moving slowly backwards, my hands held up in front of me in both protest and defence.

"What's all the noise?" To make matters worse Stacey now appeared. "Dan? What the hell are *you* doing here?" she said with all the contempt she could muster.

"You know him?" Toni said as she poured herself another drink. "He's a frigid little sod."

"I'm not frigid," I snapped. "You just need to learn to treat the male organ with a little respect." Probably not the best response I could have given under the circumstances.

It is often said bad things happen in threes and right on queue 15-year-old Chloe appeared at the doorway, in her pink pyjamas, looking every inch the schoolgirl she really was now all the make-up had been washed off. "He tried seducing me as well," she said with an accusing finger point.

"What?! I did no such thing," I tried protesting my innocence for a second time, but knew I was barking up the wrong tree if I thought Dave would take any notice.

"You're a dead man," Dave said and lunged at me. I fell back against the armchair and the force of Dave landing on me somehow enabled me to flip him over my head in the process and send him crashing into a cabinet.

"Get up, Dave! Get him!" Stacey hollered, and I started to wonder if Stacey would always be urging someone on to beat the hell out of me whenever our paths crossed.

With Stacey and Chloe blocking my exit through the front door, I made a dash for the kitchen. Toni simply sat on her chair, a fag in one hand and a glass of whisky in the other. In amongst all the chaos I couldn't help but think it's how she would have wanted to be remembered.

Dave was up on his feet and right behind me. I ran through the kitchen towards the back door, knocking down a stack of plates to stall Dave and buying myself precious seconds. They crashed to the floor behind me and shattered. Dave couldn't stop himself and slipped on the broken crockery. I grabbed and pulled the door handle. It was unlocked – the first piece of good luck I'd had so far this night.

I flung the door open and stopped almost dead in my tracks, squeezing my eyes tightly shut. From nowhere a snarling Rottweiler leapt at me from the darkness of the garden. Its sharp canine fangs were coming straight at my throat and I simply froze in pure terror.

But then nothing.

Instead of the sound of snapping neck bones under the force of the beasts rampaging jaws, I heard a yelp, which released me from my paralysed state. I forced myself to squint open one eye and thanked my lucky stars that I had been saved by a large metal chain attached to the dog's neck, preventing him from reaching me. I whistled a huge sigh of relief.

But I had no time to contemplate my good fortune as close behind, Dave was charging towards me. Stacey was now in the kitchen and threw a piece of broken plate in my direction while screaming at me. I ducked and slammed the door shut, catching Dave full in the face. I quickly made my move, scaling the wooden fence. The Rottweiler was not going to give up that easily and snapped at my heels, and clamped its teeth into my arse as I was halfway over the fence, causing me to scream out in pain.

Dave staggered out of the back door. He shook his head and started making his way in my direction, a bloody great big kitchen knife in his hand. With all my strength I made one final effort to pull myself over the fence and kicked out at the snarling mutt forcing him to release me from his grip. One final shove got me over as Dave hit the fence, the knife piercing through the wood and just missing my head by inches on the other side.

It was enough to scare me back up to my feet and for the second time in six weeks I found myself sprinting through the streets to escape one of Stacey's hired hitmen. Surely break-ups had to be smoother than this?

## Chapter 9: Visiting the Folks

*Sunday, March 1, 2009 - 12.32pm*
*Drought Clock: 59 days, 0 hours, 5 minutes*

I had been having this recurring nightmare. I'm standing on a stage in nothing but my pants. There is a huge crowd of people staring at me. From nowhere appears a man who informs me he is a Guinness World Records adjudicator. He is immaculately dressed in a black pinstripe suit, slicked back hair, and a thin hairline moustache. He is holding a certificate in one hand and a microphone in the other, and is addressing the sea of people that just seems to go on forever.

"It gives me great pleasure to award the Guinness World Record for the longest period without sex to Mr Daniel Hilles," the adjudicator proudly announces to the crowd in an annoying nasal monotone accent. Polite applause starts up as he continues. "Mr Hilles has not come into contact with the female genitalia for two months, eclipsing the previous record held by 97-year-old Hubert Grayson."

A wrinkly bald old man with huge floppy ears – resembling a cross between Dumbo and a scrotum – starts to celebrate. Hubert Grayson dances around his walking stick, showing great delight that his long-standing sexless record has been eclipsed by yours truly.

The applause grows louder, aided by heckles and taunts such as "cobweb cock" and "dusty dick'. Not content with the indignity he has already imposed on me, the adjudicator congratulates me by shaking my hand and presenting me with the certificate before he continues his verbal assault.

"Mr Hilles coined the phrase 'couldn't get laid in a brothel'. No matter how hard he tries, here stands a man with a complete lack of skills to get any ass. He will use any means necessary to obtain it yet he constantly fails at every attempt to get the pussy."

I stand there gasping, speechless and wide-mouthed. I can't get the words out to end this humiliation I am being forced to endure, and he continues: "Mr Hilles faces an uphill task to ever see a real vagina in the flesh again, let alone get near one. Ladies and gentleman, please show your appreciation to a truly sexless individual – Mr Daniel Hilles!"

By the time he has finished berating me the applause has broken into hysterical laughter. In fact the only person in the crowd not wailing in delight at this mortifying scene is my mum. She stands there, clutching both hands to the side of her face with a strange look of pride in her eyes. My dad is standing next to her shaking his head, his arms folded across his chest. I can hear his words echoing in my head from the day when my mum had found my porn stash under my bed when I was 13 years old.

"You have to see it from your mother's point of view," he explained to me in the aftermath of the horror that was the great porn discovery of 1998. "In her eyes you have gone from her sweet innocent little boy to, well, a perverted little wanker."

That's it! I snatch the microphone out of the hands of the smug adjudicator and launch into my defence. "Sexless is not technically true," I proclaim to the stunned audience. "Yes, I have not had sex for many months now, but I have in fact had self-sex in the last 24 hours." I pause for just the right effect, "Twice."

A hushed silence falls over the crowd. For a brief moment, victory is sweet.

But this is soon replaced by the reality of the utter ridiculousness of my statement. Who in their right mind would refer to masturbation as self-sex? I might as well have just pulled out my penis right there-and-then and started to stroke one out to the rhythm of the crowds roaring laughter ringing in my ears.

My mum bursts into tears at the realisation of her worst fear – her little boy is in fact a perverted little wanker. She buries her head into my dad's chest, who simply stares at me, disgusted in the knowledge that I am his spawn.

*

"Tickets please," the ticket inspector roused me from my sleep. I handed him the ticket and watched as he scribbled a strange scrawl on to it before handing it back and making his way down the carriage.

I shook my head and rubbed my face to wake myself up. It had been over two months since I had last seen my parents at Christmas, and I decided a nice break out in the sticks would do me good.

I had pretty much kept a low profile over the last few weeks since the Valentine's Day disaster, especially as I was now in hiding from Stacey's new knuckle-head boyfriend. Being the arsehole ex-boyfriend wasn't enough for me; I had to go and add chatting-up his schoolgirl sister and attempting to shag his mum to the list of reasons of why Dave wanted to kill me. Kicking his dog can't have helped either.

Yeah, a bit of home cooking and some pampering from mum was just what the doctor ordered. After dinner perhaps I could stroll down to the village pub for a pint or two with the old man.

My parents had moved to the small village just outside of Horsham in West Sussex while I was still at university. Instead of returning home from university to the hustle and bustle of inner city life I had left behind, I returned to fields of green for as far as the eye could see. The familiar sound of police sirens, traffic, and drunken ramblings I had become accustomed to outside my bedroom window had been replaced by deathly eerie silence. It was like being stuck in a Walt Disney cartoon with all the ducks, pheasants, geese and deer strolling around.

It took me about 15 minutes to walk from the train station to my parents' house. I spotted my dad in the drive washing the Range Rover he had bought when they moved here because he felt it would suit the rural landscape. What he hadn't banked on was the tiny country roads.

"Hello boy," my dad greeted me, his roll-up cigarette hanging from his mouth.

"Hello dad," I said and he patted me on the arm. I had always been close to my father. Growing up, he had been my source of inspiration. He was also the first person who offered me my first real insight into the world of the fairer sex. He would often say things like:

*Women are like parking meters; if you don't feed them with enough money you face serious consequences.*

*Women are like refrigerators; they're always cold and never seem to have a beer when you need one.*

*Women are like blue jeans; they look good for a while but eventually they fade and have to be replaced.*

I remember when I was about 16 he took me to one side and gave me what I guess was his version of that classic father-son contraception talk.

"Son," my dad started with his hand on my shoulder. "When you meet a girl, whatever you do don't tell her your real name. That way if you get her pregnant she won't be able to find you."

Of course, he had a back-up plan in case that little nugget of gold didn't help me out.

"If you are stupid enough to knock someone up, then I have a little money set aside for an emergency, and we'll fly you out to Spain where you can lay low for a couple of years until it blows over."

That was my dad. He had solutions and advice for real problems and real situations. He finished hosing the soap off the car. "How have you been, son?"

"Not bad," I told him. It was a lie, but my father was a real man's man and not the type of man that would react well to knowing that in the last two months I had run away from a fight with a girl, and had tried pulling a schoolgirl and her mum in the same night. Actually, he probably would have been quite impressed with the latter.

"Good, good," he said taking his rollie out of his mouth and stubbing it out on the floor with his foot. Suddenly his face went dead serious and he put his hand on my shoulder. "Look, I've got some bad news."

This wasn't good. The last time my dad had started a conversation with me like this was the time my pet goldfish Chips had died. I loved that little fella. Luckily my dad had eased my pain with four *Ghostbusters* action figures. I would later find out when I was older that my mum had grown bored of having to clean the tank all the time and had flushed Chips down the toilet, thinking he would be flushed out into a river somewhere. My dad would often make the crude joke that Chips was down there in the sewer somewhere holding on to a *'Richard the Third'* for dear life and paddling to safety.

But this time there wasn't a Peter Venkman or Egon Spengler figurine in sight. This had to be bad. Maybe my grandmother had died, or the dog had been run down. Maybe a 10-foot goldfish had been found in the sewers and was hell-bent on revenge against the family that had cruelly discarded of him down the toilet all those years ago. Some fish hold grudges. Did you ever see any of the *Jaws* sequels?

"Hey, what's up *cuz*?"

100

No, this was worse. Much worse.

I stood completely still, not knowing what to do. I looked at my dad for help, but he just shrugged his shoulders and went back to leathering off the car.

"Hey *cuz*, I said what's up?"

There it was again – a voice that conjured up an abundance of emotions that boiled deep inside me. A voice that cut through me like an icy blade. A voice that made my teeth itch.

"*Cuz?*"

A voice that belonged to my cousin Charlie.

"Hey Charlie," I said turning to face the boy who had once replaced all of the cream from my Oreo cookies with toothpaste. The boy who spun me on the roundabout for 11 minutes straight causing me to throw up four times. The boy who once handed me a tampon and let me unwittingly pretend it was a cigar so I could be Hannibal from *The A-Team*.

"Good to see you *cuz*."

The boy who called me *cuz*. I hated it when he called me that. But what I hated the most about my cousin Charlie was that he always had to go one better than you. If I bought the latest Eminem CD, then he had just got front row concert tickets. If I had front row concert tickets, then he had a backstage pass. If I had a backstage pass, then he had actually performed with the man on stage and knew him well enough to call him Marshall, or Marsh for short. I actually did get a backstage pass to an Eminem gig once and to this day Charlie still has a fake number in his phone assigned to Marsh.

Charlie was four years older than me and the most pretentious idiot I had the misfortune of knowing, let alone being related to. He was the type of guy that wore sunglasses to a nightclub, and wore big fake diamond stud earrings. He would boast of his many conquests with girls.

101

To complement his overbearing personality, he was also a compulsive liar. He once told me he had given the Pope a lift home after his "Pope mobile" had broken down in Bethnal Green.

He reckons the Pope needed to get to Catford.

And he was wearing a denim jacket.

A *sleeveless* denim jacket.

We made our way inside where my mum greeted me with a big hug. "It's lovely to see you, dear," she said.

"You too, mum," I replied and then whispered into her ear through gritted teeth. "What is *he* doing here?"

"Your aunt and uncle called and asked if they could pop by," she pulled away and shook her head apologetically. "It was all very last minute."

I said my hellos to my Aunt Maggie and Uncle David. Maggie was my mum's sister; a slim woman who smoked too much and always seemed to smell of cats. David was a heavyset man who had the ability to rub my father up the wrong way just like Charlie was able to do to me. Like father, like son.

"Everyone sit down," my mum ushered us towards the dining table. "Lunch will be served shortly."

My dad came back into the house as my mum served up generous portions of lamb, roast potatoes, cauliflower cheese, and vegetables, all smothered in lashings of thick onion gravy. The small talk concentrated around the usual subjects: the incredible snowstorms that had brought the country to its knees, how the banks had screwed the economy up for everyone, and a story that had appeared in the local paper story about the three-legged dog that had saved his owner from drowning. My mum was a sucker for pet stories.

Of course, the men talked about sport; it was a safe subject. My mother tried getting involved by commenting how much she thought Andrew Flintoff looked like his brother Freddie when she had seen him interviewed earlier that day on the news.

But secretly, I knew my mum had been dying to grill me more about the Stacey situation and it wasn't long before she subtly brought the conversation round to my now infamous break-up.

"So, I was telling your Aunt Maggie that you and Stacey are not courting anymore," was about as subtle as my mum got. *Courting.* It was such a parent word to describe relationships. It was up there with *mating.* Nobody used words like that anymore to describe relationships or sexual experiences. In fact, I am pretty sure that words like that died out the day swimming pools took down the *No Heavy Petting* signs.

"Yeah, what happened *cuz*? Did Stacey finally see sense?" Charlie laughed, nudging me in the arm. I smiled and resisted taking the bait. "So, how does it feel being single again?"

I thought about it for a second. What word would best sum up my re-entry into my newly found unattached status? Distressing? Disastrous? Desperate? Whatever word it was to describe how I felt obviously started with a D. "It's been okay," I lied. "I have been out on a few dates and meeting new people." Technically part of that was true. I had been on one date, albeit an unsuccessful date, but a date nonetheless. The actual details weren't important.

"That's nice, dear," my mum said. "I'd hate to see you lonely."

"I'm not lonely, mum," I reassured her.

"Leave the boy alone," my dad said waving my mother away. "Your mother was a little upset when she found out, but I told her you were too young to settle down."

"Especially when you see the way some of these young girls dress today," my Uncle David said, inhaling and shaking his head with a disturbing smile on his face.

"When I was a boy, you were lucky if you got a grope after walking her home before her old man chased you halfway down the street," my dad shared with us, laughing. "I was born too soon," he said picking up a piece of meat with his fork.

"I know what you mean," my Uncle David butted in. "I used to tell Charlie that if you sneak any girls into the house, don't let me catch you because I'll make you share."

"And he did once!" Charlie said grinning and then high-fived his dad. It was an awkward moment. I glanced towards my Aunt Maggie but she just shrugged with this *what can I do* look on her face. "Boys will be boys," she said and then went back to her conversation with my mum.

"Hey *cuz*," Charlie started nudging me on the arm again. "I saw this bloke chatting up a cheetah the other night. I thought to myself, he's trying to pull a fast one!" He burst out laughing. "You love it, don't ya," he kept saying, still nudging. "Yeah, of course you bloody love it," he finished off rustling my hair like I was a five-year-old, with a mouthful of roast potato spilling from his mouth.

We finished the rest of the meal with my dad doing his best to avoid any conversation with my Uncle David, while Charlie insisted on prodding and jabbing me every five minutes with some quip.

"Why don't you take Charlie down to the pub in the village," my mum said as she cleared the table. I stared at her in disbelief. This is the woman who carried me inside her womb for nine months. The woman who put a plaster on my knee when I tripped and fell. The woman who used to sew my name into the back of my underwear. Here she was, selling me down the river.

"Get your coat, *cuz*," Charlie said before I had the chance to answer. "You've pulled."

*

"I'm not meant to be in a pub," Charlie suddenly announced to me.

"Why is that?" I asked half-heartedly. I really didn't care, I had been trying to drown out his annoying voice the moment we arrived at the pub.

"Well, a couple of weeks ago we were in this pub and I saw this guy I recognised. This fella had taken liberties with me in the past, so I went over to front him out."

If I had a pound for every time I heard Charlie start a story like this in the past year I would probably have about £608. Granted that is not a lot of money, but you try sitting through 608 of his bullshit stories.

"Anyway, he gives it the large and before you can say Reggie Kray, it has all kicked off. There are punches flying everywhere, and the last thing I remember is connecting with a beautiful right hook," he paused. "And then I blacked out."

Charlie went quiet, shaking his head and looking to the distance, trying his best to look contemplative. "So what happened?" I begrudgingly asked.

"I woke up in a police cell. I banged on the door and demanded to know what had happened. Old Bill comes in and tells me I've nearly killed the bloke – he's in a coma." He took a drink and sat back with his arms folded. "Anyway, they had to let me go because there wasn't enough evidence."

"They let you go because there was no evidence?" I said cynically. Charlie simply nodded, leaving me to wonder how the hell I was related to this guy. "Unbelievable," I said shaking my head with a degree of ambiguity that he expected me to believe this.

"Tell me about it," Charlie said.

"And what exactly had this guy done to deserve such a savage beating at your hands?" I asked sarcastically.

"He knocked my chips out of my hand when I was 12," Charlie announced. "That'll learn him."

"Unbelievable," I uttered under my breath again.

"So *cuz*..." Charlie started. I bit my lip, fighting back the urge to smash my glass over his head. "...talk to me about your sex problems."

I almost choked on my beer. I looked around the bar and saw an old man at the next table across giving us a strange look. "Keep your voice down," I said wiping the beer away from my chin. "And I don't have any sex problems."

"Sure you do," he said. "You're not getting any at the moment, are you?"

"That is none of your business."

"Look, we're family," Charlie said. "Maybe I can help."

Everything inside screamed at me not to listen to him; to change the subject. But the truth was I was desperate; I was willing to try anything. Besides, he *was* family. Maybe he could help.

"Okay," I took two huge mouthfuls and plunged straight into my story. I explained the whole sorry tale; the unbearable strain of two sexless months. No matter what I tried I couldn't even manage a conversation with a girl, let alone get one into bed. He listened attentively, his face twisted in deep thought. He scratched his chin and made *hmm'ing* noises and would say "I see" in response to what I was telling him.

"I think I know what your problem is," Charlie finally said after I had finished. I studied his face. Maybe I had been wrong about my cousin. Maybe he did have the answers. They say that salvation can be found in the most unlikely of places.

"Your problem," Charlie said taking another sip from his beer, "is a common one."

My God I thought – it was a common problem! I was so relieved. This meant I wasn't alone. I grabbed my pint and took a large mouthful. "Tell me," I said staring deep into my cousin's eyes. "What is it?"

Charlie sat his pint down. He looked at me and for the first time I could see the family bond between us. Maybe this would be the start of a different relationship for us. This is the moment we would look back as the day we became more than cousins. We became brothers.

"The problem is," his eyes softened as he spoke, "that you are a massive gaylord and prefer bum love." Charlie burst into uncontrollable hyena-like laughing. "You should see your face!"

Why had I allowed myself to be taken in by this fool? "I knew I shouldn't have listened to you," I said sitting back in my seat. I was so annoyed at myself.

"Oh come on. *cuz*," Charlie said. "Don't sweat the petty things – pet the sweaty things!" And queue the second bout of hyena-esque laughter.

What an idiot. Here was a guy who was probably getting even less action than me. Once again I was left wondering how I was related to this moron sitting opposite me. If I did have to sit here with this simpleton then I decided that I might as well have some fun myself. I decided to turn the tables. "Tell me then, Charlie, if you are such an expert, what is the best sexual experience you have ever had with a woman?"

"What?" Charlie looked stumped, the laughing almost coming to an abrupt end. He took a swig of his pint. "There have been too many," he said trying to wave me away.

"Come on, *cuz,* you must have some stories you can share?"

I could see the cogs slowly turning in his head as he mulled over what piece of bullshit he was going to try and sell to me. He slammed his pint down. "I once gave a girl shin burn."

107

"What the hell is shin burn?" I asked with a smile, knowing full well he meant carpet burn.

"You know, shin burn?" he said with a slight look of panic across his face.

"Tell me what position you have to have a girl in to give her shin burn." I leaned forward watching him squirm. I was starting to enjoy this.

"How did it go again?" Charlie started to try and position his body in a way in which he could have inflicted shin burn during his imaginary sexual encounter. "The burn was on the outside of the leg, I remember that," he mumbled.

"That's good," I said with a wicked grin and a large dose of sarcasm. "So we know it wasn't an internal burn."

Charlie stood and tried to bend his body into a position to show me how shin burn worked. Finally he slumped back down into his chair. "I can't remember, it was so long ago," he finally conceded. "Drink up, let's head back."

I laughed and shook my head. Charlie didn't say a word on the way home. No *cuz,* no nudging, no more ridiculous lies. In fact, he must have been pretty embarrassed because he managed to talk my aunt and uncle into leaving about 10 minutes after we arrived home.

I decided to take off as well. It was getting late and I needed to catch my train home. My dad said he would give me a lift to the station. I hugged my mum and we said our goodbyes.

"I'm sorry I didn't get the chance to have a proper chat with you earlier, love," my mum said. "Are you sure you are okay?"

"I'm fine, mum."

"Because you can always talk to your old mum about relationships and meeting new girls," she said with a hopeful smile that I would suddenly cave in and tell her my innermost secrets.

"If I had something to tell, I promise you I would."

"Alright then," and she pulled me down to kiss me on my forehead. "Remember this – don't spend a lifetime looking for someone you have already found."

I looked at her, unconditional love in her eyes. It was the type of advice that only the woman who had carried me for nine months could give.

"I'm not getting back with Stacey," I replied bluntly. She may have carried me for nine months, but she really didn't have a clue what she was talking about. Did she not understand that I just wanted to get my leg over?

## Chapter 10: Office Dares

*Friday, March 27, 2009 - 11.42am*
*Drought Clock: 85 days, 0 hours, 55 minutes*

"Here are the rules," I said holding court to Kelly. "To make this day a little more interesting we are going to play a little game." The game was simple. I'd found a website that listed a host of office dares. I printed them out and then cut them into small pieces of paper and placed them in my coffee mug.

"We take turns to pull out a dare. Whoever completes the most dares in the next hour will be declared the winner. Are you in?"

"I'm in," Kelly said without hesitation. "You go first."

I pulled out a small piece of paper from the mug and a cheeky grin appeared across my face. "What is it?" Kelly said excitedly, clasping her hands together.

"Patience, my dear," I said to tease her and started to type away. I printed out the document I had created and tucked it into an envelope. "Now we play the waiting game," I said, locking my fingers together under my chin.

"Tell me what it is," Kelly said again. I put my finger up to my lips. I looked around the office and spotted my victim: Pete Crowford. Pete had been the butt of many an office prank. He was perfect. I once took his coffee mug home and drilled a hole in the bottom of it. I then filled the hole with melted candle wax, and watched in great childish delight as Pete managed to get two or three paces away from the kettle before the wax melted and coffee started pouring through the hole.

"Pete," I called out as he walked past my desk.

"What do you want, Hilles?" he scowled at me.

"Are you going into Dick's office?"

"Yes, what do you want?"

"Can you give this to him please?"

I handed Pete the envelope. He looked at it suspiciously and then sneered at me before carrying on towards Dick's office.

"What have you put in that envelope," Kelly enquired again, a big smile on her face. "Tell me!"

"Good things come to those who wait," I told her and then had to duck to avoid the piece of rolled up paper she threw at me. We continued with our work but within five minutes Pete came storming out of the office, holding the envelope and piece of paper in his hand.

"Hilles, you idiot," Pete said waving the piece of paper at me. "This is a resignation letter," he stated sternly.

"No Pete, it's *your* resignation letter," I replied, smiling.

"Not funny, Hilles. It took me ages to convince Dick not to accept it," and he slammed the resignation letter down on my desk before storming back off to his cave in the IT department.

"That was awesome," Kelly said clapping her hands. "My turn!" Kelly gleamed and dug her fingers into the mug and pulled out a dare. "I can't do this," she squealed and handed me the piece of paper.

"Are you kidding me?" I said reading it. "This is easy. You can't back out on the first one," I told her and handed it back to her.

"Just five songs?" Kelly asked.

"At least," I told her. "You must get at least five Madonna song titles into your next phone call."

Kelly quickly scribbled down as many Madonna songs as she could and then looked up at me. "I'm ready." Kelly picked up the phone and dialled.

**Kelly:** Hello, could I speak to Mr Thomas please?
**Mr Thomas:** This is Mr Thomas.

111

**Kelly:** Oh, Mr Thomas. I thought you were still on *Holiday.*

**Mr Thomas:** I haven't been on holiday this year. I'm sorry, who is this?

**Kelly:** *Who's That Girl* I hear you say? This is Kelly Campbell from Maxwell Media. I wanted to talk to you about your advertising plans this year.

**Mr Thomas:** I'm sorry, I don't advertise.

**Kelly:** But I haven't even got *Into the Groove* with my pitch yet Mr Thomas. You haven't even listened to what I have to say.

**Mr Thomas:** Nothing you can say will change my mind. I have never advertised in my life – I don't believe it works. Good old word of mouth is all I need to promote my company.

**Kelly:** *Papa Don't Preach* is what I always say to my dad when he tries to tell me that advertising doesn't work.

**Mr Thomas:** He sounds like a very smart man.

**Kelly:** Not really, he's like you in that he's just *Like a Virgin* when it comes to advertising. He has never done it either.

**Mr Thomas:** I beg your pardon?

Kelly slammed the phone down and burst out laughing. "I can't believe I just did that!" I gave Kelly a high-five to show my appreciation at a job well done.

"Excuse me, Don," Shaila said from behind me. I looked up at her and wiped away the tears of laughter from my eyes, trying to compose myself.

"Shaila, how are you?" I asked. For the last three months I had tried everything to break the ice with this girl. The flirtatious emails I had sent to her during lunchtime had not warranted any response. Any attempt at banter at the water cooler had gone down like a lead balloon. I had even poked

112

her a few times on Facebook. But nothing worked. It was ironic that someone so hot could be such an ice queen.

"Dick needs your monthly report by 4pm today," Shaila said completely ignoring my enquiry into her well-being.

"No problemo. I'm all over it. You can count on me. Call me Mr Reliable." Shaila merely stared at me as I continued with my verbal diarrhoea. "I always deliver. That's why they refer to me as the Milkman. Because I deliver. Not milk obviously, but things like this."

"If you could just bring it over to my desk at 4pm, that would be great," Shaila finally interrupted me. "Thanks Don," she half-smiled and walked away.

"That was too smooth for words," Kelly mocked me.

"What can I do to get her to notice me?" I asked still staring at Shaila. "She is amazing. I think I'm in love."

"Get a grip on yourself, *Don,*" Kelly said smiling and threw a pencil at me that bounced off the top of my head, and snapped me back into reality. "It's your turn to pick a dare."

For the next hour we performed all manners of immature and playground pranks to amuse ourselves. This included me walking around the office with my zip open and telling anyone who pointed it out, "Sorry, I prefer it this way." And whenever anyone in the office asked me to do something I had to ask if they "wanted fries with that."

Kelly now had to say "*Mon*" after every sentence in a really bad Jamaican accent, and when Dick came over to our desk she had to shoot him with double-barrelled fingers and say "I like your style". The funniest part was when he thanked her and spent the next 15 minutes explaining his inspiration behind his look. Apparently he was going for a classic 1970's influence fused with modern urban culture.

We were having so much fun that 1pm arrived in record time. I knew it was lunch because Pete Crowford was excitedly making his way to the door with three colleagues

113

from IT. He had received a call 15 minutes earlier from a local Italian restaurant called *Giuseppe's* who told him he had won a lunch for four people. I knew this because I had made the call myself as a dare. I had even booked a table for four in Pete's name at the restaurant so he wouldn't realise it was a prank until he was presented with the bill.

"Shall we?" I said to Kelly nodding after Pete and his IT gang.

"I thought you would never ask," Kelly said grabbing her purse so we could follow our victims and get a front row seat to watch our planned humiliation in action.

"We are so bad," Kelly said as we followed the happy foursome.

"I know," I said. "Isn't it great?"

Approaching Liverpool Street I saw something that left me with knots in my stomach – Carla the charity street worker. I had tried avoiding this part of town in recent weeks purposely so as not to bump into her. Every time she had seen me she had taken great delight in announcing to anyone within earshot what a cheapskate and insensitive twat I was.

I tried putting my head down, but it was too late. She had clocked me, and already had that look on her face. "Let's go this way?" I said to Kelly, diverting her in a different direction.

"Why, what's wrong?" Kelly asked. So I explained what had happened. How I had tried asking Carla out and she had taken things completely the wrong way. Carla had branded me as some sort of charity street pimp who was buying her affection by donating money for poverty-stricken children. I was a desperate Lothario who knew no boundaries in trying to get a girl into bed. I was the lowest of the low. Even I had to admit I was starting to side with Carla.

"What are you like?" Kelly said as we grabbed some chips from the fish and chip shop, and sat on a bench opposite *Giuseppe's* just in time to see Pete and his IT pals take their seats and order some wine.

"I don't know," I said popping a chip into my mouth and then juggling it around on my tongue as it was too hot. "I have just forgotten how to talk to women."

"We're not aliens."

"I wouldn't be so sure," I said as Kelly cuffed me round the back of the head. "All I'm saying is that women work in a much more complicated way than men."

"Please explain, I'm intrigued," Kelly said as we watched Pete and his friend's clink their glasses together as the waiter brought their starters over.

"Okay," I turned to face Kelly. "Men are not mind readers. If something is wrong then you should just come out and tell us. It is not fair to presume we don't care because of our lack of mind-reading abilities."

"Well maybe you should try harder to understand," Kelly said nicking one of my chips. "We are complex creatures. Women speak indirectly and men speak directly. If we were the same it would be boring." Kelly popped the chip in her mouth and wore an expression as to say she had won the argument.

"Not boring, it would be *easier*," I said matter-of-factly. "If women are complex creatures, then men are simple creatures. Come out and ask what you want. Subtle hints don't work. Strong hints don't work. Obvious hints don't work. Just say it!"

Kelly held her mouth wide open in mock shock. As she started to speak I shovelled a chip into her mouth to allow myself to continue talking.

"We don't work in the commodity of hints – tips work with us. So if you have a tip on the Grand National, we're all ears."

The main courses were now being served to Pete and his team of competition winners.

"We only give you hints so when you *finally* work out what is wrong it makes you feel special – like you worked it out all by yourself," Kelly poked her tongue out. "Most of the time, women already know the solution to their problem, we just want you to show some compassion and not try to solve it for us."

"You should only come to us with a problem if you want help solving it. That's what we do. Sympathy is what your girlfriends are for."

Pete and his friends continued to tuck into their plates of pasta, and ordered a second bottle of wine to go with their meal.

"We agree on that," Kelly said. "After all, there is only so much sympathy you can get out of a man while he is playing on his computer and constantly rearranging his man bits."

"If it itches, it will be scratched. That's what we do."

Kelly laughed. "I am going to have to start introducing you to people as squirrel then."

"And why is that?"

"Because I'll tell people you are always playing with your nuts!"

"Thanks, that should help me win over the girls," I smiled and gave Kelly a friendly nudge. Meanwhile, it looked like Pete and his friends were finishing their meals.

"Dan, I don't know where you have been going wrong but I wouldn't worry about it too much. You're a nice guy. You just need to be yourself and stop worrying too much about it."

"Maybe you're right," I said, watching as Pete was now in a conversation with the waiter who had brought him the bill.

"Of course I'm right; I'm a woman. We're always right, remember?" Kelly winked at me. The conversation Pete was having with the waiter had got quite heated and it looked as though the manager was now involved.

"I'll put your advice to the test next time then."

"No time like the present."

"What do you mean?" I asked. By now Pete had gone all red and flustered as he argued his point over the bill, while the manager was waving his finger in his face.

"Go back over to that girl and ask her out again," Kelly pointed at Carla. "But this time be yourself."

"Are you out of your mind?" I said. "She hates me."

"She doesn't even know you. Just try. What is the worst thing that could happen?"

The sirens grew louder as they approached from the distance, and within seconds a police van screeched to a halt outside *Giuseppe's*. Two burly police officers got out and entered the restaurant.

"I could end up making a fool of myself. Again!" I told Kelly.

"I dare you to go over and ask her out. We are still playing the game, aren't we?"

I looked over at Carla and thought for a second. Maybe Kelly was right, but I didn't want to walk straight into another embarrassing situation. My attention swung back to the restaurant as I heard a commotion. The two officers now had Pete in handcuffs and were marching him towards the van.

"But I am a competition winner!" he squealed as they tried to usher him into the van. Suddenly he looked up and saw us sitting on the bench across the street. "Hilles! You bastard! This is your doing, isn't it?"

"Hey, at least you are not Pete," Kelly said finishing her chips and throwing the wrapper in the bin next to the bench. "What have you really got to lose?"

I looked over and waved at Pete as he was finally bundled into the back of the police van. They slammed the

117

doors shut and I watched as the flashing sirens disappeared into the lunchtime traffic.

"You're right," I finally said. "I'm going to do it."

"Just be yourself," Kelly advised as I took a deep breath and started my way over towards Carla.

"Hi," I said as I reached her.

"Oh, it's you," Carla didn't even try to hide her disgust. "What do you want?"

"I just wanted to come over and apologise, for last time I mean. I have the tendency to say stupid things when I get nervous," I told her and she gave me a curious look. "I just wanted to say hello, not bribe you, or blackmail you. Just hello."

She stared at me for a while longer as if she was examining my expression. "Just hello?"

"And maybe coffee sometime? I just want to talk and maybe get to know you."

She gave me another look, her eyes narrowed as though she wasn't too sure if she should believe me or not. "What if I said yes, will you sign up for the charity?"

"Now who is blackmailing who?" I said with a smile.

Carla lowered her clipboard as though she was letting her guard down, and smiled back at me. "But if you don't sign up how will I get your phone number?"

I took her clipboard off her and wrote my name and number down on the piece of paper and handed it back to her.

"Thanks..." she looked at the clipboard, "Dan."

"I need to get back to the office, but maybe you'll give me a call sometime?"

"Sure," she said twisting a lock of hair around her finger. I said goodbye and as I walked away she called out to me. "How about tomorrow afternoon? If you really want to get to know me then perhaps you can come help me out tomorrow?"

"Sounds good," I told her. "Text me where and when and I'll be there."

I made my way back over to Kelly, keeping a straight face trying not to give anything away.

"Well?" she asked.

"Oh that," I said nonchalantly. "It's in the bag, there was never any doubt, was there?"

"Shut up," Kelly said punching me in the arm. "I never doubted you for a second, Romeo. So when are you meeting her?"

"Tomorrow afternoon."

"And where are you going?"

"No idea. She is texting me later with the details, I think."

"That's brave of you."

"I'm just that type of guy, Kelly," my tone suddenly taking on a newfound air of confidence.

"Oh please," Kelly said, punching me in the arm for a second time. I pretended it didn't hurt.

"Come on," I said. "We'd better get back to the office and let Dick know that Pete might be on an extended lunch break."

# Chapter 11: Up in Smoke

*Saturday, March 28, 2009 - 11.15am*
*Drought Clock: 86 days, 1 hour, 12 minutes*

*Meet me at 1pm outside Charing Cross station. We're going to Trafalgar Square. Carla xx*

That was all the text had said. I didn't really question it; I didn't need to. Trafalgar Square seemed the perfect place to meet for a first date. We could take a stroll through the square, take in some of the fine art at the National Gallery, enjoy a romantic walk under Admiralty Arch, and there were plenty of bars and cafes along Charing Cross Road if we wanted to meander on up to Leicester Square. Hold on, mental note to self – do not use the word *meander* if you want to get laid.

And that was the whole point of today. Nearly three months had passed since my penis had experienced human contact, other than that of my good self and the assault I received at the hands of Toni the mum. Neither experience was worth boasting about. I knew that if I played my cards right, I could win Carla over. I was going to take things slow and be myself just as Kelly had told me. There was no need to rush things. I'd waited long enough – I could last two or three dates.

Now what to wear for a lunchtime date? I decided to give Rob a call. He worked in fashion. Well a clothes shop anyway, or a *boutique* as he would constantly remind us. It was one of those obscenely expensive outlets where you were required to remortgage your house just to buy a sweater.

"First of all you need to decide what sort of tone you want to set," Rob said when I called him. "You want to make sure you are smart, but not too smart."

"Right, not too smart," I said as I worked my way through my wardrobe.

"Go for a casual look, but not too casual. Smart casual. You want to make an honest impression and a statement about your style and attitude."

"Okay, style and attitude," I repeated his words as I pulled out a horrible yellow and purple flower patterned shirt Stacey had bought for me for my birthday last year.

"Pick from the classic basics unless you have a specific side of yourself to express," Rob continued. "Wear neutral colours if you want your conversation to do the talking."

What the hell does that mean? I held up a Bart Simpson T-shirt and Bermuda shorts and even I realised that wasn't going to work here.

"Footwear is important. Girls notice things like shoes," Rob said as I dusted off an old pair of stained black suede Wallabies that hadn't seen the light of day since the 90s. "Personal grooming says more about you than your clothes."

"Good point," I said. I hadn't showered yet.

"Remember – clothes make the man, so create the man you want to be. And Danny?" Rob trailed off. "Whatever you do, don't wear white socks like you normally do eh? Just promise me that one thing."

I promised and Rob clicked off. Brilliant, I was even more confused than when I first started out.

I thought back to Kelly's advice: *just be yourself*. Yeah, sod listening to the guys. It was time I started listening to advice from a woman. So I pulled on a pair of jeans, a blue and white hooped polo shirt I had bought in New York last year, and a pair of plain white trainers with Velcro straps. I looked in the mirror. That will have to do.

I set off just after midday to travel the Tube to Charing Cross. I arrived 10 minutes early. I walked outside of the station and stepped out onto the Strand. Crowds of pedestrians hustled and bustled as they went about their business. London taxis and red buses zipped up and down the bus lanes whilst the rest of the traffic crawled along at a snails' pace. A few hippy types walked past flashing me the V sign for peace. At least I hope it was the peace sign.

I walked back to the station entrance. I had only been waiting a few minutes when Carla appeared. She was wearing a pair of khaki combats, a grey vest top, and a black hoodie top. It wasn't quite the short skirt look that I had been initially attracted to, but I could work with this. Maybe she was going for the *GI Jane* look. Yeah, that was it and I was her *Action Man*. How I wished I had worn my camouflaged patterned boxer shorts. I'd have to remember that for our second date.

"Hey," Carla greeted me with an air kiss on the cheek. "You look..." she paused, searching for the words as she studied my white and blue hooped polo shirt. "...like a sailor!"

Not quite the response I was hoping for. *Style and attitude* Rob had said. Apparently my interpretation of that was *Popeye*-chic style with Village People attitude. Good job I had left my can of spinach at home.

"Thanks," I hesitated in response, trying to search her tone as to whether that was a compliment or not.

"Come on," she said grabbing me by the hand. This was good, this was female contact. The way she was dragging me through the crowds made it feel more the female contact a mother would give her child when she was in a hurry, but I was hardly in a position to complain.

"What's the rush?" I asked.

"We're running late," Carla replied without turning around to face me. Instead she continued to weave her way through the crowds and built up speed.

We were *late* for something. Maybe she had a surprise planned for me. I wondered what it might be. Perhaps she

122

had booked a table for a nice romantic meal. Or it could have been the theatre – we were in the West End after all. My mind raced at the possibilities. I was excited. If I was lucky it might be a visit to the Trocadero in Piccadilly Circus.

Or maybe, just *maybe,* she was one of those direct-and-to-the-point type of girls and had booked a hotel room and we were late for check-in. You hear about these girls who like to get straight down to business. Granted, most of those girls normally require payment up front. No matter, Carla was forthright and a headstrong girl. She knew exactly what she wanted.

And she had said that I looked like a sailor. Maybe she was into that sort of thing. This could be some sort of twisted, erotic, role-play. Carla could be one of those girls who fantasised about men in uniform. And hello, we were heading in the direction of Nelson's Column. She didn't see me as *Popeye* or one of the Village People – she saw me as some sort of Admiral Horatio Nelson type, and before long she'd be asking to see my very own version of Nelson's Column.

As we approached Trafalgar Square, I could hear chanting and whistles sounding off. Perhaps Carla had arranged a party for me. Hell, after three months of celibacy I probably deserved a party. Wow, I really had hit the jackpot with this girl.

"This way," Carla said and pulled me through the crowds towards the noise. Over a wall of bobbing heads and a sea of tourists I could make out a line of police officers. Surely she hadn't arranged a police escort for us. Beyond the line of police officers was what looked like a 500-strong group of people, all looking like the hippies that had passed me earlier.

123

"This is it," Carla said excitedly and pulled me towards the crowd. I could see many of them were holding signs and posters. "Are you ready to make a difference, Daniel?"

My face told the story of confusion and pure bitter disappointment. "What is going on here? What are we doing?" I asked. What I really wanted to ask was where is the bloody hotel?

"The G20 summit takes place in two weeks. It is time world leaders started to listen to us," Carla started. "It is time to stop the wars, end world poverty, and help the starving families all over the world."

"But I wanted to be an Admiral," I whined under my breath, my head bowed like a child as I drew circles with my foot.

She held both of my hands and tilted her head as she gazed into my eyes. "This is important to me," Carla went on. "It is vital we build a different future, one that fights recession by making the world a fairer and a greener place. Do I have your support?"

I didn't care about world peace, or saving the ozone layer. I didn't sign up for this. I just wanted to get naked with this girl and give my usual 6-out-of-10 performance under the sheets. I swear it never used to be this hard. Had the rules changed since the last time I was single? Did women grant you sex for every good deed done? This was confusing.

"I guess so," I finally conceded. Maybe it was a test and if I passed my prize was that we left immediately and headed around to that hotel.

"Brilliant!" Carla threw her arms round me. "Put this on." And she pulled out a bright pink T-shirt with the words *Hug Me. Hug the World* written across the front in black. "You look a bit too much like a supporter of capitalism in those clothes."

But I look like a *sailor*!

124

I reluctantly pulled on the T-shirt. Someone patted me on the back. A woman with greasy hair wearing a brown woolly jumper and fingerless gloves gave me a massive hug. It was then that I realised the crowd was actually much bigger than I first thought. Spread all around Trafalgar Square were protesters of some kind, all supporting a different cause. Before long the crowd seemed to have grown tenfold and the banging of drums and whistles grew increasingly louder.

*What do we want? WORLD PEACE! When do we want it? NOW!*

That ought to do the trick, I sarcastically thought to myself, rolling my eyes. I stared up at Lord Nelson perched on top of his column and I could have sworn he was looking down on me with a mocking grin on his face.

Carla screamed at the top of her lungs, waving her fists and joining in with the crowd's chants. I kept looking for a way out, but by now I was well and truly penned in.

Over the next hour the crowd grew in numbers, and like a tidal wave I was swept along from Trafalgar Square towards Piccadilly. Someone handed me a signpost to carry. I didn't even bother to see what it said. I didn't care. I'd had enough of this. We got about halfway down Haymarket and I pulled Carla towards me. "How much longer does this go on for?" I shouted to her over the noise.

"You can't put a time on making the world a better place to live, Daniel," she responded before rejoining the chanting.

I pulled her towards me again. "No, I meant do you think that perhaps we could sneak off for half hour and grab a drink or something?"

If looks could kill I would have been brown bread at that moment. "A drink?" Carla said in a tone so disgusted you would have thought I'd just confessed to duetting with Gary Glitter on his comeback song. "I was right about you the first time. You don't care about saving the planet or ending poverty. You just want to get into my pants."

And before I got the chance to respond she shoved me as hard as she could. I went flying back, still holding the signpost, and crashed into the wall of police officers who were lined up along the street.

"You're nicked," I heard one copper say and before I knew it, two riot cops pounced on me. A camera crew appeared from nowhere and a news reporter shoved a microphone under my nose asking me something about this being an injustice.

"Yes! Yes!" I shouted. "I haven't done anything!"

"Leave him alone," I heard a cry from the crowd and suddenly there was a surge from the protesters. I found myself in the middle of a tug-of-war between the chanting crowd and the police. I was helpless and spread-eagled as both sides wrestled with my body, and with one final heave a huge cheer went up from the protesters as they prised me away from the clutches of the Old Bill.

Like a rock star crowd-surfing at a gig, I was lifted to safety out of reach of the police. Two stocky guys with cropped hair hoisted me on to their shoulders and the cheers grew louder.

"Daniel!" I heard Carla cry out as she ran towards me. The two men lifted me down and Carla jumped at me, wrapping her legs around my waist and started kissing me passionately. "I was wrong about you," she said kissing me more. "What you did there was amazing! You really made a stand." She kissed me some more. "I'm so turned on."

"You don't understand..." I suddenly stopped myself, realising I was about to put my foot in it again by admitting the truth.

"Understand what?" Carla said between kisses.

"Understand..." Think Dan, think. "How much saving the planet and the monkeys and the..." I started to run out of

126

things to save and just blurted out the first thing that rhymed with monkeys. "...and the donkeys means to me."

"Oh, Dan," Carla melted and kissed me more. The police were now starting to make their way through the crowd towards me. "Quick," Carla said taking me by the hand, "we need to get you out of here."

The protesters opened up a pathway for us, like Moses parting the Red Sea. They cheered for me and gave me congratulatory comments before closing their ranks as I passed to make it difficult for the police to get through.

We snuck out of the crowd and made our way down Jermyn Street and then quickly to Piccadilly Circus tube station. We ran down the escalators and jumped onto the carriage just before the beeping doors closed. We sat back in our seats catching our breath. Carla turned to me. "I'm sorry for judging you, Daniel," she said before grabbing me by the head and pulling me towards her to kiss me again.

"Where are we going," I managed to ask as she smothered me.

"My place," Carla said, straddling me on the seat. Out of the corner of my eye I noticed two pensioners looking at us, shaking their heads in disgust.

"Hey, it's been three months," I said to them and then returned Carla's kisses.

*

Carla had a little flat in Waterloo. She opened the door and didn't hesitate in taking me by the hand and leading me to her bedroom. She pinned me up against the wall, her hands all over me. If this was a sign of things to come then three months had been well worth the wait. I decided to seize the moment and moved her over to the bed. I climbed on top of her and moved my hand up her top. Yes! This was boob action. This was progress. Carla wrapped her legs around me and arched forward to kiss me.

But suddenly she pulled away. "Wait," she panted. "Let's take things slower."

*No, no* I thought to myself. Why do we need to take things slower? Please don't do this to me, not now. "But why," I asked holding back the tears.

"Don't worry," Carla said, obviously noticing the look of concern on my face. "I just want to take our time. I promise you won't be disappointed," she leaned in to kiss me and moved her hand up my thigh. "Let's have a drink and *relax* before we get started." And she kissed me once more, biting my bottom lip as she pulled away.

We went into her living room and she got two bottles of beer from the fridge. She reached down beside the armchair and pulled out a small tin box. She mischievously bit down on her bottom lip as she opened the box. Immediately the strong sickly smell hit me.

"A little appetizer?" Carla said, waving a bag of weed at me.

I hadn't smoked weed since I was at university, but perhaps having a little relaxing stimulant might not be a bad thing. I was anxious enough as it was about this moment. I didn't want to get too over-excited and end up disappointing Carla. After all, I was a hero now. And a sailor. In your face Nelson!

"Sure, why not." I casually replied like I had been smoking marijuana my whole life, and I gulped down my beer. "Can I grab another one?" I asked shaking the empty bottle. Carla pointed me in the direction of the kitchen. I came back and sat opposite her, watching her roll up the monster of all spliffs. The weed was a much lighter green than I remembered, and she sprinkled about half the bag into a Rizla.

She lit the joint up and took a couple of puffs before passing it to me. I took two puffs and then held it out to Carla, but she shook her head. "You have it," she said. "I'm going to roll another one."

Was she kidding? I couldn't smoke this whole thing to myself. I took another puff and then placed it down in the ashtray and went back to my beer as Carla rolled another spliff that Bob Marley would have been proud of.

"Take another hit," Carla urged me, but already I was starting to feel light-headed. Not wanting to lose face, I picked the joint up and tried to steady my hand as I lifted it to my lips. I took another puff and eased back in to the chair. The room had already started to fill with a thick fog of smoke. My eyes felt heavy. Four puffs and I was already in trouble. I tried to look relaxed, like I did this all the time, but even blinking was taken a huge effort. Carla finished rolling her joint and sparked up. She took two massive puffs and then held it in front of her, admiring her work.

I don't know why, but I decided I could ride this out and took another puff, this time trying to not inhale. Instead I ended up looking like a teenage boy who was smoking for the first time and couldn't quite take the smoke down.

"You don't have to smoke it if you don't want to," Carla said grinning. I wanted to stop so badly, but my male ego wouldn't let me. Instead I waved Carla's suggestion away with a crooked smile and took another puff.

The room started to spin. I gripped on to the armrests of the chair hoping the room would stop swaying from side to side like an episode of *Star Trek*. I broke out into a cold sweat, and fell into a state of extreme nausea and dizziness. I was stoned.

"Are you okay?" Carla asked. She must have seen the colour drain from my face. It made me feel ill just to move, so I nodded with minimal of effort. I placed the joint back into the ashtray and tried sitting forwards. The rush of such

129

a simple task nearly made me pass out. It was then I realised my worst fear. I wasn't buzzing. I wasn't just stoned.

I had greened out.

I started to panic, which only made the situation worse. Carla took another drag of her joint and then got up and moved towards me. She pushed me back into the armchair where I was sitting and it took all my effort not to throw up. She pulled her vest off and straddled me topless. Why was this happening to me? Why now? I hadn't seen a real pair of breasts for months, and now here were two right in front of me and I didn't even have the energy to brush my hand across one of them. Even looking at her perky erect nipples made me want to vomit. I tried concentrating on a corner of the room, hoping I could somehow cure myself by staring blankly at her CD collection.

"Do you not like what you see, Daniel?" Carla asked, lifting my hand up to cup her right breast. "Don't go shy on me now."

Carla started to kiss me, but the best I could return with was some strange kind of gurning movement of my lips. She reached over and picked up my joint and inhaled a dark cloud of grey smoke, before moving in to kiss me again. I closed my eyes and hoped I could just ride through this storm.

Carla moved her mouth over mine and without warning did something I was not prepared for. Instead of kissing me she exhaled the smoke into my mouth. I coughed violently, forcing myself forward and in the process sending Carla flying backwards.

She landed on her arse with a bump, but simply started to giggle. I leaned forward trying to get some air, but that is when it happened. I felt it from the pit of my stomach, but I was powerless to prevent it. Before I knew it the contents of my lunch covered Carla, who had abruptly stopped giggling.

She paused and didn't say a word. I looked at her through dazed eyes. For a split second I hoped that maybe Carla was so stoned she might not even notice.

"You sick bastard," she shrieked.

I could only flop back into the chair, my forehead soaked in sweat. "I'm sorry," I muttered, desperately concentrating to try and halt the spinning feeling that was still swirling around my head, not to mention my stomach.

Carla leapt to her feet and pulled at my arms to drag me up. "Get out!" she screamed. I slumped forward on to my knees, head butting her naked left breast before I slumped against her midsection.

"Please let me rest for a little while," I pleaded in my glazed over state. She side stepped, leaving me to flop to the ground in the foetal position. Everything seemed a blur. I just wanted to sleep.

Carla had other ideas and started dragging me by my feet towards the door. I could hear her shouting, but I didn't know what she was saying anymore. I simply stared up at her ceiling. The sensation of being stoned had truly gripped every part of my body. And although my mind was failing me, part of it still reminded me of how much I would regret this whole sorry event in a couple of hours when I sobered up.

I felt the cold breeze as she opened up the door. "Get up!" Carla demanded and helped pull me to my feet.

"I'm so sorry," I managed to say again before Carla gave me one final shove and slammed the door shut.

131

## Chapter 12: Beer Talk

*Sunday, March 29, 2009 - 3.22pm*
*Drought Clock: 86 days, 23 hours, 15 minutes*

"So what happened next?" Rob asked, furiously tapping away at the console controller.

"I blacked out," I said, making a fantastic last-ditch tackle on the football game we were playing. "Next thing I know, I wake up on a park bench with two little kids poking me with a stick, asking me if I was still alive."

"You idiot!" Jack shouted. "She was gagging for it, and you go and green out."

"That's pretty poor form, mate," Rob said, "even by your standards."

"What a loser," Ollie said, snatching the controller from my hands.

If I was looking for sympathy then I was barking up the wrong tree. This is another fundamental difference between men and women. After experiencing the type of trauma my date with Carla had caused, a group of girls would rally around their friend and offer their complete undivided support. My lot had just come round to take the piss as much as possible and play *Fifa 2009*.

Allow me to elaborate. If a girl calls her friend at three in the morning to tell her about a fight she has just had with her boyfriend, that friend will immediately be able to tune in and not only be a good listener, but will listen for as long as it takes and offer solid advice. If a guy called another guy at stupid o'clock in the morning he would:

a)   Be lucky if his pal even answered the phone

b)   Or if he did answer, he would be told in no uncertain terms to go *do one* because the only reason to call another man at that time in the morning is to inform him

132

that you have hooked up with Brazilian twins and you need a wingman

That is not to say that guys don't offer good advice in situations like this. We just have our own methods of delivering advice in a way that only a man can really appreciate and understand.

"Dan, your problem is that you're a bit like a striker who is low on confidence," Jack said.

"How do you mean?" I asked, reclaiming the controller back from Ollie who had made the mistake of putting it down to light a cigarette.

"What I'm saying is that you haven't scored for a long time now. You are on a drought," Jack said.

"Tell me something I don't know."

"You are missing the point," Rob interjected, and he cursed after missing a golden opportunity to score with just minutes left on the clock.

"Okay, explain it to me then," I said stealing the ball away from Rob and knocking a long pass out to my left-winger.

"Everyone knows goals breed confidence in strikers, right?" Jack continued.

"Right," I agreed, dribbling past a couple of Rob's defenders, my tongue poking out of the left side of my mouth.

"So you are trying too hard at the moment to score," Rob said, attempting a last ditch tackle before I managed to pull the trigger and watched as the ball crashed against the post.

"You couldn't even hit a barn door or pull the pig inside the barn on current form," Ollie said, and the sight of him inhaling cigarette smoke brought back too many painful memories.

"I still have no idea what you are going on about," I managed to nick the ball from Rob's defence.

"You just need a goal," Rob said. "It doesn't matter if it hits you on the backside and trickles over the line, you just need to get the ball into the back of the net by any means necessary."

"A penalty will do!" Jack shouted as Rob brought my player down in the area and the referee signalled for the spot kick in the dying seconds.

I stared intently at the screen as the ball was placed on the penalty spot. "So you're saying I just need to score once and then all the pressure I am putting on myself will disappear?" I suddenly understood.

"That's right," Jack patted me on the back. "You've got it."

I stepped up to take my penalty; a goal which would surely seal victory. But then a scary thought hit me. "But what if I miss the penalty?" I am English after all.

"Then you'll only ever be good enough to play for Scunthorpe, or at very best maybe get a sniff with Ollie's sloppy seconds," Jack said.

"Nothing wrong with my sloppy seconds," Ollie informed me before a hush fell across my living room. I stared at the controller, knowing full well that a nation's hopes rested on my shoulders. Put this one away and I'd be back on the score sheet. Miss and my drought would continue.

I turned the controller away from Rob, not wanting to give anything away. I took a deep breath and puffed out my cheeks as I exhaled. I wiped my clammy hand down my jeans. The ref blew his whistle and I made my run up. I struck the ball to the right. Everything turned to slow motion. Rob sent his keeper the right way. But it didn't matter – this one was out of the keeper's reach.

So much so that it ended up in Row Z.

"And the drought continues!" Ollie said, stubbing his fag out in the ashtray.

I slumped back into my chair as the final whistle sounded. Yet again, I had come so close to scoring only to mess it up at the last minute. "Who wants another beer," I mumbled with defeat lingering on my breath. All three shot their hands up.

"What am I going to do, lads?" I asked as I handed out our third lot of drinks of the afternoon. "I need to score soon. This drought is seriously starting to play on my mind."

"Try staying sober for a start," Rob said leaning forward. "Twice you have been in a situation to get your end away, and twice you have got yourself wasted."

"It's basic first date knowledge, Dan," Jack said. "The bloke needs to keep a clear head so he can get the girl drunk enough to convince her that sleeping with him on the first date is a good idea."

"Otherwise, how else can you expect to perform with her in the bedroom if you're plastered?" Rob said.

"It has the reverse effect on me," Ollie piped up. "I can go for hours when I'm hammered."

"That's because you have more alcohol in your bloodstream than a boozer has in their pipes," Jack said slapping Ollie across the back of the head. "But Dan is a Larry Lightweight and needs to pull it in a notch."

"Maybe you're right," I said putting my beer down on the table. "I'm at the point where I've resorted to praying, but I'm starting to think that even God has it in for me."

"God doesn't have it in for *you*," Jack said with authority, like a man with inside knowledge of God's innermost thoughts.

"He doesn't?"

"No, of course not. He has it in for Ollie, but not you."

"What are you going on about Jack?" Ollie asked.

"When God was handing out talent and looks, you must have got stuck behind David Beckham and God gave him

135

your share. That's why you have the type of face only a mother could love. Plus you have a chode." Jack wiggled his little finger at Ollie.

"Shut up," Ollie threw a cushion at Jack as Rob and I laughed. "What do you think God looks like?" Ollie said with a deep thoughtful look on his face.

"I have no idea, mate," Rob said.

"Long hair and a beard?" was my guess.

"Wrong," Jack said. "Long hair, yes. Beard, no."

"And what makes you an expert on God's appearance," Rob enquired.

"Because God is a *woman*," Jack said and drunk some more of his beer, before sitting back and letting out a satisfying *Aahh* noise, and offering no further explanation.

"How do you know God is a woman," Ollie asked with a quizzical look on his face.

"Because my ugly jolly green giant friend, if God was a man then why would he put his G-spot up his arse?"

There was an awkward silence in the room as everyone sat thinking about what Jack had just said. It wasn't exactly a question you would get on *Mastermind*, but you had to admit Jack might have had a point. "Only a woman could play such a cruel trick as to put the male G-spot in the rectum," Jack went on.

"Maybe God is gay," Ollie said, before he excitedly added, "God could be a lesbian. Now there is a God I could pray to."

Lazy Sundays and bullshit conversation. Did it get any better than this? Ollie got up and went to the fridge to grab some more beer. This is what I needed. Proper lads' chat about football, women, and beer.

"Where the hell did you get this beer from?" Ollie said as he handed out the Chinese beer I had bought from my local offie because it was on special offer.

136

"Whoa, hold on there, Ollie," Rob said before I could answer. "Are you complaining about the beer?

"No, I just..."

"Because you know there are rules about moaning about the beer in a man's fridge," Jack joined in.

"There is?" Even I wasn't aware of this.

"Oh yeah. It is forbidden to complain about the brand of *free* beer in a mate's fridge," Jack said.

"You can complain if the temperature is unsuitable though," Rob added. "It's simple beer drinking etiquette. You can find this stuff on the internet. It's the same as never hesitating to reach for the last beer or the last slice of pizza, but never take both."

"Because that would be greedy," Jack finished the sentence off for Rob. "You didn't know that? It's like an unwritten man rule."

"A bit like not having to ever have to buy a mate a birthday present?" Ollie asked.

"Exactly," Jack said. "Even remembering your mate's birthday is strictly optional."

"I've got one," I said. "Two men should never share an umbrella."

"Unless you're at the footy and your pies are getting wet," Ollie said and we all nodded in agreement.

"Talking of the footy," Rob started, "any woman who claims they love football should be treated suspiciously until they can demonstrate knowledge of the game, and by that I mean fully explaining the offside rule."

"On that note," Jack said, "when stumbling upon other blokes watching a sporting event, you can ask what the score is, but never ask who's playing."

We all chinked beers, but I quickly held up my hand as I swallowed to signal I had one more. "We missed an important one," I said. "Let us ogle. We are going to look anyway."

137

"Fact," Jack said holding up his drink to me. "Why do girls always bang on about going on diets?"

"And why is it the stick-thin girls who go on about them the most?" Ollie said. "Personally, I can't do diets."

"How come?" Rob asked.

"Because every time I shag Jack's bird she gives me a biscuit," Ollie said laughing and pointing his beer towards Jack.

"You wish," Jack responded.

We all laughed, and I was starting to relax again. Maybe because there was no pressure to go out on the pull, or maybe it was because I knew there was little chance of bumping into Dave the Neanderthal in my living room. Whatever it was I sat back and drunk my beer like I didn't have a care in the world. I was already starting to forget about what had happened with Carla. Heck, it had even been quite funny when I looked back. The way I was starting to see it, a lot worse things could happen than not have sex for a few months. I started flicking through the channels. I switched over to the BBC1 News and my heart stopped. I pumped the volume.

*Metropolitan Police are pleased that yesterday's G8 demonstration in the capital passed off peacefully. The only disturbance noted came when a gay rights protester clashed with a section of police.*

And there I was in my pink T-shirt, carrying a *gay & proud* signpost. Why the hell had I not taken any notice of what the banner had said? I watched in horror as the reporter shoved the microphone in my face and asked: *Do you feel a sense of injustice as a gay man living in the UK?*

"Yes! Yes!" I shouted. "I haven't done anything!" The news report concluded as I watched open-mouthed and wide-eyed. I could feel my friends staring at me; their stifled laughter about to explode.

"Gay *and* proud?" Rob said with a smirk. Queue the fits of laughter.

"I always had a feeling about you, Dan," Ollie said, shifting his way down the sofa away from me.

"I have to hold my hands up and admit when I am wrong," Jack said. "God must be a man, because only a man could come up with something as golden as this."

"How did this happen?" I managed to say, staring blankly at the screen. "I swear to you I didn't know what the sign said."

"And the pink T-shirt?" Rob asked.

"This is a disaster." I drank my beer, slammed the bottle on to the table, and sat with my head in my hands.

"If you had problems getting girls into the sack before, you are going to really be up against it now," Ollie said.

"No, this could help," Rob said laughing. "Girls love gay guys. You could make this work for you."

"Yeah, you could discuss fashion, haircuts, what boys you fancy," Jack said.

My friends were no longer hiding their delight, and were howling with laughter. An hour ago I was a striker who just needed to find the net again. Now I was a young gay fugitive.

"This isn't funny," I barked, but the angrier I got the funnier they found it. My house phone started to ring and snapped me out of my state of shock.

"Hello," I answered the phone. "Oh, hi mum," and I raised my finger to my lips to shut the boys up.

"Yes, that was me on the television," I paused. "No, I'm not gay, mum." The laughter now roared back into life. I shot them all a look, but the last thing on their mind was to take any notice of my feelings. In fact, Ollie had Jack bent over the sofa while Rob thrust his groin into Jack's face.

I stormed out of the living room and into my bedroom. "Look, mum, it was just a big mistake."

139

"Is that why you broke up with Stacey?" My mum asked. "Because you like boys now?"

"No, I don't like boys!"

"I don't mind sweetheart, I will always love you unconditionally. Your father might take a bit of getting used to the idea, but he'll come round."

"Mum, you need to listen to me," I said. "I am not gay." I proceeded to explain what happened, and how I hadn't realised what the sign said that I was holding. It took a while, but I finally convinced her.

"This wouldn't happen if you spoke to your old mum a bit more, and told me what was going on in your life once in a while," she said as she explained away her fantastic mum logic.

"I know mum, and I promise I will keep you in the loop more often from now on," I lied just to get her off the phone.

We said our goodbyes and I walked back into the living room. I fell back onto the sofa and sighed. I closed my eyes waiting for the onslaught but... nothing. I opened my left eye and scanned the living room. Jack and Rob were playing the football game, while Ollie had lit another cigarette. They said nothing. If anything, they were being suspiciously quiet.

"What's going on?" I asked. But they all just shrugged their shoulders and carried on what they were doing. "Seriously, what's going on?" I asked again, this time with a little more authority in my voice. I had known this lot for too long. They would have never let this joke die as quickly as this. No way had they decided this gag didn't have any more legs. I scanned all of their blank expressions. What were they hiding?

Then, out of the corner of my eye, I spotted it.

"No!" I shouted as I grabbed my mobile and saw the words *Message Sent* flash up on the screen. "What have you done?" The worst possible scenarios were running through my head.

The laughing started up again. Then Jack answered through stifled laughter: "We just wanted to put the message out there that despite national news coverage, you are 100 per cent confident in your sexuality."

"What the hell have you done?" I anxiously started clicking through sent messages, and that's when I saw it:

*I'm in a bad place right now, but I just wanted to let you know that I'm all man, and I have never stopped thinking about you. It's always been you.*

"No, no, no, no," I kept saying over and over again as my so-called friends cackled like a pack of hyenas. How could I have been so stupid? Leaving my phone with a bunch of booze-fuelled friends was the most basic of schoolboy errors. Then the replies started to come through.

*Tina Russell*
*Who is this?*

Okay, damage limitation. I hadn't seen Tina Russell since college. I was a little hurt she didn't have my number anymore, but I could live with that.

*Callie McDowell*
*Very funny Dan. Are you drunk? Xx*

*Jenny Hoxley*
*Hi Dan. Did you mean to send this to me?*

This was good. Maybe everyone would see this as a drunken joke or just a simple case of a text being sent to the wrong person.

141

*Craig Daws*
*Saw you on the news earlier and just got your text. Don't take it personally but I am deleting your number. I am not that type of bloke – don't contact me again.*

Now I was getting nervous. Sending it to a bunch of girls in my phone was bad enough, but sending it to a guy? This was getting ridiculous.

*Stacey Cunningham*
*You think you're so funny don't you? Let me tell you something now – you are not all man. Don't ever text me again you moron.*

*Unknown number*
*You are a dead man. Dave.*

"What's wrong with you lot?" I said, rubbing my brow. "Of all the people you could have sent it to, why the hell did you send this to her?" My only saving grace was that things couldn't get any worse.

*Dick Mussel*
*Is this your idea of a joke? I want to see you in my office first thing tomorrow morning.*

I was wrong. "Are you fucking kidding me?!" I was livid. "You sent it to my boss? This could cost me my job."

The laughing stopped. Everyone shifted awkwardly in their seats. "We're sorry, mate," Rob said realising my tone was deadly serious. "We didn't think."

I was furious with them. I could take a joke, but this had gone way over the line. They all avoided eye contact with me, knowing full well they had gone too far with this one.

My phone beeped with another reply.

*Grace Ellison*

*Hi Dan, it's Grace here. I accidentally deleted your text before reading it. What did it say? I'm glad you contacted me as I feel bad about running off and leaving you that night. How about I make it up to you? Why don't you come round to my place one night and I'll cook. Text back xx*

I stared at it in silence. This was unexpected. This was a total surprise. This was fucking brilliant! "Check this out," I said to the guys, shoving the phone towards them. They looked nervous to read it at first, but then they all started smiling.

"Get in there, my son," Jack said.

"But what about your boss?" Ollie asked.

"What?" I asked, completely forgetting about the message from Dick. "Oh that. Nah, I'll just tell him I lost my phone and some nut job has been texting people in my address book."

"Good work," Rob congratulated me.

It's funny how the prospect of sex can make even the most dire of circumstances simply seem like a mere blip. I was starting to see much clearer now. I would simply text everyone back (apart from Stacey and Dave) and say it was a prank. In a matter of seconds my friends had gone from zeros to heroes. Without their utter stupidity I would not have a second shot at Grace.

My phone beeped again.

*Kelly Campbell*

*I can't stop thinking about you too babe! What are you like? Let me guess, your friends got hold of your mobile? I can't believe you fell for the oldest trick in the book! x*

## Chapter 13: Amazing Grace

*Wednesday, April 8, 2009 - 5.12pm*
*Drought Clock: 96 days, 19 hours, 15 minutes*

Rob got the low down from Katie. Grace had seen her ex kissing another girl and was on the rebound. "This could really work in your favour," Rob said down the phone. "But you have to make sure you play the game correctly."

"What do you mean?" I asked, sitting at my desk at work, shining an apple on my shirt before taking a bite.

"All you have to do is come across as a better man than her ex. She is on the prowl to prove that she is still desirable. She wants to make sure in her own mind that she did the right thing leaving her ex in the first place," Rob paused. "Are you taking notes?"

"No, of course not." I put down my pen.

"You could get some very dirty sex here, you lucky bastard. I'm actually jealous of you for once," Rob chuckled. "If you play your cards right, you can kiss goodbye to the drought tonight, Danny boy."

"That is not all I plan on kissing," I said. Kelly looked up at me and shook her head. "I've got to go. I'll talk to you later."

I put the phone down and sat back. Tonight was the night. After 15 weeks without sex I was finally going to put that ball into the back of the net. I couldn't miss. I didn't even have to try and convince her to let me in for coffee at the end of the date. I was going to be in her house. I would probably be able to see the bed from the dinner table.

"So, the big date is tonight," Kelly said. "Are you ready?"

"As I'll ever be," I replied, trying to play it cool before realising this was Kelly I was talking to. "Actually, I'm a little nervous."

144

"I'm sure you'll be fine," Kelly said to reassure me. "Just try to avoid making the ten o'clock news this time."

"Very funny."

"So what is she cooking for you?"

"I'm not too sure. But I'll be bringing dessert if you catch my drift," I said with a wink.

"And when was the last time you had any dessert," Kelly said grinning. "If you catch *my* drift."

"Okay, point taken." Note to self – no more dessert references when talking about sex. "Should I take anything with me?" I was thinking a couple of cans of Stella would do the trick.

"A nice bottle of wine, although try not to drink *too* much this time."

"Bottle of wine. Check. Don't get pissed. Check."

Everything finally seemed to be clicking into place for me. I had a second shot at Grace, I had managed to avoid any further contact with Stacey and Dave, and my mother had not called for at least 16 hours to ask if I was feeling lonely. Or if I was gay.

"Hilles! My office!" Dick bellowed across the floor.

Everything was clicking into place except for work. Ever since Dick had received *that* text he really had it in for me. Kelly watched as I got up and covered her mouth to stop her laughter.

The morning after the text incident I immediately went to his office and explained how my friends had sent the text as a childish prank. I apologised profusely, admitting it was extremely unprofessional and that it would never happen again. I anticipated the anger, the shouting, and the potential disciplinary I faced from HR. I was ready for anything.

Anything other than how he had actually reacted.

"Sit down, close the door," Dick said as I entered his office. "So how have you been?"

"Er, fine," I hesitated. "I've been fine."

145

"Good, good," he said looking me up and down. "You look well."

I suddenly felt very dirty, but in my panic I blurted out the first thing that popped into my mind. "So do you."

"Thanks," Dick said getting up from his chair and walking round to sit on the corner of his desk. "I've been working out. Can you tell?" He was stroking his bicep through the sleeve of his expensive designer suit, extending his arm back and forth. I didn't know what to say so I just shrugged my shoulders and nodded.

"Would you like to feel?" Dick asked holding out his flexed bicep for me to touch.

"No, God no," I held my hands up. "I mean, I can see the bulge from here."

There have been moments in my life where I had regretted my actions or the things I had said. Telling my boss I could see his bulge would rank right up there. Dick smiled and nodded his appreciation. Realising the horror of my blunder I tried to rephrase my sentence. "What I meant was..."

"I have something for you," Dick said, cutting me off. I sat completely still as he lent over his desk to pull something out of his draw, turning to face me as he did it. I didn't know what to do. Maybe I could make a break for it, leap out of the window to make my escape. *James Bond* would do something cool like that. Then again, I couldn't exactly remember the last time Bond had to escape from a potential homoerotic encounter.

"Here you go," Dick said handing me a rainbow coloured scarf. I looked at it for a second, puzzled. Dick bent down and whispered into my ear: "I know, I saw you on the news."

My mouth went very dry and I couldn't breathe. All week his comments included innuendo, making me uncomfortable in his presence. Now I knew why. My gay

146

boss had a crush on me. I needed to set this record straight. Literally.

"Dick, I'm not..."

"Shhhh," Dick put his finger to my mouth. "Don't say another word." He had my lip pressed up against my left nostril. He somehow managed to guide me up from my chair and out of his office before finally removing his finger from my mouth, and slowly shutting his door, seductively waving me farewell by gently closing one finger at a time over his palm.

I slowly turned around and felt as though everyone in the office was staring in my direction. Did they know what had just happened in there? Had they somehow heard? I glanced down at Shaila who was sitting at her desk, a blank look on her face. Had she *seen?* Did she *know?*

"Dick was just showing me something," I stuttered.

"It's none of my business, Don," she replied.

Realising how my sentence might have sounded I tried to correct myself. "What I meant was that he wanted to give me something." She looked at the scarf and raised her eyebrows. I decided not to say anything else and cut my losses.

"Why are you holding a gay pride scarf?" Kelly asked as I returned to my desk.

I quickly stuffed the scarf into my jacket pocket. "I don't want to talk about it," I said. I wasn't too sure what had just happened. Okay, that's a lie – I knew exactly what had just happened. I had just had my first gay experience. It wasn't the best preparation for my date with Grace. Don't get me wrong, I don't have anything against gay people – I have gay friends. Okay, I don't have any gay friends, but I know gay people. Okay, I know Dick. And the guy that gave me the *Gay & Proud* sign, but he was more of an acquaintance.

*Get a grip,* I told myself. Concentrate on tonight. I had more important things to deal with and I couldn't let myself get distracted. This was just God's way of testing me, to see how badly I wanted to end this drought.

*

I stepped out of Tooting Broadway tube station clutching a nice bottle of Pinot Grigio. I only say nice because it cost me a tenner; all wine tastes the same to me.

I'd printed out a map from the internet to direct me to Grace's flat on Henry Doulton Drive. My phone battery was nearly dead so quickly sent Grace a text to say I was on my way.

"Hi, Dan," Grace greeted me at her door 15 minutes later. I handed her the bottle of wine. "Oooh, this looks like a good one."

"You look fantastic," I gave myself a mental pat on the back for remembering to compliment her. And she did look fantastic in dark jeans and a midriff-revealing top.

"Come in," she said. Her flat was very girly with lots of pink and white. There was a candlelit dining table in the middle of her living room, while Usher played in the background. And I could see the bedroom!

"This is a really nice place," I said. It was evident once the small talk was out of the way that if this night went any further we needed to talk about *that* night.

"Look, I'm really sorry for how I behaved when we first went out," I said as sincere as possible.

"I should apologise," Grace said. "I kept making you drink to get you to dance. It was my fault really."

"Why don't we agree to draw a line under that night and start again?" I proposed.

"Deal. I'll drink to that." Grace went into the kitchen to open the bottle of wine. "Dinner will be ready in about five minutes. I hope you like spaghetti bolognaise."

"Sounds great." Okay, so far so good. I was even starting to feel quite calm and collected. Grace walked back over and handed me a glass of wine, and we made a toast to a fresh start.

*A fresh start.* It was exactly what I needed. It was a poignant moment for me. There was a connection between us; I could feel it. It started at the bottom of my feet, and then started to wrap itself around my ankles. And purr?

"Smokey!" Grace said picking up her pet cat. "I think he likes you." I couldn't help but wonder if Smokey had seen the news as well. I gave him a look as if to tell him not to get any funny ideas – I wasn't into boys. Or cats.

"Sit down and I'll get dinner ready."

I did as I was told and took my place at the table. Grace brought over two plates of mince beef and spaghetti pasta with a delicious aroma from the home-made tomato sauce. "It smells great," I said.

We eased into conversation. Grace told me how she had nearly text me on a number of occasions but was worried I might not reply. She laughed so hard when I told her about my brush with the law as the gay rights campaigner that I thought she was going to fall off her chair. We finished dinner and the conversation moved over to the sofa. I knew I had to make a move so I kept looking for the signs – flirting, playing with her hair, touching my hand, laughing at all of my jokes – even the unfunny ones. Grace was doing it all, but I just froze. I was so close I could feel it.

Over three months of sexual frustration built up inside me. This was my moment, I had to take it. I looked deep into her eyes, moved forward and...

"Another glass of wine?" I found myself leaning forward to pick the bottle up. I could see the disappointment in her eyes.

"Sure," she said trying to hide her impatience and holding her glass out. I groaned inside. She was ready, and I

149

missed my opportunity. My shot. My moment! What if I had blown it? This was getting beyond ridiculous. I started to overthink things. What if I got the signals wrong? What if I tried to kiss her and she just wanted to be friends? What if I couldn't get it up? Oh why did I plant *that* seed of doubt into my mind?

The single biggest fear men have is not being able to get it up. This is a bigger universal fear for mankind than nuclear war or al-Qaeda. The pressure can be immense. A girl has nothing to worry about – she has to just lay back and hope the guy lasts longer than 30 seconds. And there is the second biggest fear. Sex with a girl for the first time leaves the man feeling he needs to prove himself and perform like a porn star, capable of lasting hours.

We live in a culture where tales of hour-long sex marathons get splashed across tabloid headlines and celebrity magazines. Telling someone you are going to shag them all night long is always said with the greatest intentions, but who seriously wants to bang away for hours on end? It's all bravado. If you manage to pull a double shift you are liable to get a dull ache in the end of your throbbing penis about 10 minutes into the second stint. And if a girl comments on how impressed she is with your stamina, it normally translates to *hurry up and finish and get the fuck off me.*

The third biggest fear? The size of your sausage No matter how comfortable you are with the size of your manhood, there is always a doubt. Whether it is fear of having a small penis or a fear of not measuring up to other penises she has encountered.

There should be support groups for men where quotes like *it is not the size of the sea, but the motion of the ocean* hang on plaques across the wall.

I could tell Grace was waiting for me to make a move. I looked at my glass of wine and took a sip, which turned into a gulp, which turned into me pretty much downing the whole glass. I wiped my mouth ready to move in for the kill and...

"Oh for crying out loud," Grace said launching herself at me, our lips locking and tongues slipping in and out like a hose that was no longer in control. She shoved me back on to the sofa and straddled me, lifting her top off over her head.

I put my arm round her, attempting the old one-hand bra release. After a few seconds of struggling, I resorted to two hands. But that wouldn't work either. I was now 10 seconds into my attempt to remove her bra. This was precisely seven seconds too long. Why don't these things come with a manual? Grace reached round to assist and I almost knocked her hand away just to prove I could do it. But I already realised I was scoring pretty low on the sexy super cool stakes so I let her remove it herself.

Now it was my time to shine. I had always considered myself a breast man and this was an opportunity to redeem myself for my so far not very impressive performance. I started with the right breast, cupping it in my hand like a stress ball and showing off my skills with my tongue. I then moved across to the left breast so it didn't feel left out.

"Careful babe," Grace said. "Gentle."

Brilliant. I couldn't even get the one thing right I thought I was good at. On to plan B. This was basically to get naked as quickly as possible so she couldn't back out.

However, I managed to lodge myself in no man's land as I attempted to lift the shirt over my head and arms at the same time. I was trapped, unable to see anything and with limited use of my arms. I could only imagine the expression a topless Grace wore on her face as she watched me attempt to escape the customised straight-jacked I had put myself into.

It was bad enough Grace had needed to help me to take her clothes off; she now had to help me take mine off too. Between us we finally lifted the shirt over my head. My hair was a mess and my face was as red as a beetroot, and we hadn't even done anything yet.

Grace didn't seem to care though as she shoved her tongue back into my mouth and yanked at my trousers. I took the hint and quickly removed my jeans as Grace stood and removed hers.

She stood in front of me in a small thong, sex in her eyes. I sat on the sofa with a boner, wearing socks. It wasn't the best look, but to hell with it. She straddled me, rubbing herself against me. I urged myself not to prematurely ejaculate, especially when the only thing that now stood in my way of sex was a piece of material the size of dental floss. I reached to pull her thong down and she whispered into my ear, "Do you have a condom?"

"A condom?" I asked. "Yes, hold on." Of course I had a condom. I was a man prepared. I reached down and pulled my wallet out of my jeans pocket. Do you really think I would come all this way, get this far, and not have a condom?

"I don't have one," I said, a look on panic in my face. "Do you have one?"

"No, I thought you would bring one," Grace said as her shoulders slumped.

"Perhaps we could..."

"I am not having sex with you without a condom," Grace cut me off.

"I wasn't going to say that," I protested, even though that was exactly what I was going to say. This was not good. This was about as far away from good as you could get. I had come so close – again!

"Wait a minute," I said. "There is a shop outside the tube station. They'll sell condoms."

Grace smiled and planted a kiss on my lips. "Hurry up then," she said. I jumped up off the sofa and got dressed in record time. I think I even had my shoes on the wrong foot and my pants inside out, but there wasn't time for small details like that. I had condoms to buy!

I raced out of the flat and weaved my way in and out of the back streets of Tooting. I ran past the local youths hanging out after dark, shot a left down the road with a telephone booth, quickly hit a right past the barking dog in the front garden, zoomed past the woman smoking on her doorstep with her neighbour, cracked a right sprinting by a guy working on his car, and navigated my way under the flickering street lamp on my final left turn before making my way out on to the High Street.

Standing across from the shop I could see the owner starting to pull the shutters down to close up. I had to get in there. Taking my life into my own hands I dashed across the busy main road, ignoring the car horns and screeching car brakes caused by my recklessness. I dodged the old lady at the bus stop and practically leapt through the front door *Indiana Jones* style. The shop assistant stared at me with a bizarre look on his face. "We're closed," he said.

"Please, this is a matter of life and death," I managed to say catching my breath. "You have to serve me."

"I'm sorry, sir, but we are closed," he reiterated.

I slammed my hands onto the counter. There was no way I was walking out of this shop without getting what I wanted.

"Look," I started. "I am sure you have had a very long day, and I don't want to keep you any longer than I have to. But you have to serve me. If you had walked in these shoes, even for just one day, then you would appreciate the sweat, blood, tears, and disappointment I have endured these past few months. My whole existence depends on this one moment." I leaned forward and grabbed him by the shirt

153

and pulled him towards me. "You have to help me. It is your duty as a fellow man."

Okay, it was slightly over the top but it did the trick. I let go of the shopkeeper and he nodded at me, straightening out his shirt. "Okay, what do you want?"

"A packet of condoms," I said it without flinching. "The ribbed ones," I continued, pointing over his shoulder to the shelf behind him.

"Are you fucking kidding me?" the shopkeeper asked.

"No," I replied. "They are ribbed for her extra pleasure."

"I am not talking about them being ribbed you idiot," the shopkeeper said throwing the condoms down in front of me. "I'm talking about that little speech."

I simply shrugged my shoulders and handed him the money. He shook his head in disgust, but I didn't care. I had condoms. I raced out and took a deep breath of the night air. After all the doubt, all the barriers, all the heartache and excessive masturbation, I was finally going to do this.

All I had to do now was get back to Grace's flat on... what was the name of her street? I had been in such a rush to get to the shop that I hadn't really taken much notice of the route I had taken. I reached into my pocket to pull out my map. It wasn't there. I must have taken it out at Grace's.

Wait, my phone! I'll call Grace and get directions. I fumbled in my pocket and pulled my mobile out. The screen was blank. I clicked the call button. Still blank. Shit, of course – the battery was dead! How could I be so foolish?

*Don't panic* I told myself. Just retrace your steps. I crossed the road and started to walk past the side streets, reading the road names to try and jog my memory. Longmead Road, Undine Street, Valnay Street. None of them rang any bells. I continued and decided to take the next left up Vant Road. I got to the T-Junction at Eswyn Road. Left or right? I craned my neck back and forth. That's

154

when I saw it – the flickering street light! I remembered that.

I took the left and stood under the flickering light; my hands on my hips scanning my options. I opted for the right up Franciscan Road and kept running. I must have been jogging for two or three minutes when I arrived at a church. I bent over, my hands supporting my body against my knees, trying to catch my breath. I was completely lost. I had no idea where to go; it was hopeless. I looked at the church in front of me. "Why God, why?" I shouted. I don't know how I thought screaming at a brick building would help. Perhaps I just wanted a sign.

Then I got it. Or at least I heard it. It was a dog barking, the same barking I had heard earlier. "Thank you, God!" I jumped for joy and started to run towards the barking on Mantilla Road. My feet pounded against the grey pavement for all of 50 yards before the barking was immediately in front of me. I stopped in my tracks; my eyes trying to adjust to the dark shadows of houses that surrounded me. I took a step forward and the bark came through loud and clear once again. I followed the sound and there it was.

Two eyes peered at me. They looked like two miniature torches glaring off the street lamps. It barked again, but this time with a much deeper and sinister tone to it. The gloss of the dog's fur beamed off the moonlight. I stopped dead in my tracks. Not 10 feet in front of me appeared the monstrous figure of a bloodthirsty hound the size of a horse, stalking its way toward me.

"Good doggy," I pleaded with my hands out as I slowly stepped backwards. The beast stared straight at me and I swear at that precise moment, he grinned at me, before stampeding in my direction.

I screamed and turned on my heels in the opposite direction back down Mantilla Road, across on to Topsham Road. I kept running, certain the hound was in hot pursuit. I

155

didn't want to look back. I felt the condoms fall from my pocket, a final condemnation that this night was coming to an end. I raced down to Upper Tooting Road and took a sharp right towards Tooting Bec tube station. My night with Grace was well and truly over.

## Chapter 14: Little White Lie

*Sunday, April 12 - 2.03pm*
*Drought Clock: 100 days, 22 hours, 18 minutes*

"Okay," Rob said putting his pint down and waving his hands. "Let's get the facts right. Tell us what happened one more time."

It was Sunday afternoon, and in my hour of need I had called upon my friends to cheer me up after the debacle of my second date with Grace. We had met in our favourite Sunday afternoon beverage establishment – the Nelson Arms in Clapham Old Town.

"Things were heating up and I was teasing the hell out of her. Really putting her in the mood," I launched into my version of events, deciding to omit the truth of how I had fumbled my way through the foreplay. "I was being real naughty, you know what I mean?"

"Like flicking the bean, and shit like that?" Jack asked, flicking his finger and biting down on his bottom lip.

"Yeah, if you like Jack," I said brushing his crude comment to one side. My made-up version was much more adventurous than that. "Anyway, she was bang up for it. Then I realised I didn't have any condoms with me."

"Schoolboy error," Rob said taking a sip from his pint and shaking his head.

"I know," I said, nodding in agreement. "Tell me about it."

"So you went bare-back right?" Ollie asked, his eyes locked on me in total concentration.

"No, I didn't go bare-back," I told him. "I played it cool. I told her that perhaps it was a sign we should take things slow. I told her I really liked her and that I respected her. I could tell she was gagging for it after that."

"You smooth-talking bastard," Jack congratulated me.

"What did she say?" Rob pressed me.

"She fell in love straight away, and told me she wanted me even more," I lied again. "I continued to play it cool and said I was going to pop out for another bottle of wine, and when I returned we would *make love* to each other."

"Make love?" Ollie said raising his eyebrows. "That's a bit gay, isn't it?"

"Yeah, even girls would find that a bit of a turn-off, mate," Jack added.

Damn it, I was losing them in my web of lies. I needed to pull them back in quickly. "Yeah, but when I said make love I was going down on her at the time."

"Why didn't you say?" Jack said. "If you are getting your knees dirty working in the *vagtable patch*, anything you say is completely acceptable."

"But I thought you had told her you wanted to play things cool." Rob chipped in. "That's a strange thing to say while you were going down on her, isn't it?"

I froze. Rob had me. My lame face-saving story was about to come crashing down around me. I took a drink to try and earn myself a bit of thinking time. Then I had a thought. It was risky but might just work. I placed my pint down as calmly as you like and said: "Hey, what can I say? That's just how I operate. I'm just that type of guy."

"Yes, you are," Jack said slapping me on the back as Ollie high-fived me. Rob didn't look as convinced as the others, but that didn't matter because the odds had swung back in my favour. Phew, that was a close one, I thought, and I dived straight back into my tale.

"I left the flat and raced down to the local shop. I had a bit of banter with the shopkeeper just so to keep her waiting a bit longer and then headed back with the condoms in my back burner. That's when it happened."

158

I picked my pint up to build the tension, and took a long gulp. Ollie and Jack were on the edge of their seats, but Rob still looked a bit dubious.

"What happened?" Rob finally asked. "Please, do tell."

That is when I realised I hadn't really thought this thing through very well. I had no idea where I was going to go with this. It was almost like I was hoping for the closing drumbeats from *EastEnders* so I could have another 24 hours to plan my next episode. I couldn't exactly tell my mates this was a cliffhanger and they would have to tune in tomorrow to hear the rest. I could feel their eyes burning into me. I had to say something. Anything.

"I decided to go home and play hard to get." Anything but that.

"What?" By the look on Jack's face you would have thought I had just revealed I was dating his mother. He was horrified.

"Why?" Ollie was baffled, and had an expression like I had just asked him to recite his 12-times table.

Rob sat back and simply took a long gulp from his pint. I couldn't quite read his reaction, but I was pretty sure it was somewhere in between Jack's utter disgust and Ollie's total confusion.

"You know, treat them mean and keep them keen," I offered weakly. "I sent her a text saying I respected her and that things were moving too fast, and we should go slow." I knew immediately they hadn't bought it.

"I don't buy it," Jack confirmed my thoughts. "After all this time of trying to get your end away, you have this sexy chick completely butt-naked ready to rock your knocker, and you decide to play hard to get?"

"That is definitely a bit gay, mate," Ollie added.

Tough crowd. This had definitely gone better in my head. Why hadn't I just told them the truth? Too late to go back now, I had to just see this through.

159

"I guess we'll just have to wait and see whether I have played a blinder or not then, won't we?" I said with every ounce of confidence I could conjure up. "I'm meeting her next weekend, and I am willing to bet that she is going to be so up for it by then that she will do anything I want in the sack." I looked at them all and then said "*Anything*" once more with real emphasis.

Slowly I saw the glow of approval grow in Jack and Ollie's eyes. It was as if I had just hatched the most amazing sex plan ever. A plan that would see me get the dirtiest sex known to man. All I had to do now was find a girl hotter than Grace who was willing to have clumsy sex with me, and then I could make up another lie about how I met this even fitter girl and shagged her instead. I congratulated myself on a job well done.

"Sounds like you have got it all sorted out, mate," Rob said. I had even managed to convince him. "But the only problem is that you won't be seeing Grace next weekend, will you?"

"I don't follow?" I said hesitantly with my pint glass held to my lips.

"You seem to forget that I am still in contact with Katie," Rob said sitting back smugly in his chair. "I spoke to her the other day and she told me that Grace had given her a slightly different version of events."

I gulped. This was not good. "Katie said Grace told her that after you left her flat to get the condoms, you never returned. You didn't text or anything."

"Maybe I forgot to text," I said. "Or maybe I was trying to keep an air of mystery around me," I offered hopefully as an explanation to try and keep up this pathetic charade.

"Maybe," Rob said. "But Grace didn't forget to send you a text, did she?"

"No," I said bowing my head, realising defeat was in sight.

"What did the text say Dan?" Rob asked.

"She texted me saying I was a pathetic little man who should not waste her time."

"And," Rob urged me on.

"And that she would have shagged the life out of me, but I had blown my chance for running away like a little wimp."

"I think you had better tell us what really happened," Rob said, patting and rubbing my back to comfort me as I sat with my head in my hands.

So I did. I told them how Grace had pounced on me, and how I had fumbled my way through the foreplay. I explained how I had stupidly forgotten to buy condoms because I was so out of practice, and that after racing to the shop to buy some I had got lost and couldn't remember where she lived.

"Hold on, let me get this right," Jack said, not even attempting to hide the grin on his face. "You were on the verge of nailing this chick and then you ran away?"

"I didn't run away," I corrected Jack. The story was embarrassing enough without adding new twists to it. "I just had a slight direction problem."

"You had a slight erection problem?" Ollie cracked much to the delight of my laughing friends. Like the old saying goes – a friend in need is a friend worth relentlessly taking the piss out of.

"Yeah, I had an erection problem because your mum is so ugly even Viagra have taken a court injunction out on her," I snapped back. No matter how old you are, mum jokes are still the best response to any type of banter.

"She must have been dripping wet," Jack started. "She could have been lying there for hours, wearing nothing but a grin and her birthday suit. And you royally screwed it up because you forgot to buy a map and pack of Randy van Warmers!"

161

"I told you that you should have gone bare-back," Ollie said finishing off his pint. My so-called friends revelled in my misery. They laughed so hard they were struggling to breathe as tears streamed down their faces.

"But that isn't all," Rob said barely able to get his words out.

"There's more?" Jack couldn't believe it.

"I bumped into Simon Peterson yesterday." Rob said. "He lives on Mantilla Road."

"So what?" I sneered. Simon Peterson was some grease monkey we went to college with. What the hell did he have to do with all this? Wait a minute – did he say Mantilla Road?

"He happened to mention that he saw you on his road on Wednesday night," Rob announced. "He was working on his car. He would have said hello, but you sprinted past him at a ferocious pace with a dog chasing you."

"Was it a poodle?" Ollie questioned.

"No it wasn't a poodle," I said. "It was a big, horrible, snarling beast."

"Simon said it was a sausage dog," Rob said and they all started laughing again.

"No way," I hit back. "It was big. It must have been a cross breed."

"With what?" Rob said through his laughter.

"I don't know," I said trying to think about it. I didn't really get a good look at the dog but it sounded big. "It was big like a German Shepherd."

"You got chased by a dog that was a cross between a sausage dog and a German Shepherd?" Ollie asked almost in disbelief.

"Was it a bratwurst?" The moment the question left Jack's lips the three of them nearly fell off their chairs amidst the eruption of yet more laughter.

"Piss off," I barked and stomped off to the toilet. I stood at the urinal, wondering whether I would ever live this new indignity down. Jeez, would I ever get laid?

"What is wrong with you?" I said looking down at my penis, standing at the urinal. "The sooner you realise we are in this together, the better. We need to start working as a team – I can't do this alone. If you help me, then I'll help you. Deal?"

It was then I sensed I was not alone, and I am not talking about my penis. I could feel someone staring at me, and I slowly turned my head to see an old man frozen in his tracks looking at me.

"I was just..." I paused. What the hell could I say? I decided that lying had got me nowhere today so I opted for the truth. "I was just talking to my penis," I decided to announce matter-of-factly.

"Bloody pervert," the old man said and then went about his business.

I washed my hands and quickly left the bathroom before I managed to get myself into any other awkward situations. I walked back into the bar and joined my friends, who were suspiciously quiet. I knew something was up because this is exactly how they had acted in the aftermath of the now infamous text incident.

"Come on," I said. "Get it over and done with." I knew what was coming next. After all, I was a bloke. If the shoe was on the other foot I would be the one dishing out the banter. I had put myself in a precarious situation and I was fully prepared for the pack of wolves to attack.

"Look, Danny boy, we have been talking," Rob said. "And we think we can help you."

"Oh, I get it," I said folding my arms across my chest defensively. "So what do you have planned? No wait, let me guess. You are going to pimp me out as a rent-boy?"

"No, not quite," Rob said.

163

"Perhaps you want to pay old Hilda who lives in that trolley under the bridge to pop out her false teeth and to give me some gum-love?"

"Nope, but that would be *absolute*," Jack said, index finger twirling.

"Well then you must be planning to slip some rohypnol into my pint and carrying my unconscious body down to the local STD clinic, where you will leave me at the feet of diseased-ravaged old hags to have their wicked way with me, just so doctors can carry out tests and discover new sexually-transmitted infections, and then put my picture in the medical dictionary next to the words 'venereal disease'."

"Dude, what's wrong with you?" Ollie quizzed, giving me a strange look.

I was really wound-up. I was ready for the A-Z of jokes, the emails with pictures of sausage dogs, the blown-up condoms left hanging in my bedroom. Bring it on, I didn't care anymore.

"We're not going to do any of those things," Rob said with a warm grin.

"Although did anyone take that last one down because as practical jokes go that would be pretty awesome," Jack said. "Has anyone got a pencil?"

"So what are you planning?" I asked suspiciously.

Rob got to his feet and spoke. "What you need is a foolproof solution. The one thing men have done for years. The one thing that breeds male bonding even more than watching England play in the World Cup. When Roman men built roads in this great country, they built them for one reason and one reason only."

This was unexpected. The suspense was killing me, and my heartbeat raced. Rob spoke with such charisma that I knew it had to be something big, something special. I had been preparing myself for the worst, but now I was on

164

tenterhooks and couldn't wait for him to reveal their big plan.

"What is it?" Ollie asked excitedly, even though he had been involved in the conversation prior to me returning from the bathroom when this great plan had been hatched.

Rob gave Ollie a funny look, but then turned back to me. "A road trip."

"A road trip," I repeated in genuine awe at the sheer genius of it.

"Think about it," Jack said. "We hit the open road and head to new untouched lands. New bars. New clubs. New women," he let the word *women* linger in the air. "A funky fuck-fest of the highest order!"

Did such a place exist? And if it did, where was it?

"This place sounds amazing," Ollie said. I guess he was thinking exactly the same as me. "Where is it?"

"Ollie, where the hell have you been for the last 10 minutes?" Jack asked. "You were here when we discussed this while Dan was in the toilet with that old man who keeps staring at him."

I looked up. Jack was right, the old man who had caught me talking to my penis was staring straight at me. I quickly turned away not to meet his gaze. "But how do you know this will work?" I asked.

"Listen," Rob said. "When a guy goes out, he has one thing on his mind – he wants to get laid."

"So true," Jack said with real sincerity and conviction. He lifted his pint to his lips and took a sip. "Even when I pop down to the newsagent I'm hoping I'll get lucky."

"The big difference between men and women is that the women have the power," Rob continued. "If a girl goes out and wants to have sex, she will have sex because there will always be a guy willing to shag her."

165

"So true," Jack repeated in the same tone, nodding to all of us with almost a combined look of sorrow and jealousy on his face.

"The thing is, a girl will very rarely drop her standards like a bloke does," Rob explained. "And rarely will they go out and end up randomly shagging some guy. It's not that they don't get drunk and lose their inhibitions like guys do, but while a guy will let his mate snog an ugly bird, a girl will never allow her friend to drop her standards."

"Cock-blockers," Ollie said bluntly, looking at each one of us.

"For blokes, it's pretty funny to get your pal smashed and then coax him into pulling some old ripper," Jack said. "Look at how many times we've done it to Ollie."

"And I think you'll find I've thanked you each and every time," Ollie said raising his drink to Jack.

"So what are you saying?" I asked. "That I need a girl to drop her standards to sleep with me?"

"It wouldn't hurt," Jack said.

"No, that's not what we're saying," Rob interjected. "We're saying we need to head to a place where the girls think like guys. Where girls *act* like guys. Where girls go out to get drunk, have fun, and get laid."

"That is the type of place I need!" I almost jumped out of my seat with excitement.

"Then my friend," Rob said putting his arm around me, "you need to visit a seaside town. A *student* town. A party capital where the girls are as wild as the guys."

Where was this place? "Tell me where?" I pleaded.

"This calls for a road trip to Brighton," Rob announced.

I was beaming. What a fantastic plan. I looked at all of them with a massive grin on my face. Despite all of the ridicule, they really did care.

But then I had a thought. What if this was a set-up? I needed some sort of reassurance that my friends were not trying to lull me into a false sense of security. "Do I have your word that you're not going to get me into any stupid situations? That you are genuinely going to help me pot the pink on the snooker table?"

"Mate, with all those women in Brighton, you will be like sheep in high heels on a night out in Cardiff," Jack said. "I promise," and he crossed his heart.

"I'll help you pot the brown if you want," Ollie said, nodding his head.

I looked at my friends. "Okay, I'm in."

"To the road trip," Rob said, and we all clinked our glasses together to toast the town of Brighton.

## Chapter 15: Jack's 10 Commandments

*Thursday, May 14 - 5.20pm*
*Drought Clock: 132 days, 19 hours, 17 minutes*

It had been a month since the foolproof plan that was
Brighton had been put in place, and boy had it dragged. It
was all I could think of. I had entered my fifth month of the
drought and I was pinning all of my hopes on the East
Sussex coastline.

I couldn't get any work done. My mind was occupied
with nothing else but getting the final 24 shagless hours out
of the way and then heading towards my utopia of sex
heaven. The possibilities in Brighton were endless –
students who were away from home for the first time and
going crazy after exams, groups of girls on hen-weekends
drinking all day long, girls who were just down for the
weekend to have a bit of fun without the risk of their
boyfriends or husbands ever finding out, and even local
girls out to pull the odd tourist or two.

"Ready for the big road trip, then?" Kelly asked as she
typed away at her keypad.

"You bet," I said, a little too eager.

"What is the plan then? I take it you must have a plan
seeing as you have been talking non-stop about this trip
since you and your friends planned it last month."

I didn't really have a plan, more of a sixth-sense. This
was Brighton after all – a place where the girls are like the
boys. What could go wrong?

"We're just going to head down there and see where the
sea air takes us," I said with a satisfying nod.

"Really?" Kelly said with a sharp tone to her voice and
narrowing her eyes. "Because that has been working so well
for you so far, hasn't it?"

168

Ouch, that was a bit below the belt I thought, and totally out of character for Kelly.

"Kelly, is everything okay?" I asked.

"I'm sorry," Kelly said. "It's Paul. We were meant to be going out together tonight after work but he has just texted me to cancel because he has a poker night with his friends. Why do you guys think it's perfectly okay to change plans at the last minute?"

"I'm sure he didn't mean to upset you," I said as a way to offer some sort of apology on behalf of all men.

"It's not your fault, babe. He is just being a typical inconsiderate man," Kelly said rolling her eyes. "I'm annoyed because I have nothing to do now."

"Why don't we go out for a quick drink after work then?"

"Yeah, that would be good. You can tell me all about your plans for Brighton."

There was that word again – *plan*. Why did I have to have a plan? Women love to have plans and structures. If this were a bunch of girls going on a road trip they would probably have an agenda or an itinerary. Maybe that wasn't such a bad idea. After all, I had pretty much been out of ideas for the last five months. Some sort of guidance or a manual of some sort probably wouldn't go amiss.

An icon popped up on my computer to say I had a new email, and like a sign from God – or Jack – my guidance appeared in my inbox.

**Subject:** Tour de Big Guns 2009
**From:** jack69@hotmail.co.uk
**Sent:** 14 May 2009 17:26:31
**To:** daniel.hilles@maxwellmedia.co.uk;
robdevlin@policy.com; ollieollie@yahoo.com

With the clock ticking away, it's time to start planning the most slut-infested, drink-fuelled, condom-wearing, STD risk-taking, non-dry-humping, two days of our lives.

Now as you all know, Dan has endured five months of torture. So once the Big Guns invade Brighton, it's time to make a pact...

## THE 10 COMMANDMENTS

1) Let's get this party rocking. As soon as we arrive, we roll the red carpet out. We let them know in no uncertain terms that the Big Guns have arrived. We dump the bags and hit the bars.

2) It's not *Groundhog Day*. No one is allowed to crack on with the same bint for more than one night. You can keep any little tart you meet on reserve in case you blow out, but I ain't having any of this meeting up two nights running like boyfriend and girlfriend.

3) Chat-up lines. They will be used. I have a list of them to hit the chicks up with! Belters like: *My name is Mr Right, somebody told me you were looking for me!*

4) The anthem. Every Big Gun should have one. As soon as the DJ plays this little number, each and every Big Gun must drop what they are doing and hit the dance floor. It's time to cut shapes.

5) High Fives. Before we go out, each and every Big Gun must line-up while I go down the line issuing high fives all round. Standard high fives will be used (nothing fancy like *Top Gun*).

6) Power ballads. Before you ask – no, I'm not gay! But there is nothing like hitting the open road, closing your eyes tight, clenching your fist, and belting out lyrics of pure raw emotion. I defy anyone to sing Bonnie Tyler's *Total Eclipse of the Heart* without a tear in your eye.

7) The way of The Hoff. *Knight Rider* and *Baywatch* – two absolute rip-snorting gems of TV genius brought to us by one man – David Hasselhoff. What is there not to love about this man? Talking crime-fighting cars, bikini-clad women, awesome super slow-mo running shots, and not to mention a chest rug to be proud of. If we use the way of the Hoff, we won't go far wrong.

8) Randy van Warmers. Dan, I've got a box full of condoms with your name written all over them so no need to worry about getting chased by sausage dogs this time!

9) The Game. When entering a different postcode, the game begins. You know how it works. You get a point for snogging some old tart, five points for flicking the bean, 10 points if she has a chat with the boy, and 15 points for rumpedy-roo!

10) What happens on tour – stays on tour. Any man who brings a camera to a road trip may be legally castrated and his man-bits thrown to the seagulls to feast on.

Let's make this one not to forget and help our friend Dan find out whether his winkle still works after all these months! Please print this off and keep it with you at all times. It is imperative that we all know the rules.

Jack

I stared at my computer, trying to take in what I had just read. It was illiterate, crude, vulgar, and completely over the top. It was perhaps the greatest and most inspiring email I had ever received. Now I felt like I had a plan. I clicked print and headed over to the printer to collect it. As I reached out to collect my print-out, my hand inadvertently brushed against a second hand belonging to someone else collecting their own print-out.

"Dan," Dick said as I quickly pulled my hand away.

"Sorry, Richard, I didn't see you there."

"No need to apologise Dan, we are both adults. And I prefer Dick, remember?" Dick said with a wink.

"What's this?" he said taking Jack's printed email from the printer and scanning the content. "Going on a trip are we?"

"Yes, to Brighton."

"Brighton, really?" he said. "You know that Brighton has a famous gay scene, don't you, Dan?" he nudged me. "Of course you do."

"Yes, I mean no," I blurted out.

"No need to be shy, Dan," Dick said, handing me my print out. "I might even see you down there. Why don't you wear the scarf I gave you?"

I politely smiled, nodded and then turned to get away as quickly as possible. I sat back at my desk. This was getting out of hand now. It was bad enough having Dick flirt with me, but now he had practically asked me out. Somehow I needed to nip this in the bud. But how? My eyes darted around the office. And then I had an idea.

I jumped up from my seat and marched straight over to Shaila. Dick was standing at her desk, holding an excel spreadsheet and giving her some sort of instructions.

"Shaila," I said, slamming my hand down against her desk. My tone obviously took both of them by surprise. They both looked at me. I cleared my throat and tried again.

"I mean, Shaila," I said her name in a strange high-pitched tone, a big cheesy grin on my face.

"Yes?" she said with a perplexed look across her face. I glanced at Dick who stood with his arms folded, and gave me another little wink. The wink gave me more desire to end this now and I turned back to Shaila.

"I just wanted to say that you are a woman and I am a man, and as a man I like women," I raised my eyebrows and nodded at Dick, who had an unsettled expression on his face. I turned my attention back to Shaila. "And as a man who fancies *women*, I think you are incredibly attractive."

Shaila didn't flinch, but Dick looked slightly uneasy and now stood with his hands on his hips. Finally he was getting the message, but just in case he wasn't totally clear I continued.

"So as a 100 per cent *heterosexual* male," I emphasised the word heterosexual for Dick's benefit, "I would very much like to take you out for a drink sometime."

There, I did it. After months of admiring Shaila from a distance, I had finally taken the plunge. And who said men couldn't multi-task? I had just managed to put Dick straight – or at least make it crystal clear that I was straight – and asked out the girl of my dreams. All in one hit.

"No," Shaila said in no uncertain terms.

"What?" I gasped, gobsmacked. I had been so sure she would say yes.

"In fact, if you don't leave me alone I am going to report you to HR."

Shaila locked her eyes on me, while Dick rubbed his chin ever so smugly. "Has this man been sexually harassing you, Ms Saxena?" Dick said.

"Yes," Shaila said, her cold eyes locked directly on me. It felt like she had pierced my chest with her accusation and ripped out my heart. "He emails me all day, makes

173

inappropriate jokes at every opportunity, and has been poking me on Facebook non-stop for months."

"Is this true, Hilles?" Dick's tone changed. "Have you been poking Shaila? Because this is a serious accusation."

I broke out in a cold sweat. How had this backfired so spectacularly? How I wished at that moment to go back to the days when Dick and I shared our bizarre – albeit one-sided – sexual tension.

"It's okay, Mr Mussel," Shaila said, pronouncing it *Moo-Cell*. "I don't want to take the matter any further as long as I have some reassurance that the emailing, the joking, and the poking stops here."

"Hilles?" Dick said looking at me over his glasses.

"I promise to stop emailing, joking and poking." I said sheepishly.

"I hope so," Dick said taking a step toward me. He was so close I could feel his breath on my face. "Because I'll be keeping a close eye on you, and if you step one foot out of line, you will face the consequences. Understood?"

I wasn't too sure if he meant he would have me sacked or he would have his wicked way with me. "I understand." I said and scuttled back to my desk.

"Get your bag and let's get the hell out of here," I told Kelly, practically dragging her out of the building.

*

We took our drinks and sat down. I pulled out the piece of paper and pushed it in front of Kelly. "What is this?" she asked.

"This is the *plan,*" I said, pretty pleased with myself.

I watched Kelly's face as she read through Jack's 10 Commandments. She held it up in front of her. "You have got to kidding, right?"

"What?" I asked, smiling.

174

"This is not a plan," Kelly said, putting her glass down on the table. "This is a recipe for disaster."

"Please present your case, Miss Campbell."

"My pleasure," Kelly said holding the piece of paper in front of her and clearing her throat. "Point one, getting the party rocking. I think you have already learned from previous experiences that getting wasted has not helped your chances with the opposite sex."

She had a point.

"Number two, *Groundhog Day*? Oooh, you wish, Daniel! If only you could find a girl who would agree to do it over and over and over again."

Two-nil Kelly.

"Chat-up lines do not work, and dancing to power ballads is a big turn-off."

Kelly was building up quite a healthy lead without reply and she was only halfway through the list.

"Randy van Warmer? I don't even know where to begin with that one, and trust me, girls know when you boys play your ridiculous transparent scoring game. And as for David Hasselhoff..."

"Now stop right there," I cut her off. "You can say whatever you like about the other things on that list but don't you dare badmouth the Hoff. The man is a God."

Kelly laughed and handed me back the piece of paper. Her phone beeped and I could tell by the expression on her face that it wasn't good news.

"Everything okay?" I asked.

"It's just Paul again. I told him I was going for a drink with you and he has got funny about it."

"Why?"

Kelly gave me a strange look, like she didn't want to tell me what the reason was.

"What is it, Kell?"

175

She put her drink down. "Remember when your friends sent me that text from your phone? The one they sent to loads of people in your phonebook?"

How could I forget? Ever since that day Dick had been trying to coerce me into some bizarre homosexual cult-type relationship with him. But I had even managed to screw that up. I was pathetic. I couldn't even seal the deal on a sure thing, even if it was a gay relationship with a middle-aged man.

"Yes," I replied.

"Paul was going through my phone the other day and saw that message. I told him it was a joke and explained what had happened, but he got really angry about it."

"I'm so sorry. Why don't you invite him down one night after work and I'll buy him a beer to apologise?"

"No, there really is no need," Kelly said. "I told him it was ridiculous – you know, you and me? Besides, I was more angry that he had been going through my phone."

"Would it really be that ridiculous?" I don't know why I said it. It just came out. Even Kelly looked as though she was blushing. "Nah, you're right – you don't even like the Hoff," I quickly said to kill the moment.

"Exactly!" Kelly replied. "Maybe I should tell Paul how much you love the Hoff and that would put all his fears to rest."

"Bloody cheek!" I joked.

And just like that we were back on track. However, I couldn't help but think about what had just happened there. I think Kelly was thinking about it as well, but neither one of us mentioned it for the rest of the evening.

# Chapter 16: Road Trip – Friday Night

*Friday, May 15, 2009 - 6.32pm*
*Drought Clock: 133 days, 18 hours, 5 minutes*

"Shotgun!" Jack called as we loaded Rob's car up with our weekend bags.

"You can't call shotgun, Jack," Ollie argued.

"I'm afraid I am well within my rights," Jack fired back. "Shotgun can be called on anything as long as you are in eyesight of the object."

"I know the rules of shotgun," Ollie said. "But you are shorter than Dopey, Doc, and Grumpy. There is no way I am squeezing into the back seat, while your short arse sits up front with all that leg room."

"Hey, I called shotgun. Rules are rules."

"What about if I take your rules, wrap them round your little head, and then shove them straight up your..."

"The back seat is fine," Jack said before Ollie could finish his sentence.

"That's what I thought," Ollie said crushing his cigarette under his feet.

I clambered into the back of Rob's car next to Jack and we prepared to set off for *Tour de Big Gun 2009.*

"Okay, gentlemen, time to establish the rules of the road trip," Rob said, putting on his *Ray Ban* sunglasses and pulling out of his driveway. "On a road trip, the strongest bladder determines pit stops, not the weakest."

"Agreed," said Jack.

"If you have to go, go in a cup," Rob continued. "If there is no cup, go out the window. If you're not *comfortable* with that, hold it."

"Out of the window it is then," Ollie said.

"Rule two, no sleeping," Rob said looking around at us all. "It is your moral duty to stay awake with me as the

177

designated driver during this journey. If you fall asleep, you will be rolled out at the nearest service station and left there."

We all nodded in agreement.

"Rule three, music," Rob turned to face Ollie. "As the co-pilot Ollie, you are in charge of the radio. This is a *very* important job. You must keep the whole car entertained and away from stations like Heart FM. Is that clear?"

"Crystal," Ollie replied.

"I think I can assist you here Ollie," Jack said handing him a CD.

"What is it?" Ollie asked.

"Put it on," Jack said with a reassuring hand on his shoulder. "I promise you won't be disappointed."

Ollie slid the CD in and we all eagerly waited to find out what would come on. The first song of a road trip is vital – it can set the tone for the whole trip. We once went on a road trip where the first song was *Saturday Night* by Whigfield. We never fully recovered after that. It pretty much ruined the whole weekend.

I was perhaps more anxious than anyone, as I desperately wanted this trip to be perfect. I closed my eyes and almost immediately my fears disappeared as that sweet music started to pour out of the speakers. It was the type of song that defined a trip. The type of song that had the potential to turn a good trip into a fantastic trip. The type of song that *deserves* to be number one on a road trip playlist.

*Here I Go Again* by Whitesnake.

Each one of us took turns to sing a line as we built up to the guitar explosion at which point we all went mental, winding down the windows and singing badly at the top of our lungs. It didn't matter if we stopped at traffic lights; you had to continue singing your heart out. This was pure power ballads at their very best.

For the next hour we listened and sung along to Foreigner, Bonnie Tyler, Mr Mister, and Phil Collins amongst others. Power ballads really are the best driving anthems in the world. We roared along the open road to our destination. Well, we popped along the A23 anyway. The key to breaking my drought would be change, and Brighton offered all of that and more.

*

I looked out at the busy streets as we drove along the seafront, and wondered if the girl to end my drought was out there. We pulled alongside a blue Ford Fiesta at a set of traffic lights. Three girls sat in the car with one guy sitting in the back.

"Hello girls," Jack said leaning out of the window. The girls all smiled and giggled. "I'll tell you what, lose the goon in the backseat and get yourself over to the Imperial Hotel."

The guy in the backseat exploded, trying to clamber into the driver seat to shout something back at us. The girls didn't seem to mind though and simply laughed. The traffic lights turned green and we sped off, all pissing ourselves laughing.

"Did you see that?" Jack managed to say in between laughs.

"That was too funny," Ollie said. "That guy looked like he was ready to kill you."

"Forget him," Jack said. "Those girls wanted us bad."

"This is going to be a good weekend Danny boy," Rob said lifting his designer shades on top of his head. "I can just feel it!"

We made it to the hotel just before eight in the evening, and true to the rules of Jack's 10 Commandments, we dumped our bags in our rooms and made our way to the nearest bar.

"I'm telling you, Dan, watch me in action and you'll have no problem getting your willy wetsuit back in the ocean," Jack said as we headed into a bar called Stripes.

"Sure," I said patting Jack on the back and laughing.

"Hey, I'm happy to do my buddy a *bro favor,*" Jack replied, pronouncing bro favor like the Spanish *por favor*.

"Gentlemen, please get your purples out for the whip," Rob said as we all handed over a £20 note. The first drink went down a treat. It had been a warm day and the girls around us were certainly dressing less.

"Great rack," Ollie commented as one girl walked past; our eyes all following her as we lifted our beer bottles to our mouth.

"You know, I nearly called Tit Monday this week," I said.

"What's Tit Monday?" Ollie asked.

"You're kidding right?" Rob questioned him, as Ollie shrugged his shoulders and curled his mouth downwards.

"Tit Monday is that glorious Monday morning when you wake up with a bit more of a spring in your step," I started. "You feel chirpier than you have in months but can't quite put your finger on it."

"All morning tremors in your pants are registering on the Richter scale," Jack took over. "They come with pleasant regularity and that is when you realise it."

"Realise what?" Ollie said, hanging on our every word.

"That Tit Monday has finally arrived," Rob said. "Tit Monday is that special day in the male calendar when, for the first time that year, the temperature rises and girls start to show off a bit more flesh."

"Oh, you mean the end of the hibernation season," Ollie said. "When fit girls start appearing from nowhere."

"Exactly," I said. "Tit Monday!"

180

It truly is a great bloke holiday. After months of covering up, women the world over suddenly dispose of the winter wardrobe of thick woolly sweaters and long skirts. Breasts of all sizes are out on display. Breasts busting out of low-cut tops, white shirts bursting at the seams, braless vest tops. Girls you would not normally look twice at suddenly appear out of your league. Life is good when Tit Monday arrives.

"This is going to be a great weekend," Jack said, finishing his bottle of beer. "Another one?"

*

We bar-hopped for a while, checking out the women and ogling at anything female with a pulse. It was all just a prelude to our final destination: Club Tropic. Rob had it on good authority that Club Tropic was the place to be if you were looking for girls who put out quicker than the London Fire Brigade could put out a candle.

"Take a look at this lot," Jack said as we entered the main room of the club. "Wall to wall fanny, Danny! You can't go wrong in here sunshine."

Jack had such a way with words, although I did have to agree with the sentiment. Club Tropic was true to its name; full to the brim of tropical-looking women of all colours. White girls, black girls, Indian girls, Chinese girls – it was like looking into a packet of jelly babies or turning up at a Playboy-themed United Nations meeting. It was heaven in Brighton.

"If you can't pull in here, Dan, then you really have got no hope," Rob said as we headed towards the bar past a group of lush-looking girls.

"No pressure, then," I said.

181

"These birds are making me bad," Jack said. "I've got to get involved soon or I'm going to do some real damage to myself."

"Which hand will you be using to do that?" Ollie said, causing Rob and I to laugh.

"Probably your sister's hand," Jack fired back with a smile and flipping Ollie the finger.

We grabbed our drinks and took a stroll around the club. The hunt was on. We were like a pack of wild dogs on the prowl sniffing out our prey. Here I was, the gunner, with three of my most trusted wingmen. I was a man on a mission to pull and get laid, in a club where it was deemed bad manners not to end the night having sex with a complete stranger.

So to find my pack standing around an hour later not really saying a great deal to each other came as a huge blow. Our stealth mode had stagnated somewhat. We had fallen into that classic nightclub trap of being rendered immobilised by hesitation, beers tightly clamped to our chests. We were just cruising on the outskirts of the dance floor, on hawker's row, staring at the female bodies gyrating to the DJ's beat. Even Rob, our great leader and very own *Don Juan,* looked out of ideas.

"What a blow-out this night has been," Ollie said.

"You said it, Lurch," Jack agreed.

"Come on, guys, the night is young," I almost pleaded looking at my watch and realising it was anything but. I was just about to concede defeat when our leader decided to take control.

"Dan is right," Rob said. "We have come all this way to help him out and we are not going down without a fight."

That was the spirit. Just like that we were a pack united again for one common cause. I knew I could rely on these guys. They were the type of friends who would lay their life on the line for you; who would stand side-by-side with you in battle.

"Go and talk to that girl," Rob instructed me bluntly, pointing at a cute blonde standing on the side of the dance floor.

"What?" I gasped. What happened to going into battle side-by-side?

"Go and talk to her," Rob repeated. "Tell her you are a dolphin trainer or something. Girls like that shit."

"Yeah, and hurry up about it Slomeo," Jack said. "It's your round next."

I couldn't believe it. My pack had abandoned me. I turned to face the blonde and sighed before making my way across to her.

"Dan?" Ollie called out to me.

I turned back to face Ollie and there was something in his voice that told me that maybe I had been wrong. I looked into his eyes and felt a warmth inside me. Something profound was about to happen. I can't explain how I knew it; sometimes with your closest friends they don't have to say anything at all. But I knew Ollie was about to speak what was on everyone's mind.

"Find out if she has got a fat mate for me?"

Or maybe he just wanted to find out if she had a fat mate. I didn't say a word. Jack just nodded in agreement while Rob pointed his beer bottle in the blonde's direction. The fear of rejection was already heavy on my mind. I glanced back at my friends, who were waving me on. I turned back to the girl and decided to take the plunge.

"Excuse me?" I said, repeatedly tapping her on the shoulder with my finger, like an annoying child trying to get attention.

"Yes?" the blonde responded, looking a touch aggrieved at the tapping. I took another deep breath, full in the knowledge that the next words out of my mouth would

183

either make or break this situation. I needed a sentence that would lyrically flow and grab her attention.

"Yes?" she asked again. Quick Dan, say something.

"Er, do you know if they sell dry-roasted peanuts at the bar?" I panicked. Her impatience had rushed me into uttering the single most ridiculous pick-up line in the history of pick-up lines.

"I have no idea," the blonde replied, slightly bemused.

"Okay, thanks," and with that I turned tail and ran back to my friends.

"Well?" Rob asked as I returned.

"She isn't sure what bar snacks they sell," I said. My friends had the same bemused look as the blonde had done just moments before. "Forget it. Can we just get out of here?"

It was finally time to concede defeat. I'd had enough. If I had to spend the rest of my life a sexless cretin then so be it. It had to be better than living a life of disappointment. Maybe I could go off and live in a convent, away from temptation. Nah, I'd probably try it on with the nuns.

"Here you go," I felt a tap on my shoulder. "They *do* sell dry-roasted," the blonde said handing me a pack of peanuts.

"She's holding your nuts," Jack whispered into my ear.

"Thanks," I said, pushing Jack away. "I don't know what to say."

"How about you return the favour by buying me a drink?" she said.

"Sure," and I walked away with her to the bar.

"So, that was a pretty good chat-up line," she said with a grin. "I mean the question about the peanuts. That was ingenious."

"You think?" I asked smiling. "It was either that or dolphin trainer."

"Good choice. My name is Jules by the way."

"Nice to meet you, Jules," I said shaking her hand. "I'm Dan."

"I'm sure you can do better than that," Jules said, signalling to the handshake and leaned in to kiss me.

Club Tropic *really* was the type of club you couldn't fail to pull in. Here I was, a bottle of beer in one hand, a packet of dry-roasted in the other, and snogging the face off a blonde in a mini-skirt I'd met just five minutes earlier. Life didn't get any better than this.

The next hour flew by. Jules told me she was in town visiting her sister who was going to university in Brighton. Then we snogged a bit more. I told her about my job at Maxwell Media. Followed by some more snogging. I managed to resist her pleas to hit the dance floor by, well, snogging instead. I only hoped that she wouldn't notice the tent I was pitching in my pants. After five months out of action you could hardly blame the little fella for trying to poke his head out and stretch a little. And *surely* this time my luck was in.

"Jules!" I felt the shake and looked up to see a girl trying to get Jules's attention. "We have to go, Tina is really drunk. I need to get her home."

"Well, take her home then," Jules said. "By the way, Dan, this is my sister Vicki."

Vicki hardly acknowledged me. "There is no way I'm leaving you here. I know what you are like. You'll end up going home with some stranger, like him," she said waving her hand in my direction.

"I'll make sure she gets home safely," I said playing the gentleman, trying not to come across too desperate.

"I'm sure you will," Vicki replied, looking none too convinced as she wrinkled her eyes at me. "I can already see you're on the verge of bursting out of your trousers."

Damn it, I'd been caught out.

"I'm not leaving you here," Vicki said uncompromisingly.

"I'm sorry darling," Jules said turning to me. "I'd better go."

"But we haven't even opened my packet of nuts yet," I said. And I wasn't talking about the dry-roasted variety either.

"I'm sorry," Jules giggled. "Take my number and drop me a line sometime and we'll hang out."

"How about tomorrow," I blurted out a little too hastily.

"Sure," Jules said. In my eyes that was as good as a binding contract.

Jules typed her number into my phone, while I tried my best not to turn my nose up at her sister who was clearly ruining my plans. "I'll drop call you so you have my number," I anxiously told her. "And then we can meet tomorrow," I just couldn't stop babbling.

Her sister dragged her away, which probably did me a favour as I was on the verge of begging her to meet me.

I took a deep breath and told myself to relax. I could hold out for another 24 hours. I knew I would have to put up with Jack chipping away at me about breaking the 10 Commandments *(Rule 2: It's Not Groundhog Day)* but I didn't really care.

I sat there for a while, contemplating how close I was to finally ending the drought, and allowing the excitement inside my trousers to slowly disappear in the process. I got up and decided to go and find the boys, but I didn't have to look far as I spotted them hurriedly walking in my direction.

"We've got to go," Jack said, his eyes darting all over the place.

"What's wrong?" I asked.

"Remember that bloke in the blue Fiesta?" Jack said. "The one who took exception to me calling him a goon so the girls he was with could get round to our hotel?"

186

"Yeah, what about him?"

"He's in here," Ollie said.

"So?"

"With about 20 of his mates," Rob said raising his eyebrows.

"Okay, let's go," I replied downing my bottle of beer and heading for the nearest exit.

## Chapter 17: Road Trip – Saturday Night

*Saturday, May 16, 2009 - 1.33pm*
*Drought Clock: 134 days, 23 hours, 4 minutes*

"Maybe you were a dare," Jack said, shoving four chips into his mouth as we walked along Brighton Pier.

"What are you talking about?" I asked, staring at my phone.

"Her mates dared her to pull you."

"You mean like when we play pull-a-pig?" Ollie asked.

"Yes!" Jack said laughing. "Dan, you were the pig! Oink oink."

"Piss off," I muttered and put my phone back into my pocket. It was already lunchtime and Jules had not replied to any of my texts.

"How many times have you texted her?" Rob asked.

"Once or twice," I lied. It was actually seven, including four I sent immediately after leaving the club last night:

*1.47am: Hi Jules, it's Dan. I hope you got home safely x*

*2.10am: I just wanted to say it was great meeting you tonight. Dan x*

*2.22am: I'm guessing you crashed out as soon as you got home! I'll give you a call tomorrow x*

*2.31am: Goodnight x*

*9.34am: Morning, this is Dan from last night – the guy with the dry-roasted peanuts. How is your head? x*

*12.29pm: I'm heading to the pier – give me a shout if you're around and fancy meeting up x*

My seventh, and final text, sent 10 minutes ago, was a picture of myself, in case she had forgotten what I looked like.

"Danny boy, put the phone away and forget her," Rob said. "We still have tonight."

Rob was right. I was coming across a little obsessive and that is never a good look. A drought will do that to a man. I needed to just relax and whatever will be, will be.

Perhaps I should make sure my phone was on vibrate as well as ring.

"Give me that," Rob said, snatching the phone out of my hand. "What's wrong with you?"

"Maybe he's taken up stalking?" Ollie suggested.

"No, I have not taken up stalking thank you very much," I said. I wouldn't even have a clue where to start if I did want to stalk Jules.

"If I've said it once, I've said it a thousand times," Ollie started. "Get yourself a large lass. Three words – Up. For. It. All the time."

"That's six words," I pointed out.

"Eh?" Ollie looked confused, counting the words on his fingers.

"Maybe Ollie is right," Rob said. "Perhaps you need to drop your standards."

"Agreed," Jack said. "Just pull some low-renter and get it out of the way. At least then you can go back to being a happy stalker."

"I am not a stalker," I said, grabbing my phone back off of Rob and checking to see whether Jules had replied. "Do you think you get service on the pier?"

"It's official. You're a lost cause," Rob said.

"Even Ollie has got more game than you, mate," Jack shook his head in disgust.

"Cheers, mate." Ollie said smiling.

"That wasn't a compliment, numbnuts," Jack reprimanded him.

I looked at my friends. It was clear they had lost all hope in me. My behaviour had descended into a farce of desperation, and that is never a cool thing to let your friends witness.

"Don't give up on me," I pleaded, shoving the phone back into my pocket. "I have got game." I looked at them hopefully.

And then looked at my phone again to make sure it wasn't on silent.

*

By the time eight o'clock rolled round I had finally given up on waiting for Jules to respond. I had allowed my bruised ego to get the better of me, and had sent her a pathetic message telling her I wasn't bothered that she hadn't replied because I didn't fancy her that much anyway.

And the ninth message was sent by Jack, who decided to take it upon himself to text her from my phone asking for some dirty pictures while I was in the shower.

Maybe I was a dare. Could it be that I was a *pig?* I tried not to dwell on it. My self-esteem had taken enough knocks over the last few months and I didn't need to add to it.

"Are you going to be ready to go in five minutes, Bacon?" Jack asked. Luckily I had my friends around to keep the Jules incident off my mind.

I buttoned up my shirt and stared at myself in the mirror. I might not have been Balham's answer to David Beckham, but I was certainly no pork scratching either. The thought that I must have been nothing but a *bit of fun* didn't sit too well. That was the man's job; to take a girls number and not call. Was I so out of touch that the roles had now reversed?

How could I have let this happen? I was nothing but a plaything to Jules; used for one night only and tossed to the side. I wasn't just a pig; I was a piece of meat. I felt used.

But then it hit me. What if I was looking at this from completely the wrong angle? After all, Rob had called

Brighton '*a party capital where the girls are just as wild as the guys*'.

I rushed into the bedroom where the boys were sitting on the bed watching television. I switched the TV off and stood in front of them, ignoring their shouts to turn it back on.

"Listen!" I shouted. "I get it." They all stared blankly at me.

"Get what?" Rob asked with a puzzled look on his face.

"I get *it,*" I repeated, hoping it would sink in this time. Blank faces. "I'm talking about last night. I got used. And I like it!"

"Well, it's about time," Jack said springing to his feet to meet me with a high five.

The thought of drunken girls out on the pull, acting like men, filled me with renewed hope. I had been so stressed out about making all the right moves that I had completely forgotten that women have needs too.

"I want to get used again." I had a taste for it now. "Tonight!"

"What are we waiting for?" Rob bellowed. "Come on!"

The four of us strutted out of our hotel into the cool night air with purpose. If our lives were a Hollywood film, our soundtrack would have been *Stayin' Alive,* because you could tell by the way we used our walk, we were on the pull, no time to talk.

We barely got 200 yards from our hotel before we arrived at the first bar. "Shall we start as we mean to go on gentlemen?" I said pointing my thumb towards the entrance. "First round's on me," I added as Ollie rubbed his hands together in anticipation of that first drink of the night.

The place was quiet. A group of lads sat in one corner while a couple of others stood at the bar. But this was okay; this was just a warm-up. I decided to set-up a tab.

"Anyone fancy a game?" Rob said pointing towards the pool table at the back of the bar.

191

Why not? A few games of pool and a couple of pints would get us in the mood and ease us into the night.

"I'll break," Jack said and he struck the white ball as hard as he could.

"This isn't a bad place," Rob said.

"They do a nice pint too," Ollie chipped in, taking the cue from Jack. "Good choice, Dan."

"I plan on making a few good choices tonight, fellas," I cracked.

"Let's hope there are a few girls up for pull-a-pig," Jack quipped as he lined up a shot, but the joke was on him as he managed to pot the white. "Oh bollocks."

"Nice shot, mate," said a guy sat the corner of the bar, smirking. We all turned around a little unsure what to say. Was he taking the piss or being friendly?

"I beg your pardon, pal?" Jack said in his best cockney accent, shifting around on the spot.

"Sorry, I didn't mean any offence," the guy said, still smiling. "I'm just waiting for some mates and I got here a bit early doors. Would you mind if I played the winner?"

We all looked at each other. London folk aren't keen on talking to strangers at the best of times, let alone letting them join us in a game of pool.

"You can play him, Jack," Ollie said. "I am going to have a go on the fruity."

We all stared daggers at Ollie as he strolled over to the bright lights of the fruit machine, but Jack saw an opportunity. "Why don't we make it interesting and play for a tenner?" Jack asked the stranger.

"Sure," the stranger said. "I'm Ethan by the way."

I moved across to Jack as he slapped a £10 note down on the side of the pool table. "What are you doing?" I whispered to Jack as Ethan hung his jacket over the chair.

"Don't worry, I've got it under control. Haven't you ever seen *The Colour of Money*? I'm going to hustle this guy."

192

Jack moved over to Ethan and shook his hand. I stood next to Rob. I couldn't put my finger on it, but I sensed that something wasn't quite right. Ethan broke and a red flew into the top right corner pocket.

"Beginners' luck," Ethan said.

I watched as he placed a second red into the middle pocket, before chalking his cue and making another excellent shot to thunder his third red ball down. That's when I realised what was wrong.

"This guy is a ringer," I said out of the corner of my mouth to Rob. "He's hustling Jack."

"Of course he's hustling Jack," Rob said without flinching. "I knew that the moment I set eyes on him."

"Why didn't you say anything?"

"Because I thought it would be funny to watch the cocky little git get a taste of his own medicine for a change."

I couldn't help but smile as Jack grew agitated, watching another red ball disappear into the pocket. Surely it was only a matter of time before his £10 disappeared into Ethan's pocket.

Ethan concentrated as he lined up his next shot, but this time the ball ricocheted against either side of the corner pocket and rolled out to safety.

"Unlucky buddy," Jack said, not even bothering to hide his delight. "Now watch an expert in action." Jack strutted around like he was Ronnie O'Sullivan, skilfully working his way around the table with that cocksure swagger of his, potting yellow after yellow. After sinking each ball he would look over at Ethan and shrug his shoulders almost apologetically. The final yellow went down and Jack lined up an easy black. This one was in the bag.

But Jack allowed his arrogance to get the better of him and he missed the easiest shot of the game, screwing the ball wide of the pocket.

193

"That's not fair," Jack said. "This table is on a slant I think." Jack bent down and closed one eye as he inspected the level of the table.

"Looks okay to me," Ethan said as he potted another red.

"Me too," Rob said with a big smile on his face.

Ethan sunk the rest of his balls until just the white and black ball remained. Jack was crestfallen, and bowed his head to accept his inevitable defeat. Ethan chalked his cue and made the shot.

But he missed.

"Yes!" Jack said, clenching his fist. "Time to pay the piper."

Jack concentrated as pulled the cue back and struck the white sweetly. It hit the black ball and with perfect accuracy arrowed the ball into the top left pocket. Jack spun round with a huge smile on his face, but Ethan simply raised his eyebrows and nodded back towards the table. We all watched as the white ball trickled ever so slowly back down the table and dropped into the middle pocket.

"I told you this bloody table was on a slant," Jack moaned.

I chuckled as Rob scooped up the money and handed it to Ethan. "You lost fair and square, Jack," Rob said.

"Thanks mate," Ethan said taking the money before turning back to Jack. "Can I give you some advice?"

"Like what?" Jack replied like a sulking child.

"You should work on positioning yourself slightly lower at the table. It will help get the right type of spin on the ball. Let me show you." Jack reluctantly watched as Ethan showed him how to play the shot. "Why don't you try?"

Ethan handed the cue to Jack who once again showed his reluctance to listen to the stranger who had just beaten him at pool and taken his money. Jack bent down across the pool table.

"No, not like that, like this," Ethan said, moving behind Jack and positioning himself across his body to help show him how to correct his shot. Jack looked more uncomfortable than I'd ever seen him as Ethan gently moved his hand across Jack's. A wolf whistle sounded from the back of the bar as Ethan held Jack in an extremely compromising position.

"Room for one more in there, darling?" the camp voice said from behind us. We turned to see a guy in skinny jeans and a tight silk shirt staring at us, seductively sipping a blue drink through a straw.

"Oooh, you've gone stiff as a board," Ethan said to Jack.

"I bloody haven't," Jack said pushing himself away from Ethan.

"Look, he has gone all shy," the man in skinny jeans said, joining Ethan at his side. "Where did you find this lot? They look a bit rough, but definitely ready."

All of us stood motionless, open-mouthed and speechless. None of us knew what to do.

"Hey guys, I just won a tenner on the fruity," Ollie announced as he joined us back at the pool table. "Result eh?"

"I'm Dominic," the friend said, extending his feminine hand for Ollie to shake. "Congratulations."

"Cheers, mate," Ollie said, completely oblivious of the situation. "I need an eyelash. Do you know where the bogs are in this place?" Dominic pointed Ollie to the end of the bar and he happily trotted off counting his winnings.

"I think I need the toilet as well," I stuttered to get the words out.

"Yeah, me too," Rob said, swallowing hard.

Jack initially froze. He looked at Ethan and Dominic who smiled back toward him. "Perhaps I can help you with that shot?" Dominic said. "Bend over that table and I'll be right over."

195

"Wait for me, guys!" Jack shouted at us, tripping on a bar stool in his panicked state, before hauling himself back up and shuffling past Ethan and Dominic, who were fighting themselves to hold back their laughter.

"Hurry back," Dominic said, pouting.

The three of us practically fell through the door. Ollie was already standing at the urinal. He looked up at us, had a little shake, and then walked over to the basin to wash his hands. Jack opened the door ajar and peered outside before giving us the thumbs up. "They haven't followed us," he said, panting. "What the hell are we going to do?"

"Okay, don't panic," I said trying to calm the situation down, while at the same time looking for a window for us to escape through.

"Don't panic?" Jack fired back at me. "We've stumbled into a sausage factory, Dan. I'm telling you, I'm nobody's *Kinder Egg Surprise*."

"What are you talking about?" I asked.

"There is no way Ethan and his boyfriend are going to get my chocolate and have something to play with."

"Will you stop it, this isn't going to get us anywhere," I said trying to reason with Jack.

"That's easy for you to say. You're not the one who just got violated out there across a friggin' pool table." Jack replied with his eyes locked on me. "This is all your fault."

"How is it my fault?"

"It was *your* idea to come in here," Rob joined in.

"What are you guys talking about?" Ollie asked as he rubbed his hands together under the dryer.

"Oh yeah?" I said ignoring Ollie and turning to Rob. "Well I seem to remember you saying what a *nice* place it was when we walked in here."

"Oh brilliant, so you're both bent as each other," Jack said with his arms crossed against his chest. "This isn't *The Flintstones* – I'm not going to have a gay old time."

"What's wrong?" Ollie shouted out, but we ignored him again as we descended into name-calling and accusations.

"None of this would have happened if you hadn't challenged Elton John out there to a game of pool," Rob said to Jack.

"Shut up, Rob, I feel dirty enough as it is," Jack said pulling at his collar. "I bet every time I bent over to play a shot, they were all watching me – wishing they could take their shot."

"Seriously, will someone please tell me what is going on?" Ollie said again as he walked over to us. He looked confused. He couldn't understand why his friends were falling apart in front of his very eyes. He had no idea of threat we faced outside these four walls.

"You probably want to stay here," Jack said to me. "You haven't had much luck with women lately so maybe you feel like taking one in the bullseye."

"Will you stop with the homophobic jibes," I fired back.

"Is that some sort of new music genre?" Ollie said, and for once his voice grabbed our attention. The sheer stupidity of the boy was outstanding. But it was enough to break the tension, and we couldn't help but laugh at how much we had blown this out of proportion.

"Can someone please tell me what's going on?" Ollie asked again. "And when are we going to get out of this gay bar and go and find some women?"

We stopped laughing immediately and let his words sink in.

"You knew this was a gay bar?" Jack said having trouble hiding his anger.

"Yeah, it's obvious," Ollie said. "This place is full of geezers and they have been playing the *Scissor Sisters* album non-stop since we got here."

"Why didn't you say anything?" Rob said turning on Ollie.

"I thought you guys knew. You all seemed to be having a good laugh with that Ethan guy, and he's really gay, but not as gay as his mate Dominic."

The red mist was about to descend. "This isn't going to get us anywhere," I said before things really got out of hand. We needed a plan so I took the lead. "Follow me."

My plan was simple. We would pay the bar tab and leave this establishment immediately. Like men. Straight men.

"You're back?" Dominic said, surprised to see us. "We were about to send the rescue team in to find you."

I ignored his comment and asked the barman if I could settle up. He wanted nine pounds and 60 pence. I fumbled around in my pocket to find my wallet. I could sense the other boys watching me, and their impatience made me panic. I searched all of my pockets but couldn't find it. Finally I felt something in my jacket pocket and pulled it out.

"Nice scarf," Ethan said. "I've got one just like that at home."

I looked down at my hands and to my horror found myself holding the rainbow-coloured scarf Dick had given to me as a gift.

"What the fuck is *that*?" I heard Jack hiss from behind me. It matched the gay pride flag hanging proudly behind the bar. How had we missed that?

I delved deeper into my pocket and felt a bank note, pulled it out and practically threw it at the barman. We turned on our heels and got the hell out of there, as Ollie waved goodbye to Ethan and Dominic.

"Wait, your change. You gave me a £20 note," I heard the barman shout out after me as the door closed.

*

We walked in silence in no particular direction; our male pride in tatters. What would people say when they heard we had been in a gay bar? How could I ever expect to get my leg-over after this setback? We were a band of friends on the brink. Something that had started out with such promise was now nothing more than a complete farce. Nothing could save this weekend.

Or could it?

From out of nowhere came hope. It might just have been the one thing that could help us rebuild the damage done; to help prove our masculinity beyond a shadow of a doubt.

Girls!

From the depth of despair two real stunners were coming towards us on the opposite side of the road. Both wore short tight skirts displaying their sexy slim legs, with their long black hair swaying in the light breeze, and dark eyes you could lose yourself in.

"Check these two out – they're absolute!" Jack said with his one finger salute and his eyes virtually popping out of their sockets. "We've got to talk to them."

"I'm bang up for this," Ollie said like a kid in a candy shop. "I've never pulled a black girl before. I might even tell them that so they are more inclined to cop off with me!"

"That statement was a little inappropriate, don't you think?" I said turning to Ollie.

"I know, but it's not like I haven't tried pulling black girls in the past. I've just never managed to seal the deal."

"That is not what I meant," I said sighing, and quickly followed as my three wingmen flew across the road to greet their targets.

"Hey, slow down," Rob was in there like a flash. "Can we talk for a second?" They smiled but kept on walking. Jack was next to try.

"Don't be shy, girls, I promise I won't bite... unless you want me too!" His tone was cheeky enough for him to get

199

away with such a comment, and even made the two girls laugh out loud. But it wasn't enough to stop them walking on. Ollie was up next.

"Please stop. I've never pulled..."

Oh my God, what was he doing? The idiot was actually going to tell them he had never pulled a black girl before. The three of us looked on in horror. I knew immediately I had to stop him putting his foot in his mouth; in all of our mouths. But what could I interject with? What would Ollie confess to never pulling before? A muscle? A sickie? A fast one?

"...his foreskin all the way back?" I spat out.

That's correct. I said foreskin. Of all the things I could have said Ollie had never pulled before I opted for the retractable, double-layered fold of skin and mucous membrane that covers the glans penis. I could have said that Ollie had never pulled the trigger before, or that he had never pulled before full stop. Hell, saying he had never pulled a black girl before would have been more appropriate and certainly less ridiculous than announcing that he had never pulled his foreskin all the way back before.

"What did you say?" one of the girls asked, as they both stopped dead in their tracks and gave me a look of disgust.

"And you say I'm inappropriate," Ollie said, raising his eyebrows at me.

I glared at Ollie, before turning back to the girls apologetically. "I'm sorry, I didn't mean..." But what could I say? How could I possibly talk my way out of this? Who uses the word foreskin in their first sentence when trying to pick girls up on the street?

"Sorry about *care in the community* over there," Jack said nodding in my direction. The two girls at least managed to avert their glare from me and at least smile in Jack's direction. "I'm Jack, by the way." Jack shook their hands and they introduced themselves as Erica and Alisha.

200

Un-fucking-believable. I was the one who saved the situation and somehow I had been labelled the liability of the group.

"So where are you girls off to tonight?" Rob asked.

"We are heading to party at the Imperial Hotel," Alisha said.

"No way, that is where we're staying," Ollie said. I shot him another look. It was his fault I was now in this situation.

"I'm sorry about the foreskin comment," I offered meekly, but at the same time realising I had now mentioned the word foreskin in my first and second sentence.

"You really can't take him anywhere," Jack said, shooting his thumb in my direction.

"We were just heading back towards our hotel, so why don't we come and join you at the party?" Rob asked.

"I'm sorry but it's a private party," Erica said.

"I'm sure you girls could sneak us in," Jack said. "Besides, we're staying at the hotel – that must qualify us for an invite?"

"It's really not the sort of party I think you would enjoy," Alisha said.

"What sort of party is it?" Ollie asked.

"A birthday party," Alisha said. "And we're already running late for the birthday girl."

"Why didn't you say so? Birthday parties are our speciality," Jack said. The two girls gave him a look. "We're exotic male dancers. We could come and put a little show on for your friend. She'll love it!"

"Come on, girls, what do you say?" Rob asked.

Alisha and Erica looked at each other mischievously and started whispering into each other's ears. They turned back to us. "Okay, you can come," Erica said.

"But you had better put on a good show," Alisha added.

I couldn't help but think that my friends were being a little too eager to agree. Were they mad? Exotic dancers? We were about as exotic as a caravan holiday in Bognor Regis. I had a bad feeling about this.

"What are we doing?" I nudged Rob as we followed the girls back towards the Imperial Hotel. "You know I hate dancing."

"Relax," Rob said waving his hand as if everything was under control. "We are just having a bit of banter with them."

"What's the problem?" Jack chipped in.

"My problem is that we're heading to a party where we're expected to put on some sort of Chippendale dance routine," I stressed. "We're going to look more like *Alvin and the Chipmunks*."

"I like that film," Ollie decided to inform us.

"Calm down, dear," Jack said putting on his best Michael Winner impression. "They know we're not really exotic dancers, it was just a bit of an ice breaker."

"Maybe," I reluctantly agreed. "But they think I'm some sort of weirdo who only talks about Ollie's turtleneck."

"I'm not wearing a turtleneck," Ollie said.

"Danny boy, think about it," Rob said. "Look at these two girls. They are gorgeous. Hot girls have hot friends."

"That is not technically true," I argued. "How many times do you see a really good-looking girl out with her ugly mate?" I had them. The hot girl/ugly girl combo is no secret in the land of bloke. The good-looking girl will hang out with her ugly friend to enhance her looks; to guarantee she is the one who will receive the compliments and get hit on all night. The ugly friend usually ends up getting ignored, so she reverts to becoming a major cock-blocker.

"Okay, maybe there will be a few facially-challenged hood rats in there," Jack conceded. "But that is why we hang out with Ollie – so he can take care of all the wrong 'uns."

Ollie looked offended for a second, but then shrugged his shoulders. "Fine by me," he said quite happily.

"Dan, you are missing the big picture here," Rob said as we got within 10 yards of the hotel. "Think about it. We are going to a party in *our* hotel. If you pull a girl, you are minutes from your bedroom. How often can you say that?"

Rob did have a point. Maybe I had been looking at this from the wrong angle. We were heading to a private party where most of the people were going to know each other. For all the single girls in there, our little group was going to be the surprise package. We really were going to be the *exotic* guests after all.

"Okay boys, here is the plan," Alisha said standing on the steps of the hotel. "The party is in the main hall on the third floor."

Erica took over. "We are going to head up now and tell the birthday girl we have a little surprise for her. You boys need to come up in five minutes and then we can really get the party started."

Rob agreed on our behalf with that winning smile of his. Erica and Alisha giggled some more as they made their way towards the lifts.

"Did you hear that?" Jack said excitedly. "We are going to be the surprise for the birthday girl. These girls are hot for us I tell you!"

"This reminds me of the time I met that girl on the way home from the pub last year," Ollie told us. "I was walking down Bedford Hill and bumped into this right little sort. We got chatting and one thing led to another, and before you know it we're back at this hotel for a bit of slap and tickle."

"Wait a minute," I said. "You met a girl on the street, took her back to a hotel, and had sex?"

"Yep," Ollie said proudly, a huge grin on his face.

203

"You paid her, didn't you?" Jack asked.

"Yep," Ollie responded with an even bigger smile on his face.

"You're a sick man, Ollie," Rob said, shaking his head and looking at his watch. "Come on guys, five minutes is up."

The lift made a *ding* sound as it arrived on the third floor. We stepped out and saw the sign for the Main Hall pointing to the right. We approached two large wooden doors with a huge "Happy Birthday" banner across the top. This was it. We took a deep breath and pushed the doors open. Confidently we waltzed into the Main Hall. The wooden doors slammed shut behind us making a huge thud. Just like in the movies, there was a loud scratch from the record needle and the music stopped. Over a hundred faces all turned in our direction. It suddenly dawned on us the monumental stitch-up that had been inflicted upon us.

There was a huge dance floor in the middle of the hall, with a massive sign that read *Happy 80th Birthday, Grandma Betty.* Not only had we gate-crashed an OAP's birthday celebration, but we had promised to entertain her with exotic dancing. But it got worse.

As the hundreds of eyes starting to burn a hole in us, it soon became very apparent that we stood out like a sore thumb, for we were the only white faces at a clearly all black family celebration. It was like Take That turning up at a Black Panther Party convention. We all pulled apologetic faces like we had accidentally walked into the wrong party and turned to walk out, but guarding the door were two huge mountains of muscle.

"You boys aren't leaving, are you?" one of the mountain men said to us.

"We got off on the wrong floor," Jack offered as our excuse.

"But you guys *are* the exotic dancers aren't you?" the second muscle man asked.

"We're not exotic, we're English," Ollie blurted out.

I elbowed Ollie in the ribs as both men growled at us. "Please ignore him, sir, he's an idiot – he thinks exotic is a country." You could hear a pin drop.

"There has been a mistake," Rob said. "We have walked into the wrong party."

"Hey Alisha," the first muscle man shouted out. We turned to see Alisha and Erica walking towards us. "Are these the dancers you were talking about?"

"Yep, that's them," Alisha said. "They told us they wanted to entertain the birthday girl."

"This one is a bit weird though," Erica said pointing at me. "He keeps talking about that one's foreskin."

"That's why you called it a turtleneck!" Ollie shouted out. We all shot him a look.

It turned out that the two behemoths who stood between us and our getaway were the boyfriends of Alisha and Erica. The one on the right with a bald head was called Andre, while the guy on the left with the huge biceps was called Leon. Andre grabbed me and Rob by the back of the neck, while Leon did the same to Ollie and Jack.

"See that lady over there?" Andre said pointing toward a sweet old lady sitting at a table across the hall with white curly hair and bottle-top glasses. "That is Grandma Betty."

"It is her birthday," Leon said, taking over. "And she has been promised some entertainment tonight. Are you going to disappointment her?"

"No, sir," I gulped.

"Good," Andre said. "Because I don't like seeing Grandma Betty disappointed. The last person to disappoint Grandma Betty was..." he paused. "Let's put it this way, *unable* to attend her birthday celebrations tonight."

"Now you are going to dance, and you are going to dance well, because if you don't, you won't be around for Grandma Betty's 81st birthday," Leon warned us.

We were thrust towards the dance floor. It was deathly silent. Someone coughed and the echo lingered in the eerie silence. We looked around at each other for inspiration, but it was clear we were up shit creek without a paddle. There was no way we were going to leave this party alive. The DJ put a record on and the sound of vinyl crackled into life. Then the beat from the track.

We didn't know what to do. We stood motionless, lifeless even. It was a train wreck waiting to happen. I looked at the others. It was best if we just got this over and done with. Songs only last four or five minutes. We would only need to suffer the embarrassment and indignity for 300 seconds tops and then we could be out of here.

"I know this one," Ollie said quite chirpily. "This is *Candy* by Cameo."

"This is not a game of name that tune, you big dopey idiot," Jack said harshly.

"No, I mean I know the dance routine to this song," Ollie said. "It's called the *Electric Slide*. Just follow me – two steps to the right."

We watched as Ollie started to move. Two steps right; one-two, one-two. We looked at each other but really didn't have any other plan. We stumbled into action, clumsily following Ollie's movements.

"Two steps left," Ollie said. I stepped on Rob's foot, who in turn stumbled slightly into Jack. We started to get heckled from the crowd, and a few boos sounded to show their contempt at our sloppy dance routine.

"Two steps back, and hold." We followed Ollie intensely as he led us into the next steps. One step with left foot forward, and lean forth. Suddenly we started to find our rhythm.

206

"One step with the right foot, and lean back," Ollie continued to work us through the routine. "Hop and kick sideways!" We moved in unison. Even I didn't look too bad, and we actually started to enjoy it. Slowly the heckling and booing was replaced by cheers and claps as we repeated the same routine but this time to a different corner of the room.

The cheers grew louder, before the whole room was up on their feet, clapping in rhythm to the funky beat. Ollie was like a pro, choreographing every move. Alisha and Erica joined us on the dance floor and we continued to grow in confidence with every dance step.

"I can't believe this is happening," I said to Rob, who had the broadest grin on his face. A middle-aged woman, a fat man, and two small children made their way to the dance floor. It wasn't long before streams of people of all ages and sizes started to pour on to the dance floor, all performing the same synchronised routine in a dozen lines. Even Grandma Betty had made it to the dance floor.

Finally, Andre and Leon made their way on to the floor and lined up alongside us to see out the final stages of the song. The four of us might not have been the best dancers on that floor, but we more than held our own.

A huge cheer went up at the end of the song with the DJ shouting over the PA system: "Give it up for the entertainment!"

"Where the hell did you learn that dance," I said as I hugged Ollie, raptures of applause ringing in our ears.

"My mum loves all those old 80's songs," Ollie said. "She used to make me do that dance in front of friends and family when I was a kid."

"I could kiss you," Jack said. "Oh sod it, come here, you big lump."

"I got to hand it to you boys," Andre said, "that was pretty cool."

"And more importantly, you entertained Grandma Betty," Leon added, pointing towards Grandma Betty who was blowing kisses in our direction.

"What do you think?" Jack nudged me in the side and whispered into my ear. "I reckon Grandma Betty looks like a bit of a goer."

"Shut your face you idiot," I said, smiling through gritted teeth.

## Chapter 18: Extreme Makeover

*Sunday, June 13 2009 - 10.47am*
*Drought Clock: 163 days, 1 hour, 50 minutes*

The weekend in Brighton seemed like a distant memory. I had failed in my quest to end the drought, but a girl had used me and that was a start. Plus, we had entertained Grandma Betty and that was pretty cool. And in a way I had been chatted up, even if it was in a gay bar. I had to take the positives.

Progress had been made, but as June arrived it was always in the back of my mind that I was now approaching half a year without sex. Half a bloody year! In that time, Iceland had appointed the world's first openly lesbian head of government, Mount Redoubt explosively erupted for the first time in 20 years in Alaska, the second G20 summit involving state leaders had taken place in London, and swine flu had just been deemed a global pandemic.

But no matter the event or story, they all just served to remind me of my own predicament. I would have killed to have explosively erupted in the company of a Scandinavian lesbian, in and around the London area, even at the risk of an infectious disease.

"Está usted bien señor?" Rosalie asked as she busily dusted, snapping me out of my daydream as I stared blankly at the television screen. "I mean, you okay, Señor Hilles?"

"Er, yes. I'm fine thanks, Rosalie," I said, putting down my half-eaten bowl of cereal on the table. But then I had a thought. Here was a woman of experience – a woman of the world. Maybe she could help me. Maybe Rosalie would be able to listen to my woes and point me in the right direction; tell me where I was going wrong and what I needed to do to get out of this rut. It was a long shot but what did I have to lose? Nothing else had worked so far.

Plus Rosalie had been coming to my flat every other weekend now for six months. That was the longest relationship I'd had with a woman since breaking up with Stacey, and she had even stayed around after the infamous duvet moment on her first day of work. It was more than I could say for any other woman in my life over the last six months.

"Rosalie?" I said nervously. "Can I ask you a question?"

"Si señor," she answered, still dusting everything in sight.

"In your country, what does a man do when he wants to..." I searched for the right word. "...be romantic with a woman?"

"Romantic?" Rosalie wrinkled up her nose. Then her face broke into a smile and she blushed. "Oh señor, Hilles, naughty boy!" And she tapped me on the head with the duster and disappeared out of the living room.

I had no idea what Rosalie thought I was asking, but obviously I wasn't going to get the answers I was looking for. Whatever it was, it was clear I was barking up the wrong tree. I picked up the remote control and started flicking through the channels. I was about to give up and go back to bed when something caught my eye.

*Extreme Makeover UK*

It was a reality TV show where ordinary men and women underwent an extensive transformation at the hands of the *Extreme Team*. The makeover process included everything from getting a new wardrobe to exercise regimes to life coaching. Did I need an extreme makeover? If I could change my ways and my look would it make a difference? I glanced up at the calendar. Six months. It had to be worth a shot. I was going to need help so I grabbed my phone and sent out an SOS.

*Your pal needs you! I am in danger of going backwards and becoming a virgin again. Before that happens I am*

210

*asking you to assist me in a complete makeover to create a brand new Dan. What do you say?*

I clicked send and watched the little envelope symbol indicate that my message had been sent to Rob, Jack, and Ollie. Content with my new plan of attack, I picked up my cup of tea and decided to get dressed. But as I stood something out of the corner of my eye immediately grabbed my attention and stopped me dead in my tracks.

Rosalie was standing at the doorway wearing nothing but a large pair of white knickers and her bra, a slight paunch exposed around her midriff.

"Romantic, señor?" Rosalie said nodding her head excitedly, her eyes wide and duster still in hand.

Open-mouthed and completely frozen, I was lost for words. To say this was not a sight I was expecting to see would be an understatement. The smash of my mug hitting the floor broke me from the trance.

"I clean, I clean," she squealed, rushing over in her underwear and dropping to her knees to clean the mess around my feet.

### Makeover with Rob: The Look

Rosalie had put her clothes back on *and* managed to remove the tea stain from the carpet by the time I left the flat. What a woman. However, I had resisted her middle-aged charms, and she didn't seem too embarrassed by the situation either. I would be lying if I said I hadn't been tempted. Had Rosalie appeared five minutes before my makeover brainwave then this story could have been over by now.

Rob had been the first to reply to my text. He had invited me to come down to his shop. He worked in a fashion boutique in Wimbledon Village called Policy. I made my way up the hill, past all the cafés and the bars where people were spilling out on to the pavements in the summer sun. I

211

arrived at the shop and entered as Rob was just finishing with a customer.

"Danny boy," he greeted me. "It's time to get to work."

Rob had started working at Policy while we were at college and enjoyed it so much he had stayed there. The job suited him down to the ground. While the rest of us would be happy with a High Street T-shirt costing 20 quid, Rob had to buy *Prada* or *Hugo Boss* costing five times that amount.

Now the assistant manager, he was often sent off to fashion capitals like Milan or Paris to pick and choose next seasons fashion stock. He would talk about trainers made of pony hair or try to preach how make-up for men would take off. At times he came across a bit gay, but always regained our respect when he would show us dirty pictures on his phone of the foreign lovelies he had met on his travels.

"Clothes make the man," Rob said quoting Mark Twain like he had done so many times before. He stood behind me brushing the shoulders of a charcoal blazer he had given me to try on. "Girls are very detail-orientated. Before deciding whether they want to be with you, one of the things they will evaluate is your clothes."

I looked at the price tag. "Fourteen hundred pounds?" I said, absolutely staggered.

"But this is *Lanvin*," Rob said, like that was meant to mean something to me or justify the outrageous price tag. "This is a blazer for 21st century man."

"I couldn't care less if it was for 25th century man," I said taking the blazer off and handing it back to him. "I'm not paying that sort of money."

Rob hung the jacket back up and selected other items of clothing for me to try on. Every time he handed me something I would look at the price tag and then hand it back.

"Look," Rob said, finally losing patience with me. "You came to me. You are the one who wanted my help. Now do you want my advice or not?"

"Yes," I mumbled, staring down at the ground and swaying. I felt like a naughty schoolboy being told off.

"Good. The first thing you need to do is be willing to change. This is the first stage of your transition and you need to let go of your dress sense." For the next half hour Rob worked his magic, mixing and matching styles to find my look. By the end of it my head was spinning.

"What do you think?" Rob said as I looked in the mirror.

"I... I think I like it." And I really did. Rob had dressed me in a dark blue shirt unbuttoned to the chest, a light grey blazer, faded denim jeans, and white trainers. It was simple but effective.

"Take one of these as well," Rob handed me a leather purse with a tiger pattern on the front in fake diamonds and jewels.

"It's a purse," I said handing it back towards him.

"It's not a purse. These are the height of fashion; all the footballers have got one of these bad boys. It's metrosexual."

"Metrosexual? It's bloody gay."

"Trust me," Rob said. I looked in the mirror again and against my better judgement I concluded that Rob had got it right so far so I would take his word on the purse.

"I've also booked you an appointment at the hairdresser across the road," Rob said. "Ask for Kim."

"But..." I attempted to argue my case. I liked my hair. I liked the fact I could pay nine pounds to the same barber I had been going to since I was six-years-old. I liked that we would talk football and all I had to tell him to do was a number five around the sides and a little bit off the top. I didn't want to pay a small fortune just to have my hair washed and head massaged before I was given the exact same haircut.

"No buts," Rob said. "You agreed to do what I told you."

"Okay," I nodded. "How much do I owe you?"

Rob punched a few buttons into the till. "That'll be £778."

"What?" I gasped, dropping my second cup of tea of the day.

### Makeover with Ollie: The Body

"Why have you got your hair done like that?" Ollie asked as he bench pressed his version of what he called a warm-up rep.

"It's my new look," I said. "Rob said girls like guys who look after their appearance."

Ollie sat up and screwed his face up at me. I don't think he was too impressed, but he didn't say anything else. Ollie had sent me a text agreeing to take me to the gym on the Wednesday evening.

I took my place on the bench as Ollie lifted the bar down into my hands. Immediately I felt my arms buckle under the weight as I pushed with all my might.

"Come on, you pussy," Ollie encouraged me, in his own special way.

"Get this thing off me," I pleaded, fearing my chest was about to cave in. Ollie lifted the bar and placed it back onto the bench. "I thought you said that was a warm-up?"

"No pain, no gain," Ollie said taking weights off the bar. "Try this."

I managed to struggle my way through ten reps, huffing and puffing as I did so. Ollie spotted me, offering slightly more positive words of encouragement this time round.

"Good work," Ollie said as I squeezed out my final rep. We swapped places and Ollie fired off his reps with ease. I couldn't help but think as I spotted him that maybe I should offer some words of encouragement. So I did.

"Come on, push that bad boy harder!"

"What are you doing?" Ollie said as he stood up to once again lighten the weight load for my set.

"Offering words of encouragement," I said with a perplexed look on my face.

"Don't ever do that again. It's weird."

"But I..."

"No," Ollie cut me off. "There are certain things you just don't say to people in the gym," Ollie explained. "For example, you should never compliment a bloke on his six-pack unless you are talking about his choice of beer."

"Okay, beer talk only," I said.

"And never let me hear you utter phrases like 'yeah baby, push it'. And under no circumstances do you say anything like 'just one more set and we can hit the showers together'."

I nodded.

For the next hour Ollie put me through my paces. There were times when I felt like I was going to pass out, but Ollie kept right on at me. It was then I realised there are two types of people who go to the gym. Insane people who have escaped from a mental asylum and seem to think going to the gym is good for you, and then you have normal people like me who know better.

Of course, you have your posers. They come in the shape of men who spend more time making love to their reflections than the weights. And girls who would turn up with a face full of make-up and spend all their time walking on the treadmill, yapping on their mobile phone. By the end of it I was ready to throw in the towel. I had never understood the attraction of spending hours on end punishing your body in the gym. But I had promised to see this makeover through, and I was determined to prove a point.

Plus I'd been conned into handing over £70 a month for the next year, and at the very least I was going to use the showers three times a week to try and justify some of that spend. I might even steal some of the towels.

"A few more sessions like that and you'll start to get used to it," Ollie reassured me. "Give it six months and you will start to notice a difference."

"Six months?" I whined. "But I haven't got six months. I need to get results now."

Ollie shrugged. This was a major setback. I had fallen into the trap of believing I would end up looking like Arnie after just a couple of sessions. As it turned out I would have to live with what I had for a while longer yet. But the worst part of this experience was still to come. As Ollie carried me back to the changing rooms, I couldn't have been less prepared for what was about to happen.

Anyone who has stepped foot in a male changing room at a gym will know of the horror story I am about to tell. If Stephen King was to ever run out of ideas then he could create a whole new genre with the terrifying ordeal that is the male locker room. For some unknown reason, certain men feel the need to walk around as naked as the day they were born. I am talking completely starkers. Bits of flesh waving and swaying all over the place. And the worst offenders are fat guys or old men. Why they feel the need to flash their tackle to other men is beyond me. Believe me when I say that the last thing you want is some fat, old guy bending over and flashing his saggy bum and wrinkly ball bag in your face.

"Beware of old man arse and wrinkly scrotums," Ollie had warned me as he dragged my lifeless body to our lockers.

216

*

As we walked back to the tube station, I felt like my body was about to give in. Ollie lit a cigarette.

"How can you smoke after coming out of the gym?" I asked. "Doesn't that defeat the whole point of exercise?"

"Duh," Ollie made the kind of noise you make after someone has made a stupid comment. "It's because I keep myself fit that I don't have to stop smoking."

You couldn't really argue with logic like that.

"I nearly forgot," Ollie said digging around in his rucksack. "I brought a DVD for you."

I looked around to make sure no one was watching. Ollie had never been the most tactful person in the world and the middle of Clapham High Street was not the sort of place you wanted to be receiving the type of DVD I'm sure he had in his bag.

"Oh," I said surprised as he handed me a copy of *WrestleRage*. "What is this for?"

"Girls like guys with good bodies," Ollie said. "But they also like guys who can look after themselves."

I wasn't sure if that was entirely true. I didn't know too many girls who made their decisions on whether to sleep with a guy or not based on his fighting ability. From my experience girls preferred a bunch of flowers to a bunch of fives.

"Okay," I said, "but how is this going to help me?"

"Duh," there was that noise again. "The main event of *WrestleRage* was the Iron Warrior vs Flex Bruiser. Two of the greatest athletes ever to grace the squared circle. You could learn a lot from these two."

I didn't have the heart to tell Ollie that wrestling wasn't real.

**Makeover with Jack: The Moves**

"Fourteen hundred quid?" Jack gasped when I told him about the blazer I had tried on at Rob's shop. "You could get yourself a hooker with that sort of money. Probably a good one as well."

I was starting to get a bad feeling about the third stage of my makeover. Upon hearing that both Rob and Ollie had already got involved, Jack insisted that he come round to teach me some "proper man moves" as he had put it. He was even referring to himself as the missing piece of my puzzle.

"What is this we're watching?" Jack asked.

"*WrestleRage*," I said as the Iron Warrior hit Flex Bruiser with a big clothesline.

"But why?"

"Because Ollie said I needed to learn how to fight."

"And he recommended you watch this?"

"Yeah," I said like it was the most obvious thing. Warrior pressed Bruiser above his head and dropped him in preparation for his big splash finish.

"And you listened to him?"

Jack was right, it *was* ridiculous. But I had been hooked since I had put on the DVD three hours ago. Watching these spandex-wearing muscle men had brought back so many nostalgic memories from my childhood.

"Shhh," I put my finger up to my lips. "The Bruiser is making a comeback!"

And he was! Shaking his head and waving his finger at the Warrior, taking everything the Warrior could throw at him. Then came the big boot and he went for his famous Knee Drop.

"That was so obvious he was going to miss," Jack said as the Warrior rolled out of the way at the last minute.

"Shut up," I said, now on the edge of my seat as Warrior bounced off the ropes and hit Bruiser with *another* big splash. "One... two... three!" It was all over – the Warrior was the new champion. I leapt to my feet and started dancing around the living room in my dressing gown, imitating the Warrior by beating my chest.

"What in God's name are you doing?" Jack said, his arms folded across his chest. "Turn this rubbish off. We've got work to do." Jack was taking it all very seriously. I took my seat back on the sofa next to him. I wasn't even too sure what man moves were. I had been too tired when he had called that morning to bother asking.

"As the missing piece of the puzzle, I will be helping you with the single most important part of your rehabilitation," Jack pursed his lips. "Man moves, otherwise known as sex education," and with that he pulled out a notepad and pen, and put a pair of glasses on.

"Wait a minute," I said. "I thought you wanted to teach me how to be cool and to get my swagger back? And why are you wearing those? You don't wear glasses." I said.

Jack ignored my question. "Hey, what impresses a girl more than being *absolute* in the sack? And after all this time out of practice, you could probably do with a few pointers."

"I really don't think this..."

"What is the best sexual position?" Jack interrupted me.

"Well... I..." The bluntness of his question took me aback.

"Too slow," Jack said shaking his head and writing something down on his notepad. "If you can't answer a simple question like that then what hope do you have when you're with a woman?"

"The girl on top," I shouted just to shut him.

"Tut tut," Jack shook his head and wrote something else down on his notepad. "Wrong answer."

"Why is it the wrong answer?" I demanded to know.

219

"Too lazy. You put too much control in the woman's court," Jack said looking at me over his glasses which were now perched on the end of his nose.

"What should I have answered then?"

"Doggy style," he said placing his notepad down like he had just come up with the solution to the perfect sexual manoeuvre. "Would you like me to elaborate?"

"Please do."

He got to his feet and cleared his throat. "The doggy position puts all of the control in the man's court. He controls the speed, the angle, and rest periods. The woman cannot direct proceedings while on all fours. She might be able to back into the man, but at any given time the man can take back control of the reins. Come here and let me show you."

I looked at him blankly for a second before realising he was deadly serious. "I am not letting you demonstrate on me. No way."

"Hey!" Jack shouted, pointing his finger at me. "You told me you had done exactly what the others told you to do. I want that same respect. Now get over here and get on all fours."

"Jack, I'm not doing this..."

"Trust me Dan," Jack said placing his glasses down on the table. "This is the only way to learn. You'll thank me."

And for the second time that day I agreed to what Jack was asking against my better judgement. Reluctantly I got down in front of him on my knees. "No funny business okay?"

"You have my word that this will be strictly professional" Jack said. "Now get on all fours, bitch." I shot him a look before shaking my head and getting on all fours. I felt him grab me by the waist and pull me towards him.

"I can't do this..." I said trying to get up, but Jack forced my head down and I sprawled on to the carpet.

"Lesson one," Jack said with one hand pushing down against my head and the other clutching onto my waist. "In the doggy position the man controls the situation."

He started thrusting his pelvis back and forth, forcing my face to rub against the carpet. "Jack, if you don't get off me..."

"Lesson two. In this position you can apply the old reach around. You can go upstairs or downstairs." Jack freed the hand from my waist to reach around to my chest and groin area.

"Seriously Jack, if you don't get off me I'll..." I turned my face to meet his gaze to let him know I meant business, but he just interrupted me again.

"Lesson three. The doggy position means you don't have to look at her face if she is fugly," he said using his abbreviation for *fucking ugly*, and with the hand that was pushing my head down he turned my face away back towards the carpet to stop me looking at him.

"Lesson four," Jack said taking a firmer grip as I tried to squirm out of the way. "The doggy position is the ideal position to switch from vagina to anal."

"Get off me now!" But as I tried pushing away I lost balance and my chin crashed against the carpet.

"And the final lesson today class, after giving the girl anal pleasure, you can play that well-known game of *taste your ass*," and with that Jack slapped my arm and twisted my hips to spin me on to my back and straddled me with his groin in my face. "Taste your ass, bitch."

"GET THE FUCK OFF ME!" And with all the strength I could muster I launched Jack across the room.

"What's your bloody problem?" Jack said rubbing his head.

"I think I've learned enough for one day thank you very much," I said hauling myself back up on to the sofa.

"Suit yourself," Jack said getting to his feet. "We'll pick this up later on in the week. Our next class will be how to perform perfect oral pleasure."

"Get out."

## Chapter 19: The Dating Game

*Friday, June 26, 2009 - 8.13pm*
*Drought Clock: 176 days, 4 hours, 24 minutes*

I had a new look. I had started to work on a new physique. And I had tried to erase all memory of Jack's lesson on *proper man moves*. Now I had to get out there and make it work. I had arranged to meet the boys in the Nelson Arms to go through my strategy. The plan was simple – I was to arrange dates with as many girls as possible and play the odds game with the hope that at least one of them would be willing to shag me.

"Where is your Little Black Book, then?" Rob asked.

In this case my Little Black Book consisted of mobile contacts, email addresses, and Facebook friends. "Here you go," I said handing them a piece of paper with a list of names I had drawn up.

"You have to take this name off," Rob said crossing out the name of Sarah Young. "We know her brother Billy."

"So what?" I said.

"If you've known a bloke for more than 24 hours, his sister is off limits forever," Rob explained. "Unless you plan to marry her."

"That reminds me, how is *your* sister Ollie?" Jack said.

"Behave yourself," Ollie said pointing at Jack with the top of his beer bottle.

"Let me ask you guys a question," Jack said shifting forward in his seat, holding out two fingers. "Why does Ollie's sister masturbate with these two fingers?"

"I'm warning you, Jack," Ollie said.

"Because they're mine!" Jack said cracking up. Even Ollie had a smile on his face.

"You probably don't want to contact this one either," Rob said pointing at Adele Tompkinson's name. "Remember the story she spread about Ryan Jefferson?"

We all nodded as we recalled of how Ryan got stuck with a nickname that still haunted him to this day. Rumour has it that halfway through sex, poor Ryan had an asthma attack and needed to stop to get his inhaler. Adele had apparently been so put out by this, that she had not bothered to help him find the inhaler. While the poor guy was gasping for breath she sat on the side of the bed sulking. To add insult to injury, she told everyone the story and Ryan became known as the *Weezy Lover,* sung to the tune of the Phil Collins song *She's an Easy Lover.*

We whittled the list down to three names. Rob handed me the piece of paper and I took a swig on my bottle of beer. I looked at the names and wondered if one of those girls could be the one to help bring an end to my drought. Only time would tell.

**Date One**
**Who:** Hannah Kennedy
**When:** Tuesday, June 30
**Where:** Dinner in Chinatown
**Background:** Old school friend who recently got in touch on Facebook.

"Do you remember Miss Clarke, the art teacher?" I asked Hannah as our food was brought to our table.

"Yes, I do!" Hannah said. "She was the one who used to disappear midway through class to have a sneaky fag outside."

It was good reminiscing about the old days and talking about things I hadn't thought about for years. Hannah hadn't changed much. She still had long brown hair and a pretty little nose. I had sent her a message on Facebook

224

asking if she fancied meeting up and she had replied almost instantly saying we should meet for dinner after work one evening.

"And how about Mr Thembury, the French teacher," I said tucking into my chicken and cashew nuts. "He used to get so worked up when he was telling the class to be quiet that he would have tears in his eyes."

"Or Mr Neal, the geography teacher, who wore that really bad wig!" Hannah said, and we both cracked up. This was going great. I kicked myself for not thinking about doing this before. Meeting up with an old friend put me completely at ease.

"I really miss those days," I said shovelling some rice into my mouth. "It would be great to go back and relive our time at school."

"Hmmm," Hannah nodded, but had an awkward look on her face.

"Everything ok?"

"It's nothing really," Hannah drunk some wine. "It's just I had a bit of a tough time at school. I got bullied."

"I'm so sorry, I had no idea," I said putting down my chopsticks and placing my hand on top of hers. "If I had known I would never have brought it up."

"It's okay, it's not your fault."

"We don't have to talk about this. We can change the subject if you like?"

"No, that's okay," she said holding my hand. "It would be nice to talk about it. I haven't really told anyone about this before."

Hannah had seemed so happy at school, but here she was looking for a shoulder to cry on. She looked so vulnerable.

I could definitely use this to my advantage.

Okay, I was a despicable human being to prey on this poor girl's weakness. But I knew it would be something

225

Jack would do, and he wasn't suffering from any sort of drought at the moment.

"Tell me what happened?"

She took a deep breath. "Things were fine until the final year. I had been getting good grades and keeping my head down."

"Go on," I said stroking her hand.

"Then one day during a science class it happened. I didn't mean for it to happen, but it just came from nowhere. And you know what kids are like at school. They can be so cruel, but I couldn't help it. It wasn't my fault."

"What happened?" I said, intrigued.

"We were set a test on the Periodic Table. It was silent apart from the noise of pencils scratching against paper. And that's when it happened?"

"*What* happened?" I asked again, this time a little too eager. The suspense was killing me. A multitude of possibilities raced through my head.

"I fanny farted."

"You what?" I said pulling my hand away in disgust. Did she say what I think she said?

"I fanny farted," Hannah said with her head in her hands. "And I did it again. And again. And again. I couldn't stop. It became a real problem for me. The kids teased me and called me Fanny Fart Kennedy. It was horrible."

"No shit," I said, and then I realised I might have been coming across a little insensitive. "I mean, you poor thing." But that didn't stop her.

"As I got older it became more of a problem, especially with boyfriends. I was with a guy who dumped me because I fanny farted while we were in the 69er position. I was horrified."

And she didn't stop there either.

"I had no control over them. They would go off at the most random of places. At the cinema, at work, at funerals.

226

It got so bad the doctor put me on antidepressants." She paused. "And then I spent six weeks in a mental institute."

You couldn't make this shit up.

"You spent six weeks in a mental institute..." I hesitated to finish, not quite believing I would ever utter this sentence to anyone. "... because you suffered from fanny farts?"

Hannah nodded. "But it's okay now. I do pelvic floor exercises, tensing the muscles down below and that keeps it under control."

I looked at Hannah and I could see the pain behind her eyes. This poor girl had obviously suffered from something that is quite natural and probably happens to a lot of girls. It wasn't her fault. My heart really went out to her. I felt guilty for judging her.

Then from under the table came a noise similar to that of air escaping a balloon.

"Sorry."

**Date Two**
**Who:** Kayleigh Marconi
**When:** Saturday, July 11
**Where:** Picnic at Hyde Park
**Background:** A former work colleague from the bar I worked in while I was at university.

"This was a nice idea," Kayleigh said as I took a bite from my sandwich.

And it was a nice idea. It was a scorching hot day and the park was packed with people making the most of the weather. The park had a lot of history. When Henry VIII claimed the land in the sixteenth century it became a royal hunting ground. It seemed an appropriate spot seeing as I had very much been on the hunt for the last six months.

"So tell me what you have been up to since we last saw each other," I asked.

227

"Where do I start?" she said, pausing to think as she chewed on her ham salad sandwich. "*Sooo* many things have happened over the last three years. Oooh, I know!" she said very upbeat. "I am now a professional singer."

"Wow," I was impressed.

"Yeah, I cut a dance track last year but it didn't get released because the DJ was doing his GCSE's."

Not quite as impressive as it had first sounded. Perhaps I was being too judgmental. Never in my life had I become remotely close to releasing a song.

"That is a shame," I said. "Why don't you sing me a few lines?"

"No, I couldn't," Kayleigh said quite bashfully.

"Oh don't be..."

And before I could even finish, Kayleigh said "Okay" and got to her feet.

"Imagine a quick beat and soft piano riff," Kayleigh said clearing her throat. "Here goes."

*In my eyes, the purple moon sky rises,*
*Soooooooo high...*

*In my eyes, the blood red sun rises,*
*Soooooooo high...*

This part of the song was accompanied by a strange dance movement which involved Kayleigh's arms dancing towards the sky like two snakes. It was kind of odd, but I smiled encouragingly.

*I wanna get high, in the sky,*
*Take a look at my face, you can see it in my eye.*

*I wanna get high, in the sky,*
*Until I do, you can't have my apple pie.*

And before you ask, yes, she did say apple pie. I even checked myself.

The dance moves speeded up and thrown into the mix included Kayleigh raising her knees one at a time at a ferocious pace. People were starting to look as she repeated the routine quicker. As far as I could see, the whole song needed to find as many words as possible that rhymed with sky. Lye, spy, necktie, thigh, goodbye, fry, hawk-eye, magpie, sand-fly. The list went on.

My favourite line was *I wanna get high, in the sky, you can be my Daniel San, and say BONSAI!* As a fan of 80's films, I thought that was a nice tribute to the *Karate Kid*.

"What do you think?" Kayleigh said, out of breath.

"That was... different," was the best I could manage.

"Would you like me to teach you the dance?"

"No, God no," I said, a little too hastily. "I mean, I don't like dancing."

Kayleigh shrugged and went back to her sandwich. It was at this point I had a flashback about Kayleigh. I remembered the time she managed to lock herself in one of the cubicles at the bar where we worked.

She spent the whole night there.

So she wasn't the brightest spark, but that was okay. I was after her body and not her mind after all. And if things didn't work out between us, I could always introduce her to Ollie.

During her routine, I'd noticed that Kayleigh had her tongue pierced. That always intrigued me, as next to a mallet to the testicles, I always considered a bolt through the tongue to be the next most painful experience you could put your body through.

"Did that hurt?" I said pointing to her tongue.

"No, not really," she replied. "Not as much as when I had my clit pierced."

"Excuse me?" I nearly choked on my prawn sandwich.

229

"I got it done just before I went on holiday last year," Kayleigh said picking up another sandwich. "I was lying on my front, sunbathing around the pool," she continued.

"Yeah?" I nervously said.

"And I slid forward to get up..."

"Yeah...?"

"And it got caught on something..."

"Yeah...?"

"And it ripped," Kayleigh said as nonchalantly as you like, biting into her sandwich. "So now I don't have a clit anymore."

I looked at one of the prawns in my sandwich and suddenly felt quite sick.

**Date Three**
**Who:** Lucy Mellor
**When:** Friday, July 24
**Where:** Drinks in South Croydon
**Background:** Met at a friend's party last year and had some chemistry but nothing was ever taken further because I was in a relationship.

We practically fell down the hallway when we got back to Lucy's flat; our lips locked together. The evening had turned out to be a fantastic success. Lucy had flirted outrageously from the get-go and all the signs were there.

Things were getting heavy. She slammed me against the wall, biting my lip. We bounced off the opposite sides of the hallway until we eventually stumbled into the living room. She pushed me down onto the couch and locked her legs around me.

This was really going to happen, third time lucky! Finally my drought would come to an end. It had been a long drawn out process. My libido had been clinging to the lifeboat for months, drifting aimlessly out to deep, lonely, secluded waters. But not anymore. Tonight would be the night I would be rescued, drained of all bodily fluids and pulled to dry shores.

Lucy was insatiable, grinding up and down against me. She moaned like a wild animal, while I could do nothing but make strange groans like a man desperate not to ejaculate while being dry humped to death. Her dry hump technique suddenly moved up a gear, and she got rougher as she took the pace up a notch. The friction was now starting to get a little too much for me so I pulled her down onto the sofa and got on top of her.

She grabbed me and pulled me towards her and started to rub herself against me again. The sensation of jeans and underwear rubbing against my genitals was now starting to take its toll. I needed to take control. So I reached down and started to unzip the fly to her jeans. She grabbed my hand and whispered "stop" into my ear.

"I just want to let you know," she said between kisses. "Nothing is going to happen tonight."

What? What was this – some sort of sick game?

"What do you mean?" I asked, trying to keep calm.

"I don't want you to think I'm the type of girl who sleeps with a guy on the first date."

Why would she say that? She had invited me back to her place. She practically molested me in the taxi ride home. She had given my penis friction burns, the scars of which may never heal. She had done everything to fill me with hope that she was *exactly* that type of girl.

"I won't think badly of you," I said. "I promise," and I took my chances to reach for her zipper again, only to be denied. Again.

"Let's take things slow," she said sliding out from underneath me so we were now laying side by side. "Let's just cuddle for a while."

Cuddle? Like the after sex cuddle? But with no friggin' sex? Men don't like cuddling after sex at the best of times. After sex our work is done. If anything we would prefer no physical contact. And if you have come to the guys place and you are a one-night stand, don't ask us to call you a taxi either. Think yourself lucky that we are even pointing you in the direction of the bus stop. You should leave immediately after the sex is over. Preferably without stealing anything on the way out.

Surely there had to be some sort of law about this sort of thing. Maybe I could take this to Parliament.

Then I had a plan. I turned into Lucy so we were face-to-face and started kissing again. I edged closer and imitated my very own form of dry humping. She was into it, this was going well. Her moans started up again and slowly I reached my hand back towards the forbidden fruit.

"Dan, I said no," Lucy said slapping my hand away. She sat up and ran her hands through her hair. Maybe I could beg, would that work? I shook my head as I imagined an image of myself, homeless and holding a sign that read *Will have sex for food*. Begging for sex was never a good look for anyone.

What I needed was a line. The type of line straight from the script of a romantic Hollywood blockbuster; a real heart-melter. I had to say something that all girls wanted to hear; something that would have her eating out the palm of my hand to rescue this situation.

Then a moment of inspiration.

"I've got to tell you, Lucy," I started, stroking her face. "Looking into your eyes, I think you could be the first girl I fall in love with since I broke up with my ex."

And the Oscar goes to…

"You think you might fall in love with me?" Lucy said. I proudly smiled back at her and nodded. "That is the most ridiculous thing I've ever heard."

Hey, I took a shot. Looking back it wasn't the best line I could have used.

"More ridiculous than inviting someone back and then not having sex with them?" I shot back.

Again, probably not the smartest thing I could have said but I was mad. I was even considering bypassing Parliament and taking my case to the European Court of Human Rights.

"I think you had better leave," Lucy said sitting up and buttoning up her blouse.

"Fine by me," I sat up ready to storm out of there, but realised I had a slight problem. The problem being I was still pitching a tent. "Can you give me five minutes?"

# Chapter 20: Shop Horror

*Friday, July 31 - 5.15pm*
*Drought Clock: 210 days, 19 hours, 22 minutes*

"Daniel!" Dick bellowed across the office. "I need to see you and Kelly in here now." It was 5.15pm on Friday afternoon. We had managed to avoid Dick for a whole week, so it was inevitable he would now attempt to ruin the start of our weekend.

"What now?" I said to Kelly as we both made our way to Dick's office. He was sitting at his desk holding a piece of paper in his hand. We closed the door and sat down.

"Can someone tell me what this is?" he asked waving the piece of paper in his hand. "I've just seen that we are forecasting to miss budget again next month."

"We are trying to drum up some new prospects, but people are being very cautious at this time of the year and not spending," I offered as an explanation. "If you look at the plan for quarter three, we are planning to make up the money when the market picks up."

Dick's expression was blank. "That's not it," Dick informed us calmly. "The problem is you are not asking for the business. I was looking in your proposals folder and found the one you sent to Collins & Spackman Limited." He just stared at me as the silence grew louder and louder.

"Yes?" I finally asked.

"It is rubbish. Every time you send a document like this to a client, you are hurting my brand," he sat back in his chair, fingers linked behind his head in that annoying power pose of his. "You are hurting the Dick *Moo-Cell* brand."

Kelly and I quickly glanced at each other, both knowing what was coming next. Dick proceeded to tell us that we needed to be more inspirational. More dynamic. *More like Dick Mussel.*

"You should be leading from the front. Let me show you," he said as he excitedly arose from his chair and started to draw some sort of diagram on his white board. "What are they?" he asked pointing at what could only be described as a group of six match-stick men holding poles. We both stared at it blankly.

"They are your competitors," Dick finally informed us. "They are holding machine guns ready to shoot you down." He then started to draw little bullets on the board. At the bottom of the drawing was a series of squares and two more matchstick men. "Who are they?" he said pointing at them.

"Us?" Kelly said making a total guess.

"Correct! That is you two down in the trenches taking on our competitors who are shooting at you from all angles." He drew a few more bullets. "You guys need to come over the trenches and start attacking because otherwise you are going to get shot down."

"Okay, I think we understand," I said in hope that he would let us leave the room so we didn't have to witness any more of this excruciating and painful pep talk.

"This is me." He completely ignored me and drew a tank. "I'm at the back, making sure my soldiers are okay. I don't want to come over the top to rescue this war, but I will if I have to." He then took a red pen and started to draw what I presumed was blood on the two matchstick characters that represented Kelly and me. "But if you die, then I will do what I have to do." He looked at us like he was waiting for a round of applause, and then back at the white board. "I've also got a fighter jet," he said drawing an airplane on the board that fired bullets down at our competitors, plus further red pen to draw blood squirting from our enemy.

"Guys, I know morale is low, but we have to win this war." He put the top back on the pen and walked around his desk to us. "At the moment morale is so low, it is down

235

here," and he suddenly dropped and laid flat across his office floor. "But we need morale to be up here," and he sprung to his feet and did some strange kind of star jump, reaching for the sky. "Do we understand what needs to be done?" he said drawing for breath.

I didn't have a clue, and I'm pretty sure Kelly didn't either. But there was no way one of us was going to admit that and risk having to watch any more of his carry on. "We understand, Dick. We'll get straight on to it Monday morning," I told him.

"Good. I'll look forward to seeing some positive results next week."

We got up and left his office as quickly as we could, both trying not to laugh until we got back to our desks. "What the hell was that all about?" I said.

"I have no idea and don't want to even try to dissect what just happened in there," Kelly said smiling. "I don't know about you, but I could do with a drink after that."

"Good idea," I replied.

People were already escaping the office for the weekend, like buffalo stampeding for the door to escape the monotony of office life. Dick stood at his door watching as his empire disappeared for 48 hours, probably already scheming how he could make his minions lives even more unbearable next week. He took one final look and then disappeared back into the shadows of his lair.

"Quick, let's make a run for it now before Dick pulls us back in to his office to give us any more motivational speeches," I said as I closed down my computer.

"Or even worse – asks if he can come with us to the pub," Kelly quipped.

We made our way down to Bishopsgate – a hub of bars packed with city suits and people with more money than sense. Some of these guys were a real throwback to the Filofax brigade of the 80s and 90s. They had swapped their

Filofax for a BlackBerry, but they still oozed that yuppie persona. A privileged education, but a complete lack of common sense. They drank champagne like it was lemonade and it would not be an unusual sight to see them stumbling around by 7pm, shirts half-untucked on one side and ties loosened, or in some cases being worn around their head like *Rambo*. Loyalty amongst some of these guys was practically non-existent, as it was not uncommon for a member of the group to be cut loose, and found staggering about alone in a nightclub in the early hours of the morning.

We grabbed our drinks and found a spot to stand in the sea of bodies who were gathered around to celebrate the end of the working week.

"So what are your plans for the weekend?" Kelly asked.

"I'm thinking of having a bit of a chilled one," I told her. "I could do with the break."

"Well, in that case, you can come shopping with me on Sunday," Kelly said.

"No way, I hate shopping." I couldn't think of a worse way to spend my Sunday.

"Please, babe, it's Paul's birthday and I need help picking something out for him," she pleaded, giving me those puppy dog eyes.

"Don't you have any girlfriends you can take with you?"

"I would, but I could really do with a guy's input and advice on this one."

The thought of having some female company where I didn't feel under pressure to try and get inside her pants did appeal. My recent experiences with the opposite sex had been disastrous to say the least. It would be good to hang out with a girl I didn't have to try and impress. It could help build my confidence up. Plus I had Rosalie coming over this Sunday to clean, and I had been trying to avoid her since the underwear incident.

"Okay," I finally gave in. "What time?"

237

"Midday. I'll meet you at Oxford Circus."

So there it was – I was committed to doing the one thing I hated more than anything in the world. I didn't even like shopping for myself. When I had to go I treated it like a military operation. I know exactly what I want and where I can get it, and I am in and out as quickly as possible. Somehow I knew this would be different.

*

By Sunday morning, I was already starting to regret agreeing to meet Kelly. The previous day I had played 14 hours straight on a new football management game I had bought the previous week. It had taken me two hours just to get through pre-season as I had taken time to carefully organise my scouting strategy and had shrewdly delved into the transfer market. As a result, I had picked up a couple of real gems in Brazil and Argentina and was sitting second in the league after 22 games. At one point, I pretended to hold a news conference in my living room to discuss my upcoming top of the table clash against Manchester United.

The thought had occurred to me to text Kelly and tell her that I was not feeling very well, but I didn't want to let her down. Manchester United and the Premier League crown would have to wait for a few hours.

I made my way to Oxford Circus via the Northern and Victoria Lines. The tubes were packed with tourists and couples heading into the hub of London's shopping capital. I got off the Tube and the crowd dragged me up the escalators to street level. My phone beeped the second I stepped outside the tube entrance with a text from Kelly: *Meet me in Top Shop xx.* I groaned inside. Top Shop on Oxford Street has to be as close to hell on earth for men as you can possibly get.

There should be warning signs for men at the entrance to let them know what they are about to let themselves in for. I took a deep breath and entered, scanning the place for the impossible task of finding Kelly. I made the plunge and started weaving in and out of the hundreds of women who had dragged their boyfriends or husbands out to go shopping.

All the men have that same pathetic look of defeat on their faces as they trail behind their women like shadows, carrying their bags, and holding up items of clothes so the women can inspect them more closely. We all share a common bond, a common misery. We could be in the pub with our mates watching the football, which is what Sundays were created for. Shopping is not a sport, and we are never going to think of it that way.

Even the layouts of these shops are designed to trip us up, like some sort of assault course which has been put together specifically for women. While the gaps in between the rails of clothes are big enough for the female physique to glide in and out of, we are left to clumsily follow, knocking clothes off rails with great frequency. Then we have the questions.

*What do I look like in this?*

"You look nice" is the wrong answer. "You look good" is the wrong answer. "You look okay" is definitely the wrong answer. You might as well get Roy Walker to follow you around and every time you answer this question he can jump in with "It's good, but it's not right." If she wanted us to respond with "amazing" or "fantastic" then she should hold up a Brazilian football shirt signed by Pelé and his 1970 World Cup winning team-mates. This is the only item of clothing we will ever get excited about.

*Which one do you prefer?*

Hmm, let me think. I don't care! Just pick that one, pick any of them! This question is designed to catch you out. On

239

the outside it might look like a simple 50/50 question, but despite the flip-of-a-coin odds, you will never get this question right. Whichever one you choose will be met by the same response: "Really? I prefer this one." If you have already made up your mind, don't ask us.

*Do you think these shoes will go with this dress?*

Let's get one thing straight here. Most guys will own a maximum of three pairs of shoes at any one time. So how does that make us even remotely qualified to choose which pair of shoes – out of the dozens upon dozens of pairs you have made us look at already – will look good with your dress?

Even when she eventually decides she likes something, the torture doesn't end. Now they have to try everything on. Whose bright idea was it to put the changing rooms bang in the middle of the lingerie department? Groups of men are forced to awkwardly stand around, trying their best not to look like pervs. The problem is, the more you try to look like you are not hanging around sniffing women's underwear, the more paranoid you become that everyone thinks that is exactly what you are doing. It doesn't help that the queue for the ladies changing rooms is normally a mile long. Don't be surprised either if after hanging around in the underwear section for 15 minutes trying not to look like a nonce, your girlfriend suddenly returns having not even tried the clothes on.

*I like it but I don't really need it.*

Why the hell did you queue up if you were never going to buy it? Of course, you can't say that. So you put up with the other pointless questions, which you neither have the answers to, nor really care about. Questions like *"Do you think I can pull this off?"* or *"does this match my skin tone?"*

With Stacey I used to just smile and nod, safe in the knowledge shops have to close at some point and I might make it home before dark if I'm lucky.

Some guys try to come up with a different strategy, but I can tell you for a fact that nothing you try will make the experience of shopping with your girlfriend any less painful. For example, the worst thing you can do is say that you are going off to the men's section. You may think this will kill a bit of time, but after you have scanned everything you wanted to see in five minutes flat, you will return to the women's section only to find that your girlfriend is nowhere in sight. Now the hunt begins, and if history tells us anything, we know that it will be a good 20 minutes at least before you manage to locate her. There is an old campfire horror tale about a guy who has been wandering around Top Shop for the last five months after letting his girlfriend out of his sight.

I really didn't want to start hunting for Kelly so I pulled my mobile out to call her. "Dan, over here!" I heard her call out and turned round to see her standing about 10 yards away, a big grin on her face. "I have been following you around for ages."

"Please, get me out of here," I begged her.

"Come on," and she took me by the arm and led me out of my misery.

We strolled along Oxford Street, her arm linked under mine. "Your face was a picture when I found you," Kelly giggled. "It looked as though you might spontaneously combust if you had stayed there any longer."

"You are not far wrong," I said. "These places should come with a warning sign, or at least a designated area for all boyfriends and husbands, like a bar in the basement or something."

"What are you talking about?" she asked with a smile.

"They should have special men-only members clubs in all female retail outlets. They would make a killing. Men would be queuing round the block to sign up. We'd gladly pay a yearly membership fee."

"So what would be in this members club?"

"They could stock it out with table football, big screen TV's, pool tables, Space Invader arcade machines. Free counselling sessions should be offered to all the men who have suffered identical shopping scenarios, so we could sit together and commiserate as we relive our horror stories while the women shopped until their hearts content."

Kelly burst out laughing. "I can't believe how much you hate shopping."

"It's not that I hate shopping, I just don't understand the way a girl shops. It takes you guys about seven hours to finally decide to buy the first thing you saw at the start of the day."

"Oh really?" Kelly said, raising her eyebrows at me. "Seeing as you think you can find the perfect present in record time, let's put it to the test today."

"Challenge accepted," I said. "I just need one or two details. What is Paul into?"

"Let me see," she pondered. "He loves his sport, and is really into boxing. *Rocky* is his favourite film of all time."

"This is going to be too easy," I said. "Come on, follow me." I directed us away from Oxford Street down Argyll Street. A quick left on to Great Marlborough Street, and then we took a right to cut through on to Carnaby Street.

"Where are we going?" Kelly asked.

"Patience, we are nearly there," and we arrived at a small shop on the corner of Carnaby Street and Beak Street called *King of the Jungle.* This place prided itself on having *Original Gifts for the Lion in Your Life.*

"What is this place?" Kelly asked as we walked in.

"Are you kidding me? This is probably the best shop in the whole of London," I told her. It was the type of shop you wouldn't find on any high street, yet it was full of little hidden gems. One side was full of football memorabilia, with framed photographs signed by some of the best players

242

in the world, past and present. Next to that was a selection of gadgets and boys' toys, like icy beer mugs, remote controlled cars, and an alarm clock with a small pole dancer figurine that would wake you up every morning with your very own lap dance. The back wall featured a selection of T-shirts with witty slogans.

But what I was looking for was in the film memorabilia section. Here you could find talking *Tony Montana* toys, a *Goodfellas* poster signed by the complete cast, and framed film cells from *The Godfather*. I resisted the temptation to start playing with the Al Pacino *Scarface* doll, and picked up a black luxury bathrobe with gold trim.

"A dressing gown?" Kelly asked with a bewildered look on her face as if I had gone crazy. "You brought me to this place to buy a dressing gown?"

"Yes, but not just any dressing gown," I said and turned the robe around to reveal the *Italian Stallion* motif and logo on the back. "This is *Rocky Balboa's* dressing gown."

She looked it up and down. "Are you sure he will like it?"

"Trust me, he will love it" I reassured her. "If he doesn't then I promise I will go shopping with you every weekend for the next six months. If Stacey had bought me this when we were together, we probably would have never broken up."

I handed her the robe and she took one more look, before she turned to me smiling, and said, "I'll get it! But it will be on your head if he dumps me for buying him a dressing gown for his birthday."

Kelly paid for the robe and had to practically drag me away from the gadgets in the corner. We made our way back up to Oxford Circus to get the Tube home.

"Why don't you come to Paul's birthday party next week?" Kelly asked as we got back on the Victoria Line and sat down. "You can bring your friends with you."

243

"Yeah, why not? I could do with a good night out."

"Thanks for helping me with this, Dan," Kelly said and kissed me on the cheek. "You've gone all red," she teased.

# Chapter 21: Paul's Birthday

*Saturday, August 8, 2009 - 8.31pm*
*Drought Clock: 218 days, 19 hours, 6 minutes*

"So what are the girls going to be like at this party?" Jack asked as we made our way to Mojo Bar in Soho where Kelly's boyfriend Paul was throwing his birthday bash. "They'd better be fit, Dan, because there are rules about taking your mates to parties where the room is full of facially-challenged women."

"I have no idea what the girls are going to be like, mate," I told him. "This is Paul's party, but I'm sure they'll be enough girls there for you. Just don't try pulling any of his relatives."

"Like his mum, you mean?" Rob joked. "Because you would never try to pull someone's mum would you Dan?"

"Or their little sister," Ollie added.

"Piss off," I bluntly replied, not wanting to be reminded of my own personal nightmare with Dave's relatives back on Valentine's Day.

"All I'm saying is that if we enter this place and all I can see is a bunch of ropey old tarts, I am going to turn straight around and walk out," Jack said just to drive his point home. "Taking us to a place like that is a bit like an uneducated midget – it's not big and it's not clever."

"Bit like you then Jack," Ollie said, lifting Jack up off his feet and carrying him about 10 yards down the road before Jack managed to wriggle free, his little legs kicking thin air.

"Get your hands off me, Lurch. Don't make me slap you," Jack said as he tugged his shirt back into place. "Seriously, Dan, I've been practising for tonight."

"Practising?" Rob asked.

"Oh yeah, I've got all my best lines prepared. Tonight the ladies had better be ready for the Jack Hammer."

"I really hope that isn't one of your lines," I commented.

We arrived and made our way to the downstairs bar Paul had hired for the evening. It was a cool and stylish venue, with black leather seats around the side, and electric blue lights to give the place a funky ambience. House music thumped over the speakers, and the bar staff served an array of multi-coloured cocktails. It was just starting to get busy and I could tell by the way Jack had his tongue almost hanging out of his mouth that he was happy with the talent.

In a sea of unfamiliar faces, I saw Kelly, but I nearly didn't recognise her. She was wearing a gold sequin dress which plunged at the neckline. She had straightened her hair, and wore a straight fringe cut just above her eyes, with her long brown hair flowing down past her shoulders. Her legs looked long and toned. She waved after spotting me and started heading in my direction. Jack had obviously noticed her as well and was tugging at my shirt. "Introduce me," he said out the corner of his mouth.

"I'm so pleased you came," Kelly said and threw her arms around me.

"You look fantastic," I said, a little surprised.

"Paul loved his present. I can't thank you enough."

"What did I tell you?" I replied, but felt a sharp pain on my shin from Jack's kick. "Kelly, these are my friends," and I introduced the boys.

"I have to dash and play hostess, but I promise I'll come over later and we can talk properly," and she made her way back into the crowd.

"Make sure you bring some friends over," Jack shouted out to her. "Come on, Ollie, help me get the drinks in."

Rob sided up next to me as Ollie and Jack made their way to the bar. I was still watching Kelly move through the crowd. "You kept her quiet, mate," Rob said. "She is gorgeous. Have you ever suggested some out of work activity with her?"

"Of course I haven't, she's just a friend," I told him. I had never looked at Kelly in that way. Besides she has a boyfriend. "She's not my type," I said, and Rob shrugged at me.

But who was I kidding? I was so sex starved at that moment in time I would have fancied the creature from the black lagoon if it had turned up in gold sequins.

"Kelly is cool, but it's never going to happen. It just wouldn't be professional," I offered pathetically as a reason, but I started to wonder if I was trying to convince Rob or myself. It had now been seven months since, well, you know what. And now looking at Kelly dressed up in gold sequins with legs that went on forever, I could be forgiven for looking longer than I probably should look at a friend.

"It wouldn't be *professional?*" Rob laughed at me. "Okay, perhaps I'm wrong," Rob said taking his drink from Jack who had returned with Ollie with the first round of the night. "In which case, you won't mind if I try tucking in then?"

"No way, you leave her alone. We're at her boyfriend's birthday party for crying out loud." I knew he was trying to wind me up, but I still took the bait.

"Who are we talking about?" Jack asked. That's all I needed – Jack chipping in as well.

"I reckon Dan likes golden girl over there a little more than he is letting on," Rob explained to the other two.

"Oh yeah, that little treacle is absolute. I'd be all over it like a rash if I were you, mate," Jack advised me.

"Me too," Ollie put his two pennies in.

"No, you would give her the rash," Jack remarked.

"Can we stop talking about her like this," I said. "There are plenty of other girls here for you lot to leer and letch over."

And it was true. The room was full of gorgeous girls. "This room is making me bad," Jack said, his eyes darting all over the place. "Check out that little splitarse over there."

The *splitarse* in question was a petite Chinese girl with long black hair, wearing a white embroidered blouse, tight dark jeans, and knee-high grey suede boots. She looked a picture of innocence with her big white angelic smile. She noticed us all staring at her and flashed a coy grin in our direction before looking away.

"Look at her," Jack said. "Look at her! Ask me if I would cheat. Go on, ask me if I would cheat," he was pulling at my arm.

"Okay, okay," I said shrugging him off me. "Would you cheat?"

"In a heartbeat," Jack said taking a big swig of his drink. "Watch and learn boys, especially you, Dan. You might pick up a few tips." And with that he marched over, bold as brass.

"I bet he strikes out," Ollie said as Jack went over and introduced himself.

"I'd like to say I agree with you, but she hasn't given him the brush off yet," Rob said looking at his watch. "I make that six seconds without her slapping him. A personal best for Jack by my records."

"She even seems to be enjoying herself," I motioned towards the fact that she was smiling.

"My money is still on him screwing it up," Ollie was adamant. We all sipped at our pints and watched. Within seconds her smile switched to a scowl and with sharp precision, she swung and landed a stinging slap across Jack's left cheek. It was loud enough to make anyone within a 10-yard radius in a crowded noisy bar turn around. Jack simply nodded and raised his hands, before strolling nonchalantly back towards us.

248

We all gawked at him, waiting for an explanation, but he simply took a swig of his pint, and even raised his glass to a stranger as they walked past.

"Well?" Rob finally said.

"Well what?" Jack replied, as if nothing had happened despite the big red hand mark on his cheek.

"What happened?"

"Oh that. It was nothing."

"Something must have happened," I challenged. "What did you say?"

"I told you, nothing," Jack paused again to take another mouthful of lager. "I was just telling her that I thought she dressed very well."

"And?" Rob said.

"And I suggested something I thought would look good on her?"

"And?" we all said in unison, growing impatient.

Jack took another drink from his pint. "I told her that I thought I would look good on her."

Laughing, we all sighed and shook our heads disapprovingly. "When will you learn?" Rob asked him.

"Hey, it's not my fault the girl is frigid," Jack said, and we all raised our eyebrows at him. "She must be a lesbian."

"You're so full of shit," Ollie said laughing. "I knew your stupid one-liners wouldn't work on girls in a place like this."

"Oh really?" Jack said, putting his drink down on the table and rubbing his hands together. "You willing to put a little wager on that?"

"I'll have some of that," I said.

And so begun the great chat-up challenge of 2009. The rules were simple: Jack had to avoid being shunned and get a phone number from just one girl using his array of one-liners to win £45. We had all bet £15 against his tenner, which meant if he lost he would have to shell out £30.

249

"Easy money," Jack disposed of the remainder of his pint and set off to work his magic. For the next 20 minutes, we watched as Jack worked his way through his jukebox of cheesy chat-up lines to a varied selection of responses:

**Jack:** Why don't we go back to my place and do the things I'm going to tell people we did anyway?
**Blonde Girl:** Piss off, creep.

**Jack:** What is a nice girl like you doing in a dirty mind like mine?
**Short-haired girl:** I don't know, but if you don't get me out, I'll punch my way out.

**Jack:** *(Licks his finger and then touches the girl's clothing)* Let's get you out of those wet clothes.
**Brunette:** Touch me again and I'll break your arm

**Jack:** The word of the day is "legs." Let's go back to my place and spread the word.
**Tall Girl:** Why don't you spread and I'll use my legs to kick?

**Jack:** Fuck me if I'm wrong, but isn't your name Gretchen?
**Gretchen:** Yes, it is actually. Do we know each other?
**Jack:** *(Pause)* I'm going to level with you – I was trying to use a pick-up line and it's backfired.
**Gretchen:** I don't get it.
**Tall Girl:** Don't talk to him, Gretch, he's a bloody pervert.

Jack was on the ropes and practically out on his feet, and like any fighter on the brink of a knockout, he looked like he was ready to throw in the towel as he sulked his way back over to us.

"Let me guess," Rob said. "They're all frigid?"

"Or lesbians," I said.

"Lesbians? Where?" Ollie said, craning his neck back and forth to scan the bar for the lady lovers.

Jack ignored Ollie's stupidity. "Whatever, the night is young," he responded, motioning that he was still up for the fight. "Those girls were just small fry before the main course. I've got bigger fish to fry yet."

We all laughed, so much so that I didn't even notice Kelly appear. "What's so funny?" she asked.

"Hi Kelly," I said. "Jack here was just trying to," I pondered before continuing, "How can I say? Get better acquainted with some of the ladies here at Paul's party."

"Ooh, really?" she excitedly said. "Show me which ones? Some of my friends are here so I'll be keeping my eye on you boys. My friends like a man who can romance them."

"I'd like to romance the shit out of them," Jack said under his breath.

Kelly's expression said she hadn't heard what Jack had said and she looked to me for help. "Don't worry," I said. "Let me buy you a drink, it's time the hostess took a break." We made our way to the bar. "So how has it all gone so far tonight?" I asked as I ordered our drinks.

"It has gone well," she said. "Paul is on his way to getting really drunk so I'll have to keep an eye on him later."

"Well, it is his birthday so he's got an excuse. Besides, I can hardly talk after my recent escapades," and I filled Kelly in with the details of my recent dates with fanny-fart Hannah, clitless Kayleigh, and dry-humping Lucy.

"Seriously, stop laughing," I told Kelly. "You are not helping with my self-esteem."

251

"Oh Dan, how do you manage to get yourself into these situations?" Kelly replied, still laughing.

"There you are," Paul interrupted, grabbing Kelly around her waist from behind, and gave her a sloppy kiss on the cheek. "Come here, gorgeous."

"Get off me, you drunk," she said half-jokingly, but with a hint of tension in her voice. "You remember Dan from my office, don't you?"

"Hi Paul," I said extending my hand, "Happy birthday, mate."

"Of course I remember Dan. He's the *funny* one you work with," Paul said. There was an edge of cynicism in his voice, but I decided to ignore it as he extended his hand to shake mine. "How are you, mate?" Paul slurred.

I could tell he was drunk by the way his eyes glazed over. Kelly looked uncomfortable with the situation, and there was now definitely tension in the air. I tried to pretend I hadn't noticed. "I'm good thanks. I hear you liked your present."

"I loved it, the best present I've ever been given in my life," and he put his arm around Kelly's neck and pulled her close to give her another sloppy kiss on the side of her face. He then turned back to me. "I *suppose* I should thank you as well seeing as you picked it out for me."

"I told Paul that you helped me pick the present," Kelly said in a tone that sounded like she was trying to avoid a potentially difficult situation. I was confused at what was happening, like there was some sort of in-joke going on and I was the one on the outside, except it didn't feel like there was going to be a punch line.

"It was Kelly who picked it out really, I just went along to make sure she didn't buy you a man-bag," I joked to try and ease the tension and divert the direction of where this conversation was heading. It didn't work.

"I wondered when you were going to start cracking a few jokes, *funny* man." Paul sarcastically remarked, patronisingly slapping me across the cheek three times.

I'd had enough of this. "Sorry, but is there some sort of problem here?" I asked.

"Problem?" Paul sneered as he removed the arm he had draped around Kelly's neck. "I'll tell you what the problem is. I don't appreciate you sniffing around my girlfriend."

"What?" I wasn't expecting that response. I had met Paul three or four times and we had always got on.

"Stop it, Paul, you're drunk," Kelly tried to push him away, but he kept trying to move towards me until he was right up in my face. I could smell the whisky on his breath as he sprayed me with his tirade.

"I saw the text you sent her. Saying how she was the *one.*" That bloody text I thought to myself. "What are you even doing here?" Paul demanded to know. "You've got some front turning up on *my* birthday and trying to crack on with *my* girlfriend."

"Enough, Paul!" Kelly pulled him away. "I'm sorry, Dan, he doesn't know what he's saying."

I was genuinely speechless, but my blood boiled inside. Not because of the ridiculous statements he was throwing around, but because I could see how this was upsetting Kelly. I decided the best thing I could do at that moment was to swallow my pride, be the bigger man and walk away.

"I think I'd better go, Kelly," I said. "I'm really sorry if I've caused any problems tonight. I'll see you on Monday."

"Yeah, go on. Get out of here," Paul said.

"Dan, please don't go," Kelly called out as I turned away. "You're such an idiot, what did you do that for? I've told you before, we're just friends." I heard her say to Paul.

"Come on, we're going," I said as I got back to the boys.

"Why, what's happened?" Rob said.

"Let's just get out of here, I'll tell you outside."

253

The boys quickly drank up and we made our way through the crowd, and up the stairs to the bar entrance.

"Hold on," Jack suddenly said as we were about to leave. "This doesn't mean I lose the bet."

"I'm afraid it does," Ollie said with a shrug of the shoulders. "You had your chance."

"No, there is still time," Jack said panicking, and looking around the room for one last target.

"What about her?" Ollie said pointing at a girl standing at the entrance door. She had shoulder-length, wavy light-brown hair. Her face was caked in make-up, and her mini skirt and low-cut top left little to the imagination.

Jack studied her closely. "Her face is butters," he commented, rubbing his chin thoughtfully. "But her body is *absolute*," he said with the usual one-fingered index salute. "Here we go."

Jack walked over to her, a little less cocky than usual, realising that his male pride and thirty quid rested on this working.

"Excuse me," he said tapping her on the shoulder. "Do you believe in helping the homeless?"

"What?" she said chewing a massive wad of gum.

"You know, charity?" Jack said straightening his collar. "Do you believe in helping the homeless?"

"Yeah, I suppose so."

"Then take me home with you," he said, a big smile on his face and his arms stretched out wide.

She looked him up and down, and then met his gaze. She chewed her gum some more, flicking it from one side of her mouth to another. Jack strained his smile and raised his eyebrows in the anticipation of her answer.

"Alright then," she finally answered. "Let's go back to mine."

Jack turned to us, his face beaming. You couldn't help but love the guy. His persistence had finally paid off. If Jack was anything he was a man who played the odds game, with him rationalising that sooner or later someone would finally give in to him. Or be drunk enough to not know what they were doing.

"That will be 45 squid please gents," he said with his palm extended out. We paid him the money. "It's a pleasure doing business with you. I am now off to do the business with old butters' face. So long, losers!"

We left the bar and watched Jack bundle his new friend into a taxi, giving us the thumbs up as he did so. "Hold up, Jack," Ollie shouted after him. "You can drop me off at Tooting Broadway. See you later, guys."

Jack's cocky expression suddenly disappeared as Ollie bounded towards him. Jack tried closing the door of the taxi, but Ollie overpowered him and forced his way in, and all three of them squashed into the back seat like a tin of sardines. We watched the taxi pull away and disappear into the busy London traffic, with Jack furiously shaking his finger in Ollie's face.

"Ten quid says they end up in a threesome," Rob said to me.

"I've lost enough money already tonight," I declined to take the bet. "Come on, let's get out of here."

We walked in the direction of Greek Street. I told Rob what had happened in the bar; the way Paul had accused me of trying to hit on Kelly.

"Have you tried hitting on her?" Paul asked.

"No, no way. She is just a friend," I told him.

"You sure?" he pressed me. "There seems to be a bit of chemistry there."

"There isn't," I paused. "We just get on."

"In that case, I'll ask again, do you mind if I have a crack?"

"Yes, I do mind."

255

Rob laughed, and slapped me on the back. I felt my phone vibrate in my back pocket. I reached in and pulled it out. It was a text from Kelly.

*I'm so sorry x*

## Chapter 22: Kelly's Hero

*Monday, August 10, 2009 - 7.57am*
*Drought Clock: 221 days, 4 hours, 40 minutes*

Kelly was already at her desk when I got in. I was surprised to see her as it was 8am and she was never normally in this early.

"Morning," I said as I approached. She turned to face me and immediately I could see she had been crying.

"What's wrong?" I asked throwing my bag down and quickly moving to be at her side.

"I broke up with Paul," Kelly said, tears streaming down her face.

"Come here," I said hugging her.

*

"I'm sure you guys will work it out," I said as we sat in the café across the road from our office. Outside, the city was alive with the usual buzz of Monday morning rush hour.

"No, we won't," Kelly said sipping on her coffee. She had managed to compose herself, but her eyes were still red and puffy. "This has been coming for a long time. The way he behaved on Saturday night was the final straw."

"I'm really sorry if it had anything to do with me..."

"It is not your fault," Kelly said. "He has always been insanely jealous. We had a blazing row on Saturday night. When we met up on Sunday to sort things out, I realised I didn't want to do this anymore."

I knew what Kelly meant; I had gone through the same thing before breaking up with Stacey. When you spend more time being unhappy in a relationship than happy, you know it is time to call it a day. I just hoped that Kelly's break-up had gone smoother than mine. She hadn't

257

mentioned any baseball bat-wielding best friends yet so the signs were good.

"How did he take it?" I asked.

"Not well," Kelly said. "He accused me of cheating. Cheating with you, and just about every other guy I have come into contact with over the last three months."

"And there was me thinking I was special," I said, trying to lighten the mood.

Kelly smiled, but I could tell her mind was elsewhere. She stared out of the window, gazing at nothing in particular. I hated seeing her like this. She was always so bubbly, but now she just looked lost.

"What am I going to do, Dan?" she looked back at me as tears started to well up in her eyes. I moved around the table and put my arm around her.

"Things will be okay," I told her. "I know it doesn't seem like it now, but everything happens for a reason." She buried her head into my chest and sobbed.

"Hey," I said. "Why don't we go out for drinks tonight to take your mind off things? You could probably do with a good night out."

"That would be nice."

*

I spent the rest of the day trying to keep Kelly's spirits up. She had been sitting quietly at her computer for the most part. I had tried everything to take her mind off Paul. We only had a couple of hours left and I decided a break was in order.

"Cuppa?" I asked.

"You read my mind," Kelly said.

I stood at the kitchen area at the end of the office waiting for the kettle to boil. I glanced back towards Kelly who was staring blankly at her computer screen.

258

"Excuse me, Don," I heard Shaila say. I turned to see her standing next to me. She looked amazing.

"Oh, hi Shaila," I said nervously. I had tried avoiding all contact with the ice queen ever since I had been threatened with sexual harassment.

"I just wanted to say..." she started. Here we go I thought to myself. What was she going to accuse me of now? I hadn't emailed, joked, or poked her in ages. I promise!

"...sorry."

"What?" I was so shocked I even burnt myself as I poured boiling water into my mug.

"I know I haven't been the easiest person to work with these last few months. I've had some personal problems to deal with and brought those problems to work with me. It wasn't fair of me to take that out on you and for that I apologise."

Even though she still remained very business-like, she managed a smile. The ice queen had finally cracked! She had a terrific smile and looked even more gorgeous. I didn't know whether to joke or poke.

"That's okay," I said. "Don't worry about it."

"So I was thinking, perhaps I could take you out for a drink this evening after work to make up for it?" Shaila said with the cutest of grins. I couldn't believe my luck. This was fantastic. The woman of my dreams was asking me – Don Hilles – out on a date.

I looked around the office. I wanted someone, anyone, to witness this moment, to make it even more real than it already was. I spotted Pete Crowford suspiciously looking in my direction. I saw Dick poking his head out of his office, trying to pretend that he wasn't watching.

And then I saw Kelly.

"I'm really sorry," I said turning back to Shaila. "But I can't make tonight."

"Are you sure," she seductively leaned in towards me.

259

"Yeah, I've already made plans but how about..."

"Fine, suit yourself," Shaila snapped, flicking her hair and storming back to her desk.

\*

Murphy's Bar was busier than usual. The new Monday night karaoke theme had brought in a few more punters who wanted to try their hand at being Michael Jackson or Robbie Williams for the night.

"Do you think I'm doing the right thing?" Kelly said nursing her pink and orange coloured cocktail.

"Well personally I would have gone for a drink in blue."

"You know what I mean," Kelly said smiling. It was good to see her smiling again. She had spent most of the day making impromptu trips to the ladies after getting text messages from Paul. Her phone beeped again. She picked it up and her expression immediately told me who it was from.

"Why is he doing this?" she said sounding stressed.

"What is he saying now?"

"He asked me earlier if we could meet up to talk. I told him I didn't think it would be a good idea and that we should give each other some space. This is what he texted back."

*Fine. I hope you have a nice life.*

"Why is he being such a dick?" Kelly said. My sentiments exactly, but I kept my mouth shut.

The evening turned into night and we knocked back cocktail after cocktail. We laughed at the poor deluded souls who got up on stage thinking they could sing, and we sung at the top of our lungs when someone got up to sing *Livin' on a Prayer*. By 10pm we were well and truly pissed.

"And do you know what else he always used to do?" Kelly slurred. "He would stick his finger up my bum during sex. I bloody hated it when he did that."

"Yeah, I hate that too," I joked.

"He had this obsession with my bum. He was forever asking me for anal sex and hovering his penis around my bum, like that was some sort of mating call I would be unable to resist. What is it with you guys and anal sex?" Kelly laughed out loud.

"I think it is the primate instinct in us. We are like hunters, or explorers. We see a hole and, well..." I chugged back my cocktail. "We want to explore inside."

"That is disgusting!" Kelly said giggling. "I told him once that we could have anal sex on one condition," Kelly paused. "That I got to do him first with a strap on. You should have seen his face."

We both started to laugh uncontrollably. Her phone beeped again and she picked it up off the table. In the background the DJ was asking for Sam Jones to come up to the stage.

"Why does he keep doing this?" Kelly said as her laughter turned to anger. "He is now saying he wants me to pick my stuff up from his place tomorrow or he is going to throw it all out."

"Don't let him get to you," I said. But it was clear her emotions, mixed with four hours' worth of drinking, were going to get the better of her again.

*This is the second call for Sam Jones to come to the stage, Sam Jones to the stage please.*

A tear trickled down her face, followed by a second, and she held her hand up to her face and carefully wiped her eyes in that way that girls do to try and prevent their make-up smudging. I handed her a tissue and offered some words of comfort, but it didn't help.

261

*Do we have a Sam Jones in here? Sam Jones to the stage please.*

I had never been the best at dealing with other people's emotions, and sitting here three sheets to the wind did not enhance my social skills to adequately deal with this situation. Her sobs were on the verge of turning into wails. I felt completely helpless.

*This is the final call for Sam Jones.*

That was it. "I'm Sam Jones!" I shouted, jumping to my feet with my hand raised in the air. Kelly looked up, bewilderment across her face, but at least she had temporarily stopped crying.

"Up you come then," the DJ said inviting me on to the stage. I got up and saw Kelly give me a look as to ask what in God's name was I doing? The truth was I really didn't have a plan. All I wanted to do was to cheer Kelly up.

"Are you sure you're Sam Jones?" the DJ asked, holding his hand over the mic. My disguise had been rumbled, but I remained calm. Whatever happened I was going to sing. I *would* cheer Kelly up.

"Yes," I answered confidently taking the microphone in one hand.

"You're *Samantha* Jones?"

Gulp. I turned to the screen and saw the title of the song flash up on the screen. I was filled with apprehension. Sam Jones was a *girl*. No self-respecting male would ever choose this song, but there was no going back now. I was going to sing. I stared at TV and followed the words on the screen.

A hushed silence fell across the crowd. Not because I was singing the song well – I couldn't hold a tune if my life depended on it. It was more in amazement that a bloke was singing such a female anthem.

*I Will Survive.*

It felt like I had a thousand pair of eyes on me, but only one pair of eyes mattered. I started to sing and just like the words to the song, at first I was afraid – I was petrified. Kelly looked shocked, but as I stumbled my way through Gloria Gaynor's words I saw a smile start to break on her face.

I was half expecting to be booed off the stage, but instead something amazing happened. Kelly raised her hands over her mouth, and tears started to flow again. But this time they were tears of joy. The sight urged me to put everything I had into the song. My effort didn't go amiss and before you knew it every single person was singing along as only a room full of drunks could.

I grew in confidence, belting out lyrics just like every wronged woman had done at some point in her life. I started to strut a strut that Mick Jagger would have been proud of. I held the mic out to the crowd and touched hands with my new adoring fans. Kelly clapped and laughed, and I could see that twinkle back in her eyes. I waved her towards me and she raced to the stage to join me in a duet. We sang it loud. We sang it proud. We sang it with passion. We sang it completely tone deaf.

But it didn't matter. It was the perfect end to the evening. At the end of the song we embraced and the cheer inside Murphy's Bar that night was deafening. Even Gloria Gaynor would have given us a standing ovation.

*

"That was amazing," Kelly said, linking arms with me as I walked her back to her flat. "I can't remember the last time I had so much fun. Thank you, Dan."

"Don't mention it," I said. We arrived outside her front door. "Are you going to be okay?"

"You know what," Kelly pursed her lips. "I think I am. Thank you again for such a great evening."

She put her arms around me and kissed me on the cheek. At that moment I felt a surge of adrenalin run through me. Kelly was the one girl I never got tongue-tied around. The one girl I always felt comfortable with. She slowly pulled her face away from me and we met each other's gaze. She smiled, and I knew what I had to do. All the nervousness I had felt with other girls had completely evaporated. I leaned forward and kissed her. And for a split second she kissed me back.

"Dan," she said startled, pushing me back. "What are you doing?"

"But I thought..."

"You thought what? Here is Kelly on the rebound so why don't I take advantage?" She was mad.

"No, that's not what I..."

"What, you thought you hadn't been able to get anyone into bed for the last seven months so you thought you would try your luck with me?"

"I promise you I..."

"I thought you were better than that," Kelly said pulling away from me, and stomping up the steps to her flat. "But you are just like all of the rest."

"Kelly, wait..." The door slammed.

*

The next couple of days were a bit of a blur. I just wanted to see Kelly and tell her how sorry I was. But she called in sick on Tuesday morning, and again on Wednesday. I had tried calling and texting her but got no reply.

I kept playing the moments of that night over and over in my head. Why had I jeopardised such an important friendship? I realised how lucky I was to have a friend like Kelly, and how she had deserved better.

264

Kelly finally returned to work on the Thursday morning, but Dick had called her in to his office before I'd even had the chance to speak to her. I was so nervous about seeing her that even my palms were sweaty. I had a horrible feeling in the pit of my stomach that I might have inflicted some sort of lasting damage on our friendship. After what seemed like an eternity, Kelly came and sat down at her desk.

"What did Dick say?" I asked. "Is everything okay?"

"He just wanted to make sure I was okay and feeling better," Kelly said sitting down. "He also asked me what you were wearing today." I looked around the office and could see Dick peering out of the glass panel on his door. He waved and I quickly looked away like I hadn't noticed.

"Look Kelly, I'm really sorry about the other night. I don't know what..."

"Dan, I need to tell you something," Kelly interrupted.

I guess this was the part where she was going to tell me how disappointed she was with me; that I had let her down. I just hoped she would let me explain. Allow me to somehow make this up to her. It was a terrible mistake and it would never again. If only she would listen to me we could go back to how things were before.

"I have just handed in my notice."

265

## Chapter 23: Jack Hammered

*Friday, September 11, 2009 - 8.11pm*
*Drought Clock: 253 days, 19 hours, 16 minutes*

Four weeks had passed since Kelly had dropped her bombshell that she was leaving. We had started talking again, but something had changed. We no longer had that natural easy back-and-forth chemistry. And I knew it was my fault.

I sat back in my armchair at my flat feeling pretty sorry for myself. Kelly's resignation had knocked me for six. My head was all over the place.

During the two days she had spent out of the office, she had booked a flight to Thailand with her friend Claire. They were going to start in Southeast Asia and then spend the next 12 months travelling around the world. I should have been happy for her but instead all it did was cement how I really felt for her and it left me feeling empty.

"Snap out of it," Jack said, handing me a beer. "What's wrong with you?"

"Are you still thinking about Kelly?" Rob asked.

"No, I'm not *thinking* about Kelly," I lied.

"Why don't you just tell her how you feel? She is leaving soon isn't she?" Rob said.

"She leaves on Monday," I said. "But what difference does that make?"

"You could get a goodbye shag," Ollie said.

"I don't want a goodbye shag," I snapped.

"Again, I will ask – what is *wrong* with you?" Jack said.

"She is leaving and that's that. There is more chance of me running naked through the streets of London than there is of me getting together with Kelly," I said, hoping to put an end to the conversation.

"I'm going to hold you to that," Rob said. "That is as good as a promise in my book."

"Fine," I replied unconcerned.

As for my big problem? Well, that didn't seem so big anymore. So I had gone eight months without sex. So what? The world hadn't stopped turning. There were bigger things in my life to worry about other than sex.

"Right, drink up because we need to get this man some action before it falls off." Unfortunately Jack didn't share my newfound sentiments.

The plan tonight was to go to a house party on the Ramsgate Estate. Jack considered going to a party where there was a bedroom just up a flight of stairs to be the ideal place to find me a shag buddy. I couldn't care less anymore about getting my leg over, but I had decided to go along just to get my mind off Kelly more than anything else. The Ramsgate Estate was not the nicest of locations in south London, and the prospect of the type of girls I might meet there frightened me more than excited me.

We left the flat and jumped on to a bus. The other lads were all in good spirits and I pretended to join in with the banter. I couldn't help but think the sooner Kelly left, the better I would feel. Out of sight, out of mind. She had a leaving do planned for tomorrow night, but I had already said my goodbyes in the office. I had seen the disappointment in her eyes when I told her I was unable to make drinks, but I felt it was for the best. There was no point dragging these things out.

The bus pulled up outside the Ramsgate Estate and we jumped off. "Okay, this is it, boys," Jack said. "Now this place can get a little bit naughty, if you know what I mean? So make sure you keep your wits about you."

"Are you talking about the girls at the party?" Ollie said wide-eyed.

"No, you idiot. I'm talking about the gangs of kids roaming around waiting to rob the first big gormless freak they lay their eyes on."

"Come on," Rob said. "Let's not hang around here."

We marched through the estate. Jack guided us around to the right, past some wino sprawled out on a park bench. We spotted a bunch of hoodies standing around by a fence in the distance and opted for a route around the back. It was after about 15 minutes when it finally dawned on us.

"You haven't got a clue where we're going have you?" I said to Jack.

"I know it's around here somewhere," Jack said, hands on his hips.

"This is stupid," Rob said frustrated. "I thought you knew where this place was."

"I do," Jack said. "It's over there somewhere," he said pointing in a south-westerly direction. We all looked blankly at him.

"That's him!" We heard a girl's voice shout from the distance. We all turned to see the girl Jack had met at Paul's birthday party.

"What a stroke of luck," Jack said to us before turning back towards the girl with a cheeky grin. "How's it going, Candice?"

"That's the one who gave me chlamydia," Candice announced to the group of hoodies who were now slowly starting to advance on us.

"Did she say chlamydia?" Jack said.

"Jack, what the fuck have you done?" Rob asked.

"Run!" I screamed.

We took off at a 100 miles per hour. Fear can make a man do amazing things. I had always thought we would clean up at the Olympics if we had a pack of wild dogs in hot pursuit of our track athletes.

The hoodies were hot on our tails as we zoomed through the park. We leapt over a set of metal railings, but Ollie got his foot caught and went down before I dragged him to his feet screaming "Get up!" like in one of those clichéd scenes from a horror film. We bolted across the forecourts of one of the high-rise towers and took a sharp left.

"This way," Jack shouted and we followed him to the right down a short road.

"This is a dead end," Rob hissed.

We quickly turned, but it was too late. The group of hoodies stood not 20 feet away. My pulse was racing. We were trapped. They gathered in numbers as though they had picked up other gang members along the way. There must have been 25 of them at least, of all different shapes and sizes. I'm sure one of them looked no more than eight-years-old. What a way to go, beaten to death by a minor.

We were in the deepest of deep shite. There was no way we were coming out of this unscathed. There have been very few moments in life when I was genuinely scared. Being attacked by Sophie was one of them, running from Dave would be another, but this topped them all. We were in a bad part of town and we were well out of our depth.

"You got a lot of nerve showing up round here, blood," one of the hoodies said in that strange accent many inner city kids seemed to have developed. "You think youse can show your face round here after what you did to my little sister."

"Great," I whispered to Jack. "You had to go and infect the little sister of the Blazin' Squad over here. If we ever get out of this alive, *I'm* going to kill you."

"I'm talking to you!" the hoodie shouted. "I'm gonna cut you blood, you get me?"

This was it. My mouth was dry and I felt sick to the pit of my stomach. Too often I'd picked up the local newspaper to read of yet another senseless knife or gun attack in

269

London. I gulped and prayed that once the dust had settled we would at least be able to walk away in one piece. But something inside me knew that wasn't going to happen. The stories and rumours about this estate were infamous. The look in their eyes told us that we were dealing with a class of people with no morals. True, we were hardly in a position to talk about morality seeing as one member of our gang had given a member of their gang chlamydia, but surely that didn't warrant a death sentence.

Then something happened that I will never forget.

"Okay mate," Ollie said stepping out. We all looked at him in disbelief. "This is the situation. I know that you boys are going to do some serious damage to us, and probably put us in the hospital."

"That's right, blood," the hoodie said much to the delight of his fellow cronies.

"But you," Ollie said in his big booming voice pointing at the one hoodie who had been making all the noise. "I promise that you will be in the hospital bed right next to me. Let's do this."

You could have cut the tension with a knife. My only hope was that no one actually had a knife to test that theory out. The hoodie looked at his friends and then back at Ollie. He paused. "Why me, blood?" he asked nervously.

"Because you are the one with the big mouth," Ollie said without even flinching. "Now come on, let's get this over with."

The hoodie stared at us. I stepped up alongside Ollie, closely followed by Jack and Rob. Every muscle in my body felt like jelly and it took a superhuman effort not to empty my bowels right there and then.

After what seemed a lifetime, but was probably only ten seconds, the stand-off finally came to end. "You boys are soft," the hoodie said. "You ain't even worth my time." And with that the hoodie slowly stepped back before walking off

270

altogether. One by one his friends followed until we were left standing alone in the alley.

"Oh... my... fucking... God!" Jack shouted, grabbing Ollie by the ears and planting a big kiss of his lips. "I love you! I would have your babies right now."

"Get off," Ollie shrugged Jack off and wiped his mouth. "You'll end up giving me chlamydia too."

"Let's get the hell out of here before they change their minds," Rob said, and we took off into the night and didn't once look back.

*

Saturday was a complete wash-out. Rob was working, Jack was at the clinic getting tested for chlamydia, and Ollie was playing rugby.

The most exciting thing I had to look forward to today was shaving my pubic hair. I had once again decided against my better judgement to listen to Jack's advice. He had insisted that girls liked it when men "shaved their bits." He also promised me it made your penis look much bigger.

Boredom had got the better of me, and now here I was standing in front of the mirror, using a pair of clippers to give myself a short back and sides. I had to admit that it didn't look too bad. But as I moved in to apply the finishing touches my phone buzzed into life, completely taking me by surprise and causing me to shave a huge bald patch across one half of my pubic region.

"Arrggh," was the only noise I could manage to express my horror looking down at my... skin head.

"Hello," I said abruptly.

"Danny boy, it's Rob. Everything okay?"

"Yeah," I said brushing the hair away from my groin. "What's up?"

271

"I've been thinking and I wouldn't be a mate if I didn't say this."

"Go on," I said.

"If you don't go tonight then you are an even bigger idiot than you look," Rob said not pulling any punches. "It is clear you really like this Kelly and if you don't go tonight, you will regret it."

"I don't need this," I said.

"But Dan..."

"I'll talk to you later," and I clicked off the phone.

I was angry. I was more than angry, I was furious, but not with Rob, with myself. I knew he was right, but I was just being stubborn.

For the next five hours I could do nothing but stare at the clock. It was almost as if I was counting down the hours until Kelly was leaving. It was 9.47pm. I tried to clear my mind of everything that was spinning around in my head. I kept thinking of what my mum would say to me if she knew how I had treated Kelly. And out of nowhere it came to me.

*Don't spend a lifetime looking for someone you have already found.*

It was something my mum had said to me. At the time I had completely dismissed it. But now it made sense. And I knew what I had to do.

\*

I made it down to The Crown in Balham in record time. I stood outside the door, catching my breath and trying to gather my thoughts. I had no idea what I was going to say. I just knew that when the time came, the right words would come too.

I took a deep breath and made my way in. The bar was absolutely rammed, just as you would expect it to be on a Saturday night. Pushing my way through the crowds I got

272

about halfway and then I saw her. She looked beautiful. Her curly hair bounced against her shoulders as she laughed. As usual she wore very little make-up; she didn't need to. Her skin was flawless and her eyes twinkled. I felt a lump in my throat. I knew instantly I had made the right choice. Here goes nothing I thought as I started to navigate my way towards her.

"Well, look what we have here," a figure suddenly stepped out in front of me. "I've been waiting for a long time to catch up with you."

It was Dave.

Before I had the chance to react he grabbed me and swung me towards the fire exit, and the impact forced the door open and sent me sprawling out into the alleyway at the side of the bar. I heard the door slam and looked up to see Dave and three of his goons looking down on me.

"You have been ducking me for a long time," Dave said. "But now I have you just where I want you."

I was completely trapped. Dave's cronies had already moved into position to block my only exit from the alley as I got back to my feet. Why was this happening, now of all times? I made a run for it, hoping I could force my way past his friends, but they grabbed me and hurled me towards Dave who caught me square on the jaw with his fist. I hit the ground like a sack of potatoes.

"Get him up," Dave said, and his three stooges dragged me to my feet. Dave grabbed hold of the top of my shirt and pulled his fist back. "I'm going to enjoy this," he said in a menacing tone.

"Let him go," a voice came from nowhere, but a voice I knew. Dave took a step back and looked to his right. "I *said* let him go."

It was Rob. He glared at Dave, his fists clenched at his side.

"You're outnumbered, mate," Dave sneered. "You think you two can take on all four of us?" Dave sniggered.

"That's why we're here," Ollie appeared, followed by Jack.

Dave looked at me, and then back at his friends. He nodded to them and the stooges released their grip, and I staggered towards my friends rubbing my swollen face. "This isn't over," Dave threatened me.

"Come on, Dan, let's go," Rob said. But I was tired of running. Just as I had to face Kelly, I knew I had to face Dave. I had to lay this ghost to rest and put this problem to bed.

"No," I said turning around. "Let's end this now."

"Are you crazy?" Jack said. "Look at the size of him!"

"I'm not going to keep running," I said to Jack before turning back to Dave. "You ready to do this?"

"My pleasure," Dave smiled and stepped out to the middle of the alleyway. I was clearly the underdog but I just didn't care anymore. So what if I took a beating? At least I would walk away with my pride.

There was just one small problem – I had no idea how to fight.

The last time I had even hit someone was in the playground when I was 12-years old, and that was because Duncan Valentine had tried stealing my yo-yo. I had smacked him in the nose and got detention for a week.

We circled each other before Dave took full advantage of my clear and apparent lack of arm-to-arm combat skills. He grabbed me in a headlock and squeezed so tight, I thought my head was going to pop off. I tried forcing him back, but he just laughed and threw me to the ground like a rag doll. I scrambled to my feet as my friends offered words of encouragement, but it was hopeless. I was a dead man.

"The power of the Warrior," Ollie shouted at me. For a moment I wondered what the hell he was talking about.

Who did he think I was? But then I remembered – *WrestleRage*!

I ran full-steam at Dave, taking him by surprise and hitting my very own version of a Warrior clothesline, catching my forearm across his throat. He coughed and staggered back. I had absolutely no chance of pressing him above my head so I opted for a fireman-carry style lift instead. I threw him over my shoulder and slammed him on to the concrete. I got to my feet and watched Dave writhing around on the floor. I took one step back and then launched myself at Dave, belly-flopping him!

I lay on top of him for a while, not really too sure what to do next. It wasn't like I had a referee to make the three count. After a few seconds I decided to get to my feet. The problem was Dave also started getting to his feet. He didn't do it with quite as much gusto as Flex Bruiser had done, but it was clear he was on the road to recovery.

"Get him," Jack shouted as I threw my best punch. Unfortunately my aim was completely off, and my fist bounced off his shoulder. Dave laughed as I attempted a second punch, merely side stepping out of the way. He even gave me a Bruiser-style finger wave to let me know I was really in trouble and crashed a hard blow into the side of my face. And another. And another!

Dazed, I fell towards Dave who grabbed me by the arm and threw me into the wall. I bounced off the brick concrete and crashed to the floor. I could hear my friends urging me to get up as Dave circled me, victorious. I had put up a good fight, but I knew I was beaten.

But Dave wasn't finished with me yet. It wasn't enough for him to win the fight, he wanted to seriously hurt me. I heard the blood-curdling scream from my friends first and in what seemed like slow motion I twisted my face to see Dave leap into the air and angle to bring his knee crashing down against my skull.

275

The last eight months flashed before my eyes; everything that I had gone through up until this point. I thought of Stacey and our break-up. I thought about my friends and how they had been at my side through the good times and the bad. And then I thought of Kelly, and how I would never get the chance to tell her how I really felt.

I couldn't let that happen. I *wouldn't* let that happen.

Summoning every last ounce of strength and energy left in my body, I managed to roll clear at the last second, just like the Warrior had evaded Bruiser's Knee Drop that night at New York's Madison Square Garden. There was a terrible crack as Dave's knee crashed against the concrete floor. I bounced off the wall and hit Dave with another big splash. This time Ollie jumped to the floor and counted – one... two... three!

I'd done it! I had defeated Goliath. I was a warrior after all. My friends hoisted me up on to their shoulders as Dave's stooges could do nothing but try to comfort their fallen friend who was howling in pain, clutching his right knee. They carried me to the end of the alley. There was a new champion in town. I jumped down from their shoulders. "How did you know I'd be here?"

"I just had a feeling you'd do the right thing," Rob said.

"Thanks, mate," I said embracing my best friend in a complete unashamed display of bromance.

It was time to make things right. I led the boys around the corner to make our way back towards the pub entrance. Nothing could stop me now.

"Thanks for tonight, guys, I'll miss you," I heard a voice say that I knew all too well. Kelly was hugging her friends and climbed into the back seat of a taxi just 30 yards from where I stood. I tried calling out to her and ran towards the taxi, but Rob grabbed me by the arm and pulled me back.

"Wait, you don't want Kelly to see you like this," Rob said pointing towards my bloodied and swollen face.

I watched Kelly's taxi disappear into the night, hoping that I hadn't missed my chance. Tomorrow couldn't come soon enough.

## Chapter 24: The Betrayal

Jack slumped onto the sofa, holding his head in his hands. His rucksack was on the floor to his left, with just enough clothes to keep him going for the next week.

"I can't believe this has happened to me," he said looking at me through his fingers.

"I take it you told Anna?" I asked, bringing him a cup of tea.

"My plan was to get down to the clinic, get treated, and get the all clear before she had a chance to find out," Jack said taking a sip of his hot tea and placing it on the table. "I thought I could then avoid sex with her for a couple of weeks and then suggest to Anna we both get ourselves checked out. You know, just so we knew we were both clean. I would obviously be given a clean bill of health, but the doc would tell her she has a dose. I could play the nice guy – tell her I'd stand by her even though she had obviously cheated on me."

"Please tell me you are not going to do that," I interrupted. I had laughed off a lot of despicable things Jack had done to that poor girl over the years but making her think she was the one who had brought an STD into the relationship was crossing the line.

"Not exactly," Jack said. "When I got back last night she was sitting in the living room and a real terrible sense of guilt came over me. I knew I had to come clean; she deserved that at least. As soon as I told her I had chlamydia she burst into tears and started to apologise."

"Apologise?" I said baffled.

"Yes, apologise," Jack said sharply. "She said she couldn't be certain where *she* had picked it up from."

278

"Where *she* had picked it up from?" I said even more surprised this time.

"Yes, where *she* picked it up from," Jack said angrily. "What is there an echo in here or something?"

I apologised and told him to continue.

"She confessed that she had been having an affair with some guy called Neil. But she also had a fling with the milkman a couple of weeks back. Then there was her ex Greg who she had done *stuff* with in the last month."

I sat open-mouthed as Jack listed the guys Anna had confessed to sleeping with. It was unbelievable. All the time Jack had been sleeping around behind her back, she had been doing exactly the same thing to him. I couldn't work out if Jack was pissed off because Anna had cheated on him, or because she had been getting more action than him by the sounds of it.

"Can you believe the audacity of the woman? To cheat on *me*?" Jack said looking completely mystified. "Anyway, thanks for letting me stay a few days so I can get my head straight." Jack said nodding towards the rucksack.

"No problem, mate."

I had never seen Jack like this before. He looked dishevelled. He resembled what I can only imagine Jimmy Krankie would look like the morning after drinking a whole bottle of Sambuca. He was putting on a brave face, but I could see how much Anna's confession had taken out of him.

"You'll sort things out," I said. It was a lie, but sometimes you say the things you think people want to hear.

"Nah," Jack said shaking his head and sitting back into the armchair, staring at the ceiling. "Not this time. She has really crossed the line. I can't trust her now can I?"

"I guess not," I responded having to bite my lip about the whole trust issue.

"The truth is mate," Jack said sitting forward, "all those times I cheated on Anna, all that meaningless drunken sex I had behind her back, it didn't mean a thing. Not really. I can see now it was nothing more than a stupid ego trip."

Jack bowed his head. I was worried he was going to cry. It's bad enough when a girl cries, but this was a bloke. What do you do in a situation like this? Is it okay to put your arm around him or is that just too weird? And what do you say? Getting a tissue and wiping the tears from his cheek was definitely not an option. There is only so far a man will go for his friends. My plan was to watch in silence until he was all cried out. Maybe I would offer him a beer. After all, that always did the trick in all other moments of sadness in a man's life.

*England have just been knocked out of the World Cup.* Let's get another round in.

*My son told me he likes playing with Barbie more than Action Man.* We'd better get you a drink.

*My uncle passed away last week.* I hope they have beer at the wake.

At least when a girl cries, you know where you stand. Whether she is genuinely upset about something, or emotionally blackmailing you, you still feel the need to comfort her. But a man crying? It is unheard of. Girls cry in front of their friends all the time, and they will rally around her to make sure she is okay. But if a bloke cries then he is on his own, I'm afraid. The only time it is okay for a man to cry is if his football team has lost in the FA Cup Final, or when she is using her teeth.

"Dan, can I ask you something?" Jack said, lifting his head.

"Of course you can, shoot," I said, while at the same time glancing towards the nearest exit in case I had to make a break for it at the first sign of any tears.

Jack took a deep breath. "You got any porn?"

280

I shook my head and sighed. Technically I wasn't lying. I didn't own any porn, but the internet is a wonderful thing. Hey, it had been nearly nine months. But I was uncomfortable watching porn in the presence of another man. I normally like to view porn on my own, for obvious reasons. Besides, Jack was the type of guy who would commentate the whole way through how he would *ruin* the girl on screen. One time around Ollie's he disappeared halfway through *Schindler's Fist* only to return and proudly announce how he had just "stroked one off" in the bathroom. I wasn't prepared to put my bathroom through that kind of horror.

"I guess I'm in the same boat as you now," Jack said. "The search for the woman of my dreams starts again."

"I guess so," I said. "Although where you are going to find a Harley Davidson riding, triple-breasted woman who urinates Jack Daniels is beyond me."

Jack laughed. "Talking of dream women, what are you going to do about Kelly?"

"I honestly don't know," I said. The decision to go to her last night was made at the last minute so I didn't have time to think about it. I had spent the whole night thinking about nothing else but what I was going to say to her today. I couldn't sleep. "Do you think I'm doing the right thing?"

"Dan, listen to me carefully," Jack said joining me on the couch. "You never truly know what you have got until it's gone." Jack looked at me square in the eyes. "If I could go back and change everything, I would. Don't make the same mistake as me."

This was amazing; it was such a poignant moment. Jack – the happy-go-lucky cockney who never took life too seriously – offering me a heartfelt piece of advice. I got a lump in my throat and turned away. How awkward would it be if *I* started to cry? I could see Jack eyeing up the exits.

"Do you really mean that?" I asked. "You would go back and change everything?"

Jack paused. He sat back in his chair and looked towards the window. He looked back at me. It took an age for him to answer.

"Of course I don't bloody mean that," he said in that cockney twang of his. "I'd still bang everything with a pulse. If anything, I would go back and do it all again!" Jack chuckled to himself.

I laughed with him, but already my mind started to wander. Kelly was leaving tomorrow. I knew there was no chance of anything happening between us. But that feeling continued to nag away in the back of my mind, like a termite eating its way through my conscience. How many times was I going to convince myself that going to Kelly was a bad idea when everything inside of me screamed the complete opposite?

"I need to go and tell Kelly how I feel," I said out loud.

"That's the spirit," Jack said waving his clenched fist at me like Andy Murray does after winning a set of tennis. "Go and get involved, my son!"

I grabbed my trainers and pulled them on without even untying the laces. I struggled with one of the arms of my jacket, leaving me chasing the armless sleeve like a dog chasing his tail. I snatched the keys off the table and bolted towards the door.

"Dan, before you go," Jack called out to me. He stood from the chair. I could tell he was trying to search for the right words; profound words I could take with me on this quest.

"Are you sure you don't have any porn?"

I slammed the door behind me.

*

282

This was it. No going back now. Sometimes a man's got to do what a man's got to do. This wasn't just about sex. Kelly was everything I could have hoped for in a girl. She was smart, funny, and easy going. It was a huge bonus that she had big boobs. Okay, so it was a little bit about sex. I didn't expect Kelly to drop everything and stay in Balham and live happily ever after, but I didn't want her to go with the way I had left things.

Against my better judgement, I had acted like a complete twat, especially on her last day at work. I had tried pretending that it was no big deal – like I wasn't that bothered she was leaving. Even Pete Crowford the IT geek had made more of a fuss over her than I did. All I offered was a lacklustre hug and wished her the best. Even if she slammed the door on my face, at least she could go away safe in the knowledge that I cared for her.

As I turned the corner of her street I felt like I was actually turning a corner in my life. Things were going to be okay. Kelly would understand. She was not the type of girl to hold a grudge.

But nothing could have prepared me for what I was about to face. Like a violent blow to the stomach, my first reaction to what I had just seen forced me to jerk backwards. The vision left me frozen, numb even. In a split second my entire body shivered with shock. What the hell had I just seen? Was it real or was my mind playing tricks on me? I quickly stepped out of sight to try and compose myself. I felt like I had been hit with a sledgehammer. My stomach churned like I was going to throw up. If I hadn't seen it with my own eyes I would never have believed it.

What I had just witnessed was Kelly opening her door, standing in her dressing gown. And she wasn't alone. Like someone with impaired vision, it took my eyes a moment to adjust, but it didn't take long for me to make out the figure exiting her flat was male. On the face of it, I had no right to judge. Kelly was a free agent and I had no one else to blame for missing my chance but me.

But this was different.

I was too far away to work out what they were saying to each other as they said their goodbyes, but I was near enough to recognise that face. It was a face I'd known since I was six-years-old.

It was Rob who had walked out of her flat. It was Rob who now kissed her on the cheek, and held on to her hand. Kelly hugged him, and my heart ached as their body language told me everything I needed to know.

My legs felt like jelly. I was deflated and tried to steady myself against the wall. I forced myself to look again, to make sure this moment was real. I watched Kelly wave goodbye to Rob as the snake walked down the street, once glancing over his shoulder and then finally disappearing out of view.

I fell back against the wall and slid down it. My *best* friend. How could he do this to me? My mind was still racing but this time in different directions. Then something stuck in my thoughts, something Rob had said to me at Paul's birthday.

Twice that night he had asked if I minded if he tried to pull Kelly. He had wrapped it up as banter at the time, but now it was all making sense. This was Debbie Chopman in the school playground all over again. This was Rob proving to me how easily he could take someone I desired so much. But this wasn't a kids' game of kiss chase. This was a betrayal of the highest order.

The bastard, he had actually done it. But how long had it been going on for? Maybe that is why she had been so freaked out when I kissed her. I bet they had been laughing at me all along, thinking that I would never find out because Kelly would soon be leaving the country. And it was Rob

284

who stopped me going to her last night. It all made sense now.

*Your best friend has just pulled the girl of your dreams.* I needed a strong drink.

*

So here we are, back at the beginning, or the end depending on which way you looked at things. I sat on the curb outside the White Horse feeling pretty sorry for myself. It was bad enough my best mate had betrayed me, but the assault from the barmaid had been the cherry on the cake.

I pulled my phone out of my pocket and started to type out a text message.

*I just want to let you know that I know what you have been doing behind my back. You call yourself a friend? If I ever see you again it will be too soon. We're done as mates.*

I pressed the send button and watched as my phone confirmed my message had been sent to Rob. I sat there for a while before my phone started to vibrate. I looked at the screen expecting it to be that traitor Rob calling me to try and squirm his way out of this one. But it was Kelly's name flashing up on the screen.

She was some piece of work. She was probably with him, and now they both knew I had rumbled them. I thought about answering it, telling her exactly what I thought of her. She would have deserved it. In the end though, I put the phone back in my pocket. I simply didn't have the energy left in me to speak to her.

It was time to head home. I picked myself up and slowly walked back to my flat. It was not like I had anything to rush home for. I put the key in the lock and opened the door. As soon as I entered I could hear the sounds of sexual moans coming from my bedroom. I figured Jack had found the computer and logged onto the internet.

I knocked on my bedroom door just to give Jack enough time to pull his pants up just in case he was doing something I really hoped he wasn't. There are some things you don't ever want to see your friends doing.

And this would be one of them. For the second time that day I found myself completely frozen, staring in the face of pure horror. First Kelly and Rob, and now this!

"Señor Hilles, so sorry!" Rosalie screeched. "I clean! I clean!"

"Where have you been hiding this little señorita?" Jack asked as he continued to hump my cleaner from behind. "Do us a favour mate and put the kettle on. I'll be done in a few minutes."

I closed the door. I could still hear Rosalie as I walked down the hall. And I could have sworn I heard Jack say "*taste your ass*" as I quietly left the flat again. I stepped outside and looked up to my bedroom window and laughed. Despite everything, I still had to smile.

"What's so funny?"

It was Kelly. What was *she* doing here?

"What are you doing here?" I asked.

"I tried calling, but you didn't pick-up. I need to talk to you. I need to tell you something."

"Oh save your breath, Kelly, I already know." I said. There was no way I was going to give her satisfaction of giving me some bullshit story about how it *just happened* with her and Rob. "Save it for someone who cares, because I've got nothing to say to you," I snapped, storming past her.

"Why are you being like this?" she cried out after me. I spun round. If she really wanted to know I would tell her. She could then carry that on her conscience as she was travelling around the world.

"I saw you, Kelly," I said. She pulled a face like she didn't know what I was talking about. "I saw you with Rob. This morning. Coming out of your flat."

"Oh," was all she could say.

"I saw the two of you. So now I know, okay."

"And you put two and two together did you?"

"Don't insult my intelligence," I said. "Just go and leave me alone." And I turned to walk away, but not before saying "Have a nice life." I purposely chose the words Paul had texted her when they broke up.

Kelly grabbed my arm. "I don't know what you think you saw, but whatever it is, you have it completely wrong."

"Oh please Kelly, I haven't got time for this..."

"If you must know, Rob came around to tell me how stupid I would be if I left without saying a proper goodbye to you."

I was stunned into silence.

"He told me you came looking for me last night," she continued. "He told me what happened." She paused as though she was trying to stop herself from crying. "He told me how you felt."

I was lost for words. It was so much to take in. How could I have been so wrong? I felt a complete fool for the way I had treated Kelly. For the way I had jumped to conclusions with her and Rob.

"Kelly, I'm so..."

"Forget it," she said. "*You* have a nice life." And she turned and walked away.

I watched as she started to disappear for the second time in as many days. But this time I wasn't going to let her go without a fight. I ran to catch up with her. I pulled her around by the shoulder. She shrugged me away, but I pulled her back.

"Please, listen to me," I said as I pulled her to face me. I could see the tears, I knew I had put them there, and I knew

287

I had to make things right. "I'm an idiot. I'm the biggest idiot on the planet. I don't know why you should give me a second chance. God knows I don't deserve one. But I need you to know something. I need you to know..."

I tried thinking of the words that would repair this damage. I needed it to be magical, something Kelly would remember for the next 12 months. This was my one and only chance. But I couldn't find the words, not words that would do this justice.

"You need me to know what?" she asked, a single tear rolling down her face.

I kissed her. I pulled her close and I kissed her. And this time she kissed me back. I felt one of her tears trickle down on to my cheek as she closed her eyes tightly, but this time I knew the tears were there for the right reason. I didn't want to stop kissing her. I wanted this moment to last forever.

But I knew eventually we would both have to come up for air.

"Wow," she whispered, almost stunned as we pulled our lips away from one another.

"That's what I needed you to know," I said wiping the tear from her cheek. "I'm so sorry Kelly."

"Shhh," she held her finger up to my lips. "It doesn't matter now."

And she was right. Everything that needed to be said, the feelings between us, had already been said in that moment.

"That was pretty impressive. Are you sure you don't have anything else you need to tell me?" Kelly asked.

"Like what?" I said raising my eyebrows.

"Something you might need to tell me back at your flat?" she said with a devilish look in her eye, wrapping her arms around me.

For a second I was confused, but I soon cottoned on to what she meant. "Yes," I finally said with some authority. "Yes, I do." But then I remembered – Jack and Rosalie.

288

There was no way I was going to get back into my bed without burning the sheets after seeing what I had seen.

"We have a small problem," I said. Kelly looked down at my trousers. "No, no. Not that kind of problem," I protested, and then explained the Jack situation.

"Let's go back to mine then," Kelly suggested.

I took Kelly by the hand and started to guide her back towards her flat. With each step my pace quickened. Kelly's place must have been a 15-minute walk away. I dragged her there in about four minutes flat.

Kelly fumbled with her key in the lock. I jigged up and down impatiently. She explained that the key sometimes got stuck. I took the key from her and tried to force it in.

"Oh shit," I said as I broke the key in the lock. I looked at Kelly who looked as horrified as me. I looked back at the door. This was not going to happen. Not to me. Not today. I stepped back and charged at the door. Nothing. I took another run and crashed shoulder first. Nothing!

I stood back rubbing my arm in quite some pain. "Shall I call a locksmith?" Kelly asked.

I was not going to let this get in my way. And with all my might I flung myself at the door, breaking through the lock, wooden splinters spraying out from the now broken door frame. I turned to Kelly and picked her up in my arms. "You might want to call that locksmith later on," I said and with that I carried her upstairs to the bedroom.

I threw her onto the bed and dived on to her. We tore at each other's clothes. I wish I could tell you I was the perfect lover, but what the hell did you expect after nearly nine months. Foreplay would have to wait for round two.

After all the waiting, all of the humiliating situations and the teasing, all of the frustration, the moment had finally arrived. This was real, this was happening. I was in! I was having sex! The drought was finally over. In my head *Celebration* by Kool & the Gang played. I had completely forgotten what the feeling was like. Jack recently tried convincing me it was like masturbating in the bath. Jack is an idiot.

I started to work up a rhythm. I was in danger of getting a little carried away but I thought Kelly would completely understand if I finished a little prematurely on this occasion.

"Don't you dare cum yet," Kelly said rather aggressively as she dug her fingernails into my back.

Shit. I had to resist. I couldn't let Kelly leave thinking I was a two-stroke, two-second wonder. You never knew who she might bump into and tell on her travels.

I clenched my eyes tight and cleared my mind completely of any sexual thoughts. I tried to think of absolutely anything that would take my mind off the task at hand. My grandparents. Different types of cheese. Bushy eyebrows. Wet socks. That reminds me, I hadn't removed my socks. That was pretty unsexy, and becoming a bit of a habit.

And then I finally crossed the line. I had gone beyond the danger zone and felt confident I had the situation under control.

Now it was time to unleash hell.

The endless hours of watching porn were going to pay off. I twisted Kelly into positions she probably thought were not humanly possible. I congratulated myself as I watched her eyes roll into the back of her head. I gave myself a little pat on the back each time I felt her leg tremble. With one final thrust Kelly nearly screamed the house down and I finally slumped on top of her, completely out of breath, and completely drained of all bodily fluid.

After nearly nine months little Dan still worked!

I clambered off of Kelly and lay beside her, completely exhausted.

"That was amazing," she finally said after catching her breath. "But can I ask you something?"

"Yeah, of course," I said holding her close.
"Why have you shaved off half of your pubic hair?"

# Chapter 25: A New Beginning

*Sunday, September 13 - 2.11pm*
*Drought Clock: Expired*

The drought was finally over. The clouds had finally opened and the rains had come. After months of psychological torture, emotional stress, and physical doubt, it was finally over. And boy was it worth the wait.

I had feared that my sexual development would have been set back years, but as the old saying goes, it's like riding a bicycle. Well, the riding part anyway. My confidence had taken a real hammering, but just like a star striker, I had finally found the net again and there would be no looking back now.

On many occasions over the last few months I had prayed for the clouds above my head to stay and bring the rain, which would end the drought. But each and every time they would pass, and simply extend the period of dry weather, or in this case, dry-humping.

My journey had seen me trudge through barren wastelands, fearing I was destined to wander the desert forever. But now my journey was over. If I was to offer advice to anyone else in my situation it would be this:

Climate change is a natural thing that no one can determine or control. You have to take the rough with the smooth. A drought is a natural phenomenon caused by changes in weather patterns, but those same weather patterns can also bring the floods. Droughts kill more people than floods because the effects are more prolonged. The best remedy for weathering a drought is to water regularly while you have the chance.

If you are in a relationship then don't take your partner for granted. Water them daily – do it two, three times if you must to help that relationship grow. You never know when that next bone-dry stretch is around the corner.

"What are you thinking?" Kelly asked me as she snuggled up to me in her bed.

"Nothing really," I said. "Just how great the weather is today."

She gave me a funny look, but I knew what I meant. I kissed her on the forehead, but couldn't help feeling I had forgotten to do something.

Then it came to me. The text I sent Rob. I reached across and grabbed my phone. I had one missed call from Rob and a text message.

*Can you call me mate? I honestly have no idea what I've done. I hope everything is okay.*

I groaned. Without Rob I wouldn't even be laying here with Kelly right now, and in return I had accused him of betraying me, going behind my back, and labelled him a traitor. What type of friend was I? I knew I had to make this up to him, but I had no idea how.

I racked my brains for the right words, but deep down I knew a simple apology wasn't good enough.

But then it came to me. The promise. The promise Rob said he would make me stick to if I ever ended up with Kelly. I knew I owed him much more, but this would be a start. I got out of bed and stood in front of Kelly completely naked. Okay, I still had my socks on. I hadn't had time to take them off in the heat of passion.

"I'll be right back," I said and ran down the stairs and out of the front door.

*There is more chance of me running naked through the streets of London than there is of me getting together with Kelly.*

I had been wrong and now I had to see this through. I waved at Kelly who was looking at me from her window like I had gone mad. And then I started to run.

My tackle flapped and swung from side to side with each stride that I made. I ran down to the High Street and watched people dive out of the way as I ambled my way through the crowds. Small children pointed and screamed as their parents covered their eyes. An old woman shrieked – I couldn't tell if it was in horror or delight.

I ran past the White Horse and spotted the chav barmaid who had served me a beating just a couple of hours ago. She almost jumped out of her skin and a huge wave of satisfaction came over me as she dropped all of the glasses she had been collecting at the shock of seeing my naked body jiggling past her.

I continued my canter up towards the Nelson Arms. As I passed the window I spotted Ollie and Jack at the bar. I made a quick U-turn and made a grand entrance through the pub door.

"Guys!" I shouted. It was Sunday lunchtime and everyone in the packed pub stopped dead in their tracks and stared at my complete nakedness, minus the socks. But I didn't care. "I've only bloody done it!" I said to Ollie and Jack. "The drought is over!"

"Get in!" Jack shouted. I ran to the bar, grabbed Ollie's shot of Jack Daniels and downed it. The whole pub, including the staff, stood in disbelief as three men – one naked – proceeded to perform some sort of strange conga in front of their very eyes.

"I gotta go," I said high-fiving them as I ran out the pub and continued my journey. I got about halfway down the road when I heard the sirens. I took a sharp left down an alleyway and at the end I jumped over a fence into someone's back garden.

But to my disbelief this wasn't just anyone's back garden. As I approached I saw a man on crutches. I must have startled him as he lost his balance and fell to the floor. I grabbed a piece of chicken off the barbie for the journey and turned to see Stacey and Sophie help a snarling Dave get to his feet.

I must have leapt over six or seven fences before I got back out on to the road. I cut down the back streets and finally arrived at my destination. I banged on the front door and rang the doorbell several times. I waved at a neighbour who had poked her head out of the door to see what all the commotion was, but she slammed it shut at the sight of me. Finally Rob answered.

"Have you completely lost your marbles?" Rob gasped. I barged past him and into his house.

"I've done it," I said, jumping up and down, hugging Rob.

"Done what?" Rob said, pushing me away, looking slightly concerned that I had just rubbed my naked body against him.

"The drought is over," I said with a huge smile on my face, talking at a hundred miles per hour. "It was with Kelly. I had to come and tell you. I thought you had slept with her, but I was wrong and I'm really sorry. That's why I sent you that text. But she told me you went round there and convinced her to see me before she left. And then I remembered my promise that I would run naked through the streets of London if I finally dipped my pen into the ink with Kelly. I probably can't do all of London but will Balham do? Anyway, you should have seen me, I pulled off some cracking moves," I continued to ramble on, demonstrating the positions I had performed.

Then I heard someone clear their throat behind me. "Hello, Daniel."

I slowly turned around to see Rob's mum sitting at the dining table. But it wasn't just his mum. His dad was sitting there too. And his grandparents, his aunt and uncle, and his cousins. All four of them. And someone I had never seen in my life before. Rob folded his arms across his chest, cocked his head to one side, raised his eyebrows at me, and half-smiled.

"Hi, Mrs Devlin," I nervously said. "Hi everyone."

"Cold outside, is it, Dan?" Rob's dad asked me.

"I better go," I said turning back to Rob. "I'll call you later," I whispered, holding my thumb and finger to my mouth and ear. "Bye everyone."

*

I made it back to Kelly's flat and hopped back into bed.

"What was that all about," she said half smiling, half looking at me like I was a crazy man.

"Just something I had to do," I told her. "Hey, you ready to go again?" Before she even had a chance to answer I jumped back on top of Kelly and moved back into position for round two. We had only been at it for a few seconds when she once again told me in no uncertain terms: "Don't you dare cum too early."

There was a pause.

"Sorry," I said.

*

The next day I took Kelly to the airport. There was no awkwardness whatsoever about what had happened. It just felt right. We hadn't made any silly promises to wait for each other or anything like that. We both knew a lot could happen in 12 months, and there was no way I could go on another drought. Besides, she had just come out of a long-term relationship. If we still felt the same when she got back then we would see where the wind takes us. But until then...

"I guess this is it," Kelly said after she had checked her bag in. We hugged and kissed.

"You're going to have a great time," I said and for the first time I realised how much I would miss her.

But something caught my attention. On one of the TV screens they were showing Sky News. I couldn't hear what was being said but I saw the image of a naked man in a pair of socks running down the high street – my naked sock-wearing image running down the high street with the headline: *Gay Rights Protester Strikes Again.*

I quickly looked away before Kelly had the chance to notice what I was looking at. I could feel my phone vibrating in my pocket. I would have to call mum back later to explain.

"I want you to have this," Kelly said handing me a plastic bag. I took the bag and pulled out what was inside.

"The Rocky Balboa robe," I said in total shock. "But this was Paul's birthday present."

"Yeah, well Paul didn't exactly deserve it now did he?" Kelly said smiling. "I want you to have it."

We hugged again. I didn't want to let her go.

"Hey," Kelly said looking at me. "You keep performing like you did last night and I don't think you'll be experiencing any more droughts."

We both laughed. I kissed her for the final time. I then watched her go through passport control. In 12 hours she would be halfway across the world. I walked back towards the train station.

I stood on the platform and thought about the last 24 hours – about the last nine months. It really had been a whirlwind ride.

"Excuse me, does this train go to Green Park?" a girl carrying a suitcase asked me as the train pulled into the platform.

"Yes, I hope so, otherwise I'm going in the wrong direction," I joked.

297

She smiled and thanked me as she struggled to lift her suitcase onto the train carriage. "Here, let me help you," I said lifting her suitcase up.

"Thank you," she said. "I'm Cindy, by the way," and she extended her hand.

I looked up and thought of Kelly. "I'm Dan," I said shaking her hand. "So where have you just come back from?"